THE CRIMINAL LAWYER

Jack Hillgate

First published in the United Kingdom by Delacheroy Books in 2010

ISBN-13: 978-1505280975

ISBN-10: 1505280974

Jack Hillgate has asserted his right under the Copyright, Designs and Patents Act 1988 to be identified as the author of this work

This novel is a work of fiction. Names and characters are the product of the author's imagination and any resemblance to actual persons, living or dead, is entirely coincidental

Delacheroy Books, Hanover House, 14 Hanover Square, London W1S 1HP, UK

About the author

Jack Hillgate is a writer of books and screenplays.

He lives with his family in Europe.

Also available by the author

The Jew with the Iron Cross

Cocaine (Volumes 1 & 2)

ACKNOWLEDGMENTS

For B & E, D, T and M&G

CHAPTER ONE

My name is Jonathan Berry. I'm a legal aid barrister. I live under a flight-path. My family tree stretches back generations, hundreds of years to Norman England when the name was *Berrie*. One of my ancestors was hanged in 1649 by Oliver Cromwell. A bishop, a knight and a succession of landowners made and squandered money through the years, buying moated Jacobean manors and trading them down to modest Farnham country houses in order to pay death duties. The Farnham country houses made way for a four bedroom semi in Roehampton with a seventy foot garden and a clear view of the underside of planes descending into Heathrow, spewing out carcinogens.

In my dream I'm sitting by my pool in the South of France wondering what the chef has prepared for lunch. My kids - all four of them - splash happily, watched by my loving and devoted wife Georgina - beautiful too. In my dream I don't have to work. In my dream I'm rich. In my dream I'm happy, and then I wake up and I'm running down the corridor of a hospital, following an orange line that a black woman tells me will lead me to my youngest daughter, my leather-soled shoes slipping on smooth white tiles. Into the ward and the nurses look at me strangely. My wife Georgina's blonde hair is matted and her make-up smeared down her face.

'Where's Sophie?', I ask.

Sophie is our two year old. The youngest of our four. Georgina screams and I shut my eyes and pray.

'Mr Berry? Mr Jonathan Berry?'

I open my eyes to a grim young doctor who puts his disinfected hand on my pinstriped shoulder.

'Is she....?', I croak.

***

I did my first rape when I was twenty-eight.

'Lovely opportunity, sir', said my clerk Jacob Potts in his best Marks & Spencer pinstripe, 'lovely opportunity.'

'I dunnit', were the first words my client Brian Dunne uttered to me in a holding cell underneath Islington Police Station. 'I dunnit, guv. Best shag I ever 'ad!'

I watched Brian pick his nose and eat the result, the handcuffs still on his wrists. Of course he was guilty. They all were. I never wanted to do rape, but, like cab-drivers, barristers couldn't turn down clients and, as my clerk Jacob Potts said, it was a lovely opportunity.

I found it difficult watching Glenys's tiny figure in the witness box, only feet away from my guilty client dressed in Jacob's M&S suit, Jacob in Brian's Sergio Tacchini. And yet, although I found it difficult watching Glenys, it didn't stop me interrogating her for nearly a whole day. I remarked on her short-sightedness, her long-sightedness, her prescription anti-depressants and Nordaz tranquilisers and all those bills from

Unwins for chianti and kettle chips. The jury deliberated for four hours and the judge fell asleep more than once, but out of the darkness came a ray of light.

'Not guilty!', intoned the foreman.

'Bloody brilliant!' roared Brian as he stuck two fingers up towards Glenys' husband.

I walked out into the fresher air outside the courthouse. I sat on the concrete steps resting my foot on a bollard and held my head in my hands. Brian Dunne ran out a free man, clapped me on the back and shook my hand. God he was ugly.

'Fanks, gov!' he spat, getting on an unlicensed, uninsured scooter behind a boy even uglier than him and crashing straight into a bus.

I didn't attend his funeral.

***

Sophie's funeral was on a Thursday. Brian Dunne's funeral had also been on a Thursday but Brian Dunne had been a rapist and Sophie was my two year old daughter.

Febrile convulsions, they said. One in twelve infants, they said. In Sophie's case the febrile convulsions had led to brain damage and death when the piece of banana she'd been eating got stuck in her windpipe. I'd been sitting in chambers doing fuck all at the time.

My family came down from Yorkshire and Georgina's came up from Hampshire. Everyone from chambers was there, half of the Middle Temple as well. My old Oxford friends were there too, Georgina's old work colleagues from Silverman Bach and the mothers and fathers of our children's school friends. Our three children were there too – they had all said they wanted to be there – and so we respected their wishes. Sophie had been their sister as well as our daughter and we didn't really care what anyone thought.

Georgina and I could not bring ourselves to say much, or even to stop crying during the service. Sophie's body was taken to a cemetery just off the A3 Kingston Road, right next to the school where we were sending two of our children.

'We have to move', Georgina whispered to me. 'I can't stay in that house.'

Our doctor put us on tranquilisers. We looked for a new house immediately but it was difficult to focus with the Nordaz clouding everything. Georgina said we should move nearer to her mum but I couldn't get much of a mortgage on my earnings. My clients were unemployed, legally-aided criminals. It was so true what they said about crime not paying.

My desk at work - 21 Wessex Yard, just off Chancery Lane - was flooded with papers. I couldn't afford a secretary and so I had to do my own filing which of course I never did because I never got round to doing it. I had a good excuse now for doing even less. I had a frayed shirt because I kept forgetting to wear the new ones that Georgina bought me and that we couldn't really afford. One of the hinges of my glasses was loose – an old gold-rimmed pair that made me look older than I was – and I had a tiny rip in my charcoal pin-stripe trousers. I earned less than my clients, most of whom were unemployed.

I had two files, but you would never have guessed it from the mess on my desk. A fraud on Customs and Excise – imported caravans filled with millions of Nicaraguan cigarettes – and a rape, a young girl from Muswell Hill out walking in Queen's Wood attacked by a Rasta with a bicycle pump.

As the whiff of Kouros hit me I looked up to see my clerk

standing there, wearing his new Paul Smith.

'Aft'noon, sir.'

'Hello Jacob.'

'Long day, sir?'

I pointed to the large pile of manila files stamped '*Customs & Excise*' next to a photograph of Sophie. I was sitting at my desk but I wasn't doing any work and I had to share my room with a young chap – Archie Macdonald - who was never there because he was so busy which made it even worse.

'If yer daant mind me sayin' so, Mr Berry sir, you look like you could do with a little pick-me-up.'

I looked out of the window. It was getting dark and I was drugged and depressed.

'Get me some fucking money, Jacob. I'll do anything. Just…you know, do your thing.'

'I'm like an Hollywood agent, sir. Steering you slowly though the waters – '

'I'm not Brad Pitt, Jacob.'

I was peed off that his suit was nicer than mine. He looked at me quizzically for a moment, studying my face carefully.

'No sir, you definitely ain't 'im.' He handed me a little card from his jacket pocket. 'Why don't yer leave yer files and 'ave a drink on me. Go on, tell 'em I sent yer.'

I looked at the card.

It had a single word on the front – *Velvet* - and a West End address and telephone number on the back.

I peered around the side of my files and up at the large clock on my wall which read ten past five.

All those lucky enough to be in court would be in the pub. You'd hear them across Middle Temple, Fleet Street, The Strand and Chancery Lane with their loud voices and thick wallets, la-di-da-di-dum and telling each other how well they'd done. Cunts. And then there was me, sitting on a mound of paper with a dead daughter.

Oh life was just so beautiful and as if it couldn't get more spectacular I remembered that Georgina's old boss from Silverman Bach had invited us round for dinner.

***

We left the kids with a babysitter for the first time since it happened and we headed into town, splitting an extra Nordaz between us.

When we arrived at Chas and Brenda Mullion's house we couldn't get out of the Volvo, just sat peering up at the enormous floodlit wedding cake mansion, double-fronted with four storeys and painted all over in creamy white like a meringue. It was huge and backed onto Holland Park. Chas Mullion's last annual bonus had paid for the whole thing in cash, Georgina whispered to me. I nodded, said 'cunt' again under my breath and watched Georgina as she looked wistfully towards the enormous windows.

'This is…this is…', she began softly.

'Oh it is, it is.'

'He's doing very well, Jonathan.'

'Don't rub it in.'

We could barely afford one of the little turrets on the top

of the Mullion wedding cake but then if Georgina were still at Silverman Bach…maybe, just maybe… and then I saw a look in Georgina's eyes that depressed me even more. It was as though her eyes were tracing a huge 'L' on my forehead.

I worked up the courage to get out of the car, walked up the steps hand in hand with Georgina, each of us steadying the other, rang the bell which chimed like Big Ben and then suddenly we were swept inside by a butler, underneath a gigantic crystal chandelier which sparkled so much that it hurt my eyes. I looked down the hall scouting for signs of life somewhere out there in the marble and mahogany.

'Bet you every day's Christmas round here', I whispered to Georgina, wondering how much a house like this cost.

'Twelve to fifteen mill', boomed Chas Mullion, walking in holding a bottle of 1990 Krug. 'But I knocked 'em down a little. That was what you were thinking, right? Right?'

'That's the spirit', I replied, forcing a smile and shaking his outstretched hand.

His wife Brenda, a plastic surgery veteran at the age of forty-three, followed him in and hugged Georgina.

'So sad to hear of your loss.'

'Ditto, guys', said Chas. 'Thought you could use a little cheerin' up!'

The cork popped out of the bottle he was holding and champagne dripped onto the gleaming floor.

I watched as a gloved hand appeared from nowhere, wiped it up and then disappeared again. We sat in a grand drawing room with tall French windows leading out to the brilliantly-lit garden. Chas stood with his back to a roaring fire, the flames licking up around his back to create a halo effect around his head.

'How's work, Jonathan?' he asked me.

'Difficult, you know, with...'

'Yeah yeah yeah. Still in crime?'

'Yes.'

'Well someone's gotta do it, hey? Hey buddy?'

'Er...something like that.'

'And you Georgie? How's my best girl?'

'Bearing up, Chas. We're still getting over Sophie, you know.'

'I know, honey, I know. Listen – here's to Sophie and the rest of your gorgeous family.' He raised his glass and we all did the same. 'If there's anything I can do...'

He was looking hard at Georgina.

'I can't go back to Silverman Bach, if that's what you mean, Chas. I must be with the kids.'

'Of course, Georgie. You know, I hope you don't mind me sayin' this but you were one of the best goddam people I had in my team. We pulled an amazin' year, last year, Georgie. There's always a place for you, if you, I mean, if you feel...you want a change, you know...'

I shifted uncomfortably on the enormous sofa. The champagne really did something to the Nordaz.

Georgina took another large gulp from her glass. She was feeling it too. Numbing.

'Money's not everything, Chas', she said.

'You're right', he replied, standing in the centre of his fourteen-million-pound drawing room holding a thousand pound bottle of vintage champagne with a cigar chomped between his teeth. 'Money's not everything.'

Chas started to laugh, joined swiftly by Brenda.

I joined in too, just to be polite.

CHAPTER TWO

Somewhere on the other side of the world there were children dying of starvation. Their mothers and fathers were being slaughtered like cattle and their homes razed to the ground. These children had done nothing more unfortunate than find themselves born to a particular religion which was out of favour with the government of their allotted State – Jadzikistan - and its ragged, ill-paid and ill-educated army. I turned another page of my newspaper and had to look away from the awful pictures, but the mess on my desk was nearly as awful.

The mess consisted of my never-ending Customs fraud case involving unpaid duty on millions of fake Nicaraguan Marlboro Lights, and a rape. The advantage of the fraud was that Customs were even less organized than I was and needed to pay someone a pittance to shuffle thousands of pieces of paper about. If they were happy to pay me a pittance to shuffle paper then that was fine by me. It meant I could always pretend that I was busy on Customs work, when in fact I might be busy on something else, like my only other case.

Colleen Marden, seventeen, was taking a lunchtime stroll in a park when a six-foot-three Rasta by the name of Desmond

Lyons knocked her to the ground with a bicycle pump, ripped off her skirt and knickers and raped her in the middle of a cycle-path. Then, after he'd raped her, he smashed her over the head with the bicycle pump, damaged her left eye beyond repair and left her requiring forty-six stitches. The police photographs were sickening, Lyons initially confessed his crime but then retracted his confession and was pleading not guilty. I had the misfortune to represent him.

Desmond Lyons was a drug dealer who lived in a squat next to a mental institution on St John's Villas in Archway, North London. Desmond was black and Colleen, the victim, was white. I wanted a black jury, but it was unlikely I'd get more than three out of twelve. The case wasn't well paid – standard Crown Prosecution Service defence rates – and to make matters worse Colleen Marden's grandfather was Lord Marden of Winchelsea, one of England's top judges, a Lord of Appeal in Ordinary. No other barrister had wanted to take the case.

I remembered meeting Desmond for the first time because he tried to garrot me with his handcuffs until I told him my name was Jonathan Berry and I was his barrister.

'Ya, riiiight. Don' fuck wi' me now, *Janny*', he said as two policemen shoved him back onto his metal chair.

'I'm not...erm...*fucking* with you, Desmond. I've got to be straight with you.'

'You is all crooked.'

'*Pardon?*'

The policemen smirked at me.

'Why I is here, *Janny*?'

'Well...they found the girl's blood all over you, they found the assault weapon – the bicycle pump - under your bed, they found your semen inside her and you had scratch-marks all over you with her DNA all over them. It doesn't look good. Plead guilty, maybe.'

'Wassat like sound like *diminish rasponsbilty…?*'

'*Diminished responsibility* might apply if you were a minor – under eighteen – or drunk, or on prescription medication or insane, temporarily or permanently or clinically depressed or something like that.'

'I sure is depressed, *Janny*. An' she *provoke* me. Da bitch *provoke* me.'

'In what way, Desmond, did *she* provoke *you?*'

Desmond stared at me menacingly. He was nearly as ugly as Brian Dunne, his face scarred and pock-marked, his hair lank and greasy. I wasn't looking forward to putting him on the stand. I wasn't looking forward to seeing Lord Marden in court.

I didn't do any work for three weeks.

I just sat at the desk in my room in chambers and thought about Sophie. Jacob kept bringing me cups of tea which were very useful in washing down the little pills.

Jacob stared at me a lot. I must have looked like shit. In fact, I was sure I looked like shit. Jacob, conversely, was immaculate, about thirty, short, not bad looking in a Nick Leeson sort of way, fairish hair and brightly-spotted tie.

'We're in', he said one day, cup of tea in hand, as the rain fell outside my grimy window.

'We are?', I asked, without much enthusiasm.

I took the tea from him and he placed an overflowing lever-arch file on my desk, smiling serenely.   It didn't look like a Crown Prosecution Service file.   I turned the spine towards me and I read one word: 'KELSEY.

'Kelsey? Jacob?'

'It's an arbitration, sir.'

'What…?'

'A *commercial* arbitration, sir.'

'But I only do crime, don't I?'

'These people like the sound of you, sir. And they pay quite well. And you did say…'

'Yes I did, didn't I.   Who's my contact?'

'An acquaintance, sir. From the club, sir'.

'Velvet?'

'Yes indeed, sir. I'll leave you to have a look sir. Brief fee's been agreed. On the back as usual.   I'll be next door if you need me.'

I took a sip of Earl Gray.

I turned over the file and looked at the cream coloured brief with my chambers address on the bottom right.

The bundle, as always, was wrapped up with violet ribbon just like a birthday present.   My eyes scanned the page. I got to the bottom where it mentioned my fee and I blinked.   In Jacob's own handwriting was a little note which he'd initialed stating that the fee was payable even if the arbitration settled, even before I'd done any work.   I looked at the pound sign followed by numbers and blinked again. And again. I opened the file and started to read.

Kelsey, a rich American, thought he'd got the deal of the century. Someone was going to sell him thirty-five million dollars-worth of Nigerian oil for twenty-two million, a bargain. It was too good to be true. He chartered a ship from Harbor Shipping, Inc. of Delaware. The ship arrived but the oil didn't, the seller turned out to be a dummy company and he'd paid up front for both, so Kelsey went crazy when Harbor took their ship away. It was adding insult to injury. He couldn't sue the people who'd scammed him because he didn't know who they were so Kelsey decided to get what he could from Harbor, my new client, for taking their ship away.

I knew nothing about charterparties and shipping law. I did know that Delaware was like Liberia, Panama or the Cayman Islands: a set of post-boxes. No-one had an actual office there. And as for Nigeria? I hoped I didn't have to go to Nigeria. I wasn't a good traveler.

I looked again at the brief fee. It was almost too good to be true but there it was in front of me in black and white.

At last someone was going to pay me properly.

I had no idea why they would want a criminal barrister for a commercial case, but all I wanted to do was kiss Jacob. I also wanted to kiss the instructing solicitor, whose name, I could see from the brief, was Hussain Tarzi of Mount Street, Mayfair, London. Never heard of him, but that wasn't unusual.

I raised my empty cup of Earl Gray to Jacob Potts, to Hussain Tarzi and lastly to Mr Kelsey and Harbor Shipping Inc. of Delaware. My new friends. Maybe I should stop taking the pills. I put in a courtesy call to Tarzi but his secretary said he was away on business. She was a little vague on the date of his return.

Georgina made me accept a knock-down price for our old house. She said we should rent. She said she thought the market was going to go lower. I took a large gulp of coffee and looked at the agent's particulars again. It had four bedrooms and it was in Holland Park, a modern house on Abbotsbury Road facing the park itself with a small garden and a garage. Chas Mullion's Silverman Bach-funded palace was thirty seconds walk away. We could peer in at his windows if we got bored of the view from ours.

The day of the move Georgina and I stood in the room that had been *hers* and we cried. Everything was gone now. We'd given everything to the local charity shop and now there was nothing left of our little Sophie's. It was easier that way.

We had our memories of her, we had the photographs, the videos and the portrait that our artist friends from Wimbledon had done. The floorboards were bare and clean, the walls a newly-painted white. I'd changed the pink quickly to get the smell of her, everything, out of my mind.

Maybe, maybe if I'd been home that evening…but then, even if I'd been home, if I was honest with myself, what would I have been doing? I would probably have been in my little office at the end of the garden, batting away the daddy long-legs and huddling by the stand-alone electric heater at my keyboard, trying to think of what I could possibly say in defence of my rapist and my cigarette smugglers.

I blamed God, whom I was sure now didn't really exist, because if he did then he wouldn't have taken my beautiful blonde-haired two year old daughter away from us. It couldn't have been punishment for anything because as far as I knew none of us had done anything wrong, apart from Ben our eldest having once sworn at his second year primary school teacher.

Moving house meant moving schools. We headed upmarket even though we couldn't afford it, not until the Kelsey brief fee was paid, but we could eat into our savings until then and of course we had the money from the sale of the house.

The red and black uniform suited eight-year-old Ben magnificently and the girls' green uniform from the Norland Square school was very fetching.

Three lots of school fees to pay. I hated myself for even starting to think that at least it wasn't four. I'd go to hell for that thought, I knew I would. And I'd deserve to.

The house was smaller than our old one but that was more than compensated for by the much nicer area. No grim tower blocks round the corner. No 747s screaming overhead to rattle our windows and clog up the sky with jet fuel dumps. A beautiful park lay opposite and the schools were both within walking distance. It was incredible how much a simple change in surroundings changed everything. Hussain Tarzi had even called me on the *Kelsey* arbitration to arrange a meeting. He played tennis and suggested, bearing in mind the location of my new home – Jacob must have told him - that we have a game on one of the courts inside Holland Park. I agreed willingly.

'I will recognize you', said Tarzi. 'I've seen your picture.'

'Oh, really? Eight-thirty then? Court four?'

'Splendid, Mister Berry.'

'Please. Jonathan.'

'If you insist, Jonathan.'

It had to be him. He was short, slim, dapper and had a thin moustache and a large smile. He was immaculately dressed in perfectly-ironed tennis whites and he had two old wooden rackets in presses. He looked like something straight out of a Coward play. I didn't know anyone who still played with wooden rackets.

'Good morning, Jonathan my dear fellow', he said as he glided towards me, a fixed grin on his face.

'Morning!', I replied, trying to rev up the old charm without much success. I wasn't really a morning person.

He shook my hand very firmly. He was much stronger than he looked.

'Hussain Tarzi. At your service', he said, pointing to his rackets and grinning.

'Ha ha', I laughed politely, 'very good.'

Tarzi might have used wooden rackets but he was a lot better at tennis than I was. We played two sets in just under an hour and he beat me comfortably, leaving the wind to freeze my sweat. In contrast, he was as dry as a bone.

We headed out of the park towards *Tootsie's* on Holland Park Avenue. I was still steaming when we sat down and I ordered a large orange juice, freshly-squeezed. Tarzi ordered an espresso and a croissant. He ate delicately, with long slim fingers. He was very neat and tidy, well-pressed, immaculate.

'I'm glad I've got you on the case', he said to me after a long chew of croissant. 'I feel I can trust you. Jacob told me you were infinitely reliable, a pillar of the Establishment.'

'It's nice of him to say so.'

'I like the fact you can trace the Berrie family back hundreds of years. You must have some interesting contacts.'

'We used to.'

'Your wife was at Silvermans, wasn't she?'

'Yes, yes she was.'

Tarzi sipped his coffee in silence and nodded.

'I do a lot of business with Silvermans', he said absent-mindedly. 'I also do a lot of business at Velvet. You are a member, no?'

'Not yet.'

'Then let me propose you.'

'That's very kind', I replied.

I finished my orange juice and ordered another. Tarzi seemed completely engrossed by his croissant, eating so carefully that not a crumb was wasted.

'Do you want to go over the Kelsey arbitration?', I asked him.

'No', he replied laconically. 'Not really. I just wanted to get a feel for the sort of man you were. I'm sorry about the loss of your daughter. Jacob explained.'

'Oh? Err...thank you.'

'I think I can trust you implicitly Mister Berry. Jacob has told me excellent things about you.'

'He's one of the best clerks in London', I replied.

'Yes he is', said Tarzi, 'but he didn't have to sell you to me very hard. I knew you were perfect for this, that your talents were right. The client would like to meet you.'

'A conference? Of course, I'll ask Jacob to set it up.'

'No no, the client has requested that we meet at the club. Tonight.'

I didn't have to ask him which club. He ordered a third espresso and the bill.

'Will a cheque be alright, do you think?', asked Tarzi politely.

'Oh please don't worry', I replied. 'You got the court. I'll take care of this.'

I searched for my wallet which was somewhere in my tennis bag. When I found it I looked up at him. He was smiling at me. I looked down at my empty glass and next to it sat the distinctive cheque of a well-known private bank in the amount of one hundred and fifty thousand pounds. Payable to me.

'I prefer to pay up front', he said.

The cab drove along Embankment, past the Inner and Middle Temples and up to Trafalgar Square. We peeled off, headed up Charing Cross Road and then cut round the back into the maze of West End streets that headed to Mayfair. In twenty minutes of light traffic at seven o'clock we were there, outside Velvet. I remembered the film and the song – *Blue Velvet* – and that is how I'd imagined it would look. Seedy. Anything to do with my clerk had to be. But it was nothing of the sort. It was terribly grand, like *Claridge's* or *The Savoy*. I winced. I bet my thirty-year-old clerk earned three times what I did and he hadn't even been to university.

'A guest of?' enquired the smartly-dressed gentleman in his sixties at the door.

'Jacob Potts. Meeting Mr Tarzi.'

'Oh! You better come in, Sir. Don't want to catch a chill.'

A fire burned in a grate by the door. The floor was dark brown and highly polished. The lighting was low. The entrance hall alone was as big as my house, a grand vestibule just like Dorian Gray's in that old Wilde film, the one where everything was black and white apart from the lurid colour portrait in the attic, the portrait that showed Dorian Gray had sold his soul. I checked my watch. Back home Georgina would be in the middle of *The Gruffalo*, or maybe a *Mr Men* book.

The plasterwork on the ceilings was very fine indeed, the rugs early nineteenth-century, the artwork a mix of Old Masters and modern pieces by Warhol, Hockney and Picasso. My ancestors used to live in places like this before they lost their money and now my clerk was the lord and I was his serf, his impoverished and grateful guest.

'Cocktail, sir?' asked a waiter dressed in white and holding a tray with two freshly-poured glasses of champagne resting on it. I nodded and he handed me one of the glasses.

'Why *Velvet*?' I asked.

'Looks expensive', he winked, 'but underneath it's just cotton.'

'Oh?'

'Do excuse me sir, Lord Willoughby is calling me.'

I turned to see the former Foreign Minister waving at us, sitting in a group of five men all with suntans and of Middle

Eastern extraction.

I turned away. I'd voted him out of office.

'*This is where it's all happening*', Jacob said to me earlier that day after I got back from tennis. Well I couldn't see much happening and I was early so I walked out of the room and down a corridor along which hung a succession of portraits of former presidents of the Velvet Committee, back to 1788. That was strange. There was Boodle's, White's, The East India Club and so on but I'd never heard of Velvet and yet it was more than two hundred years old. I stopped by an unmarked wooden door, looking for cotton, pushed it open and walked inside.

Groups of men stood at roulette wheels and blackjack tables. The croupiers were all men. Every time the bloody wheel went round the school fees swam before my eyes and then I remembered Tarzi's cheque.

'Sir?' asked a croupier, shaking me out of my thoughts. 'Cocktail?'

I nodded and he handed me another champagne cocktail from a tray. I took it. It was free.

'*Chemin de Fer*?' he enquired.

'*Non merci*', I replied. 'I just like watching.'

'Mr Tarzi's in the Red Room, sir', said a distinctive voice. I turned and looked up at a tall bowler-hatted gentleman who looked like one of the porters at my old Oxford college. 'That way, sir', he added, indicating the corridor leading down a flight of stairs and to the right.

I glanced at the papers sitting on a large leather-topped desk on the landing. There, under *The Times*, was the *Daily Mail*'s story on my disastrous client, Desmond Lyons. I vaguely remembered Jacob saying media bias might be the only way to win the Lyons case, but then I wasn't sure if Jacob had seen the photos of Colleen Marden that I and no doubt Lord Marden of Winchelsea, her grandfather, had seen. I wondered how the press had got hold of this one.

"TWELVE INCHES OF HORROR!" ran the headline, referring, I hoped, to the bicycle pump. I picked up the paper and carried it downstairs with me, taking a quick glance at the story. Apparently a posse had formed in Lord Marden's village of Blockley. A bunch of farmers, pensioners and shopkeepers - anyone with access to a shot-gun - had got together to hunt down Desmond Lyons and blow off his bollocks, hopefully not with me standing right next to him.

I folded *The Daily Mail* under my arm and checked myself out in the long mirror just before the entrance to the Red Room. I was wearing a black Ede & Ravenscroft pinstripe, a high white collar and a Middle Temple tie, gold cufflinks, polished Church's Oxfords and the simple metal Rolex that my father had given me on my twenty-first. I adjusted my tie, pulled my cuffs slightly more out of my jacket and opened the door.

The Red Room was more gold than red, ornate with deep velvet curtains, a thick red and gold rug on highly polished oak and a large chandelier which hung directly over a large oval table. There was one spare seat at the head of the table which Hussain Tarzi ushered me towards.

'Good evening, Jonathan', he said warmly.

'Good evening, Hussain', I replied.

We shook hands and I looked behind him at the ten men around the table.

'Are they *all* with Harbor Shipping?' I asked, suddenly a little nervous.

'No', he replied in a whisper, '*one* of them is a representative of Harbor Shipping, the rest of them are my other clients.'

'Your other clients?'

'That is correct. Why don't you take a seat and I'll introduce you to everyone.'

'Ten clients?'

'Always ten. I give a very personal service.'

I nodded and sat down. Hussain Tarzi whispered something to a waiter and a few seconds later someone was opening a Nebuchadnezzer of pink champagne and handing out twelve bubbling glasses.

'To happy times!' said Tarzi.

'Happy times!' I replied, and took a drink. No-one else said anything. They stared blankly at me. I stared blankly at them.

They knew who I was, but I hadn't the faintest idea who any of them were.

'What's our strategy, Berry?', asked the Corona-smoker in an American accent.

'You're with Harbor Shipping?', I asked.

He nodded.

'I don't care what you say, son, in front of these people. Just tell me your strategy.'

Eleven pairs of eyes trained themselves on my face, waiting for an intelligent reply. I knocked back my glass and looked at my jury. I cleared my throat and then I heard the distinctive '*Beep! Beep!*' of my mobile telling me it had a text message for me from Georgina - '*I want u 2 fuck me l8r – I only charge 150k*' it read. I looked up at the eleven pairs of eyes looking at me and quickly put my phone away.

'So? What's our strategy?' repeated Corona-man.

'Well…I haven't read all of the papers yet, but it looks to me - but I'm not an expert - like a Nigerian flake deal.'

Everyone looked at me blankly.

'Go on', drawled Corona-man.

'A flake deal is just a fraud. Very common in Nigeria. It works like this. Kelsey bought twenty-two million dollars of oil but the oil didn't materialise. He was defrauded by someone. Not you, obviously. So when *you* took your ship away he didn't suffer any loss, because there was nothing to put on your ship in the first place.'

'So why's he suing us?', he replied. 'Sounds pretty clear. We didn't sell him the oil. We just lent him a boat.'

'He's got no-one else to sue. The people who took his money have vanished. But - technically I think - you may have been in breach of contract for taking your…your *boat* away.'

'Not if there ain't no oil to take. What's his loss?'

'I agree', I said. 'But Kelsey wants to sue you anyway. He says, I think, that if you had left your ship there in Lagos then the oil would have turned up eventually.'

'We did leave it there. For a month. There was no oil.'

'Well, if that's right – '

'There was *no oil*. Read my lips. We had another offer on the vessel. We refunded Kelsey the charter money. What more could he want?'

Everyone around him nodded.

'Perhaps I can explain, Mr...?' He didn't offer his name. I looked over to Tarzi for some help but he averted his eyes. So did everyone else.

'So what's the damage?', asked Corona-man.

'Errm...yes...well it's difficult to assess, very difficult.' I nodded sagely, desperately trying to give the impression I knew what I was talking about.

'Okay, okay, so what are we talking here? How much, Mr Berry, will Harbor have to fork out in damages if we lose hands down?'

'I'd have to read all the papers again before I could give you a proper estimate', I said, willing Tarzi to say something helpful.

He didn't.

'Alright, Berry', said Corona-man. 'I'm gonna tell ya what you're gonna do. You draft a bullshit defence and then ask to meet with counsel for the claimant. Just the two of you, in private. We'll give you a wire.'

'A *what?*'

Tarzi was looking at me now.

'Look, Berry. You're gonna be just great. You look so...I dunno...English.'

'Mr Berry is respectable', said Tarzi. 'This is his first commercial case. I'm sure he'll make it a successful one.'

'Perhaps I should discuss this with my clerk...?'

25

'Once they have seen your defence', said Tarzi, 'you will offer them one million dollars to settle.'

'One *million*?', I said, puzzled.

'Yes. That's our maximum and we want it settled. That is', Tarzi paused, 'if you feel up to it. We can always approach another…'

'No', I said as firmly as I could, thinking about the hundred and fifty thousand that would soon clear into my joint account. 'I can do this.'

'And if you settle it for *less* than one million dollars', Tarzi continued, 'I have instructions from my client to split the difference with you.'

I nearly choked on my champagne.

'We're not litigious people', said Corona-man. Everyone else in the room nodded in agreement.

'More champagne, sir?' asked someone, handing me a napkin.

As a waiter filled my glass, Hussain Tarzi slipped a shiny Velvet membership card into my pocket. I remembered my father saying to me once that one should never join a club where they actually wanted you as a member.

'Life membership', he whispered.

'I don't know quite what I've done to deserve it.'

'No', he said, somewhat absent-mindedly, 'I don't suppose you do.'

CHAPTER THREE

Jacob Potts looked at me slightly differently the next morning.

'Everything alrigh', sir?', he asked.

I thought about the client conference the night before. When I went back to Georgina afterwards I failed to live up to her text message. All I could think about was professional ethics, wire-taps and maybe, just maybe, splitting one million dollars with my client. It would certainly make looking for houses a lot easier.

'Everything's fine', I replied to Jacob.

'Good meetin' last night at the club?'

I made myself look busy. It wasn't difficult with all the mess in my room.

'Not bad', I replied as nonchalantly as I could.

I could sense Jacob lingering by my desk.

'If you need to discuss anything, sir, bearin' in mind this is your first commercial case, I've got a lovely lady who'll 'elp you draft a crackin' defence.'

'That's very kind, Jacob.'

'Er name's Kate Bowyer.'

I looked up.

'I know her', I replied.

'I know yer do, sir. Thas why I suggested 'er.'

'I better get on, Jacob.'

'Right you are, sir. Make sure you get some lunch though. Yer look pale. I 'ere Middle Temple's doin' a a nice roast beef and Yorkshire.'

'Thank you, Jacob.'

Dining at Middle Temple Hall was something you had to do when you were starting out as a barrister. To earn the right to wear the wig and gown and address a court you had to eat a certain number of dinners at an Inn of Court, in my case Middle Temple, and sometimes dinner was accompanied by a lecture. The idea was based on osmosis, the knowledge of the experienced lawyers rubbing off on the less experienced ones. No-one really listened to the lectures. In my experience it was difficult to learn much with your mouth crammed full of apple crumble and custard. I don't think lunches counted.

It was a beautiful old room. It reminded me exactly of hall at Oxford, large high-ceilinged rooms with large old paintings on the walls, huge stained glass windows, long benches and ugly servants ladling out soup and mushy peas to spotty students. Fifteen years on, the food was better, alcohol was less frowned-on and everyone was a lot more smartly-dressed. Gowns weren't obligatory either.

'Ever been to Blockley?', said an old man's voice into my right ear. I was miles away, thinking about wire-taps and professional ethics but I knew who it was without looking up.

Lord Marden of Winchelsea – 'Bill' to his friends, which definitely didn't include me - had appeared on radio and television many times over a long and illustrious career. His voice was very distinctive, gravelly and somber. His eyebrows were thick and bushy, his face heavily–lined with hooded eyes and his nose, I noticed from my seated position, sported a bristling brush of nostril-hair.

'I don't know you, Berry', said His Lordship. 'But I heard about your daughter. I'm very sorry.'

'Thank you sir', I mumbled into my food.

'Dreadful business you getting this case with my grand-daughter'.

I chewed my meat slowly.

'You've seen the photographs, I take it?'

I knew he'd have got hold of them somehow. I nodded, hearing the crack in his voice.

'Man's a menace to society', he continued in a low whisper.

I nodded again and shut my eyes. Suddenly I could see the 'TWELVE INCHES OF HORROR!' headline together with the Blockley posse led by His Lordship, wielding a pair of double-barreled shot-guns.

'I know I can count on you', he whispered, squeezing my shoulder tightly.

I watched him walk slowly to the other end of the hall, glad-handing as he went, seemingly without a care in the world.

I looked down at my roast beef and Yorkshire pudding and suddenly didn't feel very hungry.

I went back to chambers after lunch and tried to draft the *Kelsey* defence just like Harbor and Tarzi had asked me to do. I tried to ignore thoughts of wire taps and hundreds of thousands of dollars from split-settlements. Still, I checked the Bar Ethics Handbook and it was very unclear on remuneration. Splitting settlement with your client wasn't specifically prohibited. I didn't bother to look for a section on wearing a wire.

I re-read all the papers that afternoon and tried to speak to Hussain Tarzi but his secretary told me he had left the country on a business trip. I needed to ask for a little more time to draft my defence but there was nobody to ask. Jacob my clerk had been right. He normally was. I picked up the telephone again and dialed the number on the back of the cream-coloured card that he'd given me that morning.

'Kate Bowyer please.'

'Just a minute, sir. Who shall I say is calling?'

'Jonathan Berry, 21 Wessex Yard'

'Just a moment, sir. I'll put you through.'

The line went quiet and then I heard her voice.

'Hello Jonathan.'

'Hello Kate.'

'I know why you're calling. It's an arbitration, isn't it?'

'You're well–informed.'

'Your clerk Jacob called.'

'Oh. He did, did he?'

'Yes. I assume you'd know?'

'Yes yes yes', I replied, unsure if I did know.

'Don't tell me. You're drafting a defence and you're stuck.'

'That's right! How did you -'

'Why don't you do a first draft and I'll come look at it this evening.'

'Really, Kate? That's very kind.'

'No problem. Seven okay?'

'Yes, yes seven's fine.'

***

The clock in my office stood at five to seven and I was on the phone again.

'When are you coming home?', asked Georgina.

'Soon.'

'You know it's the kids' Christmas service tomorrow?'

'Oh, er, yes. What time?'

'Four, Jonathan.'

31

'I'll be there. Just got to do this damned arbitration.'

'Are you OK, darling? You sound a little strained. You know last night…is that why you couldn't…?'

'Um, yes', I replied, just as Kate Bowyer walked into my room.

'Got to go', I whispered down the phone hurriedly. 'Catch you later. Bye.'

Kate Bowyer was from 16 New Square, a maritime arbitration specialist who I'd gone to law school with. She was going to look at the defence I'd drafted in exchange for one hundred and fifty an hour, and she was here now in my chambers in her black suit, legs crossed, poring over my type-written words.

Kate was very attractive. I could feel the old *Berrie* charm stirring as I noticed she was wearing stockings rather than tights. I also noticed she had a wedding ring but, judging from her figure, no children. She crossed her legs one way, and then the other, her skirt a little higher than before. She was probably thirty-four or thirty-five – the same as me – but she looked a good six or seven years younger. I was paying her a hundred and fifty an hour. In my life I'd only paid one other woman in stockings with a hot body more than that and she'd been no barrister.

'Why are you looking at me like that, Jonathan?', she asked. I blushed and looked down. I'd been staring. I saw the bulge in my trousers and promptly crossed my legs.

'Nervous', I replied. 'Commercial work's not my thing.'

'You always were more attracted to crime, weren't you Jonathan?'

She turned to me and removed her black-plastic-framed

glasses.

'I saw your name in *The Mail* – a rape case, wasn't it?'

I smiled.

'Sex and violence sells papers.'

'This is a good piece of work, Jonny', she said as she handed me my defence. 'I'll get my clerk to send yours a fee note tomorrow. One hour OK?'

'That's very good of you, Kate.'

'That's what friends are for.'

'Thanks'

Kate smiled and shook my hand. I resisted the temptation to peck her on the cheek. I watched her walk around the piles of files on my desk, navigate the umbrella stand and head out onto the street, towards the lamp-lights of Wessex Yard, a freezing mist covering her that made the condensation trickle down my windows. I'd happily pay Kate Bowyer a hundred and fifty plus VAT to come and sit in my office every day and do that thing she did with her legs.

I held the slim set of papers in my hand, the defence in the *Kelsey* arbitration. It wasn't half bad. I'd dredged up a few useful things from the file and they were all in front of me now in twelve point type.

Mr Kelsey had thought he was buying thirty-five million dollars of oil for the bargain price of twenty-two million. The only catch was that he had to pay up front, but as he believed he was dealing with Shell Nigeria he had thought he could trust them.

He also paid about a quarter of a million dollars of port

charges.

He voyage-chartered a ship from my client, Harbor Shipping, to carry the oil. The ship arrived but the oil didn't, even after a week and Mr Kelsey was steaming.

'Attn Harbor Shipping, Inc, Delaware', he wrote, *'what the goddam hell have you slimeballs done with my goddam oil?'*

My client, Harbor, was rightly losing faith. They contacted Shell Nigeria themselves. *'No oil'*, said Shell. *'Never heard of Kelsey.'* Harbor telexed a message to Kelsey's 'Shell Nigeria' telex answerback and discovered that Kelsey hadn't been dealing with Shell Nigeria. He'd been dealing with someone using a telex at the King Midas Kebab House in Tufnell Park, North London. The only oil they had would be for frying onion rings.

Harbor asked Kelsey if they could take their ship away bearing in mind there was no oil and surely Kelsey was more interested in finding out who'd scammed him. Kelsey's reply to Harbor was succinct: *'Get me my fucking oil you scumbags.'* Harbor took their ship away and paid back Kelsey all his charter hire as a gesture of goodwill. There was no way Kelsey could possibly think of suing Harbor. My client had behaved impeccably. Kelsey was just shooting in the dark, trying to find someone to sue because neither Interpol nor Shell Nigeria nor the FBI had any idea who'd gone walkies with Kelsey's twenty two million two hundred and fifty seven thousand dollars and eighty cents.

I couldn't understand why my client was happy to offer Kelsey a million dollars to go away.

Why offer anything at all? Kelsey would be lucky to get *ten* dollars. And Harbor was going to split the difference with me for every penny I could get a settlement *below* a million dollars. Christ, all it would take would be one telephone call to Kelsey's counsel – I checked for his name on the Points of Claim –

Duncan Markson of 144 King's Bench Walk, a sensible chap of twelve years' call - and the whole thing would be done and dusted. I could do that tomorrow morning. One telephone call and I might be a lot richer than I was now. It was very exciting just thinking about the possibility.

It was eleven o'clock and and I'd spent long enough at chambers for one day. Outside it was misty and I turned up the collar of my thick woolen coat. I didn't like taking the tube when it was late, even though it was only a straight westward ride home on the Central Line for one pound eighty. I hailed a cab instead, and I got the driver to stop at Charing Cross station so I could pick up the first editions of next day's papers. I bought *The Mail*, *The Telegraph*, *The Guardian* and *The Times*. I opened up *The Mail* and breathed a sign of relief. The day was finishing nicely.

I was in a very good mood when I got into chambers the next morning, buoyed by the visions of Kate Bowyer that had kept flashing into my mind whilst I'd been in *flagrante delicto* with my wife the previous night. I'd also been rather pleased with *The Mail*.

On page five, next to a story about the atrocities in Jadzikistan was a picture of Lord Marden wagging his finger at the Blockley posse – the one champing for Desmond Lyons' bollocks. The posse had been asked to stand down by his Lordship himself.

'*I know you'll do the right thing*', his Lordship had said, his hand resting paternally on my shoulder. It was comforting to think his Lordship trusted me to do the right thing. I slipped the Bar Code of Ethics into a drawer and pressed the button on my telephone that Jacob had shown me how to use. It was the one that recorded the telephone call. I could hear a faint hiss in the background but Jacob assured me that no-one else would be able to hear it.

'It's Jonathan Berry for Duncan Markson, please.'

'Just a minute, Mr Berry sir.'

The phone crackled for a second and then Duncan Markson's velvety tones came on the line.

'Berry my dear fellow. How are you?'

'Fine thanks, Duncan.'

'Good show. Sorry to hear about your youngest. Terrible thing. Terrible.'

I paused, remembering Sophie.

'Thanks', I replied slowly.

'Got your defence this morning, old bean', he said brightly.

'I thought you might have', I replied.

Silence. Neither of us wanted to be the first to speak.

'Has your client seen it?', I asked after a long pause.

'Yes. Yes, he has.'

'And?'

'And what?'

'And surely he doesn't want this to go all the way.'

'My dear Jonathan. Kelsey will not settle.'

'Erm...but we'll win, Duncan. Seems an awful waste of everyone's time, all those costs...'

'Off the record, I know that, my dear fellow.'

'So you've advised Kelsey not to go ahead?' I asked rather a little too eagerly.

'Off the record, Jonathan and if I may speak candidly, my client is rather headstrong. He doesn't care if he loses. If there's a chance, a small chance he might win something of the twenty two million back from your client –'

'But the two events are completely unrelated – '

'Doesn't matter old chap.'

Fuck it, I thought. *Fuck, fuck and double fuck.* I took a deep breath.

'Duncan?'

'Yes?'

'Without prejudice to my client's contention that it has done nothing wrong and has acted properly towards Kelsey...'

'Yes?'

'I have instructions to settle the matter now for...for a hundred thousand dollars.'

I could hear Duncan breathing down the telephone.

'Duncan? Duncan? What do you think? We can settle this, collect our brief fees and go on to the next one. What do you think?'

The line went silent.

'Duncan? Duncan? Are you there?'

And then I heard an awful sound, the worst sound I could

possibly have heard, coming at me loud and strong down the telephone line.

It was the sound of laughter.

CHAPTER FOUR

I had less than twenty minutes to get to the carol concert.

'You're late', whispered Georgina as I sidled next to her near the back of the pews, thirty minutes later.

'Sorry, darling. Damned traffic.'

In front of us Mollie and Amy stood in a row of thirty, all in their green uniforms. Ben, our eldest, had his concert later that afternoon and was sitting next to Georgina in his magenta and black stripes, his cap perched jauntily on his head. I looked out at the girls, heard the thin reedy sound of the organ that accompanied them, filled my lungs and sang a rousing chorus of '*Good King Wenceslas*' together with all the other mums and dads, nannies and grandparents.

'*When the snow lay round about, deep and crisp and even...*'

A very loud baritone voice was belting into my ears.

'*Brightly shone the moon that night...*'

I turned round and directly behind me, hammering out the

carol was the fourth-richest man in Britain – according to *The Sunday Times* at least – serial entrepreneur Martin Hotson.

He was tall and athletic with a gleaming smile that adorned a number of cheesy television advertisements. His hair was dyed blond and he had a rather striking beard.

Next to him, in a cravat, stood our Silverman Bach neighbour Chas Mullion and his plastic wife Brenda.

They nodded and smiled as I turned round and saw them. Chas mimed raising a glass to me and winked. I faced forward, my voice getting louder and louder, trying not to think of the wall of money standing less than two feet behind me.

When the music petered out I kissed Mollie and Amy on the forehead and told them how wonderfully they'd sung. Georgina looked at me lovingly and hugged me.

'We're getting through it all, darling, aren't we?' she whispered into my ear. 'I mean…Sophie.'

'Yes,' I replied. 'I think we are.'

'Jonathan, Jonathan, Jonathan', said Chas Mullion in his hearty American accent, 'give me a hug you ole' softy.'

He gripped me tightly and nearly lifted me off the ground, then turned and kissed Georgina square on the lips.

'What could have been', he said, winking at me. I winced as he beckoned over his own wife, the perfectly plastic Brenda with her perfectly seamless smile of laser-blasted enamel. I looked down at the enormous diamond on her finger and grimaced. Our house, right there, on her perfectly-manicured digit.

'Hi y'all', said Brenda, letting her ring sparkle under the lights.

'Say', said Chas, 'let me introduce a good friend of mine. Martin Hotson.'

He stepped forward and reached for my hand.

'Jonathan Berry. Delighted to meet you', I said.

'Pleasure's all mine', he replied with a smile. 'Hope my singing didn't deafen you. I like a good rouser and, well...'

'Mulled wine?' said Chas, grabbing a tray.

We all took one and raised our paper cups in a toast. I was the poorest one in our little clique by a factor of a thousand and I couldn't take my eyes off the glitterball on Brenda's finger. I sipped my mulled wine, livid that my ancestors had squandered the *Berrie* fortune.

'Listen Jonathan, I know you're a busy man', said Chas, 'but Martin here has a problem he wanted some advice on, and, well you know how it is, buddy, right? I kinda thought we might have a drink somewhere more private to discuss it, maybe iron it out for him? Could be a lot of money involved.'

I looked up from my mulled wine.

'Oh?'

'Jonathan is the best goddam lawyer in this miserable country of yours', continued Chas. 'He managed to talk his lovely wife out of a career at Silvermans where believe me she'd've cleaned up. He's the best.'

I smiled but I didn't like the way he always mentioned Georgina and the money she could have earned if she'd have stayed at Silvermans and not married me.

'Where do you go Jonathan?' asked Martin Hotson. 'I mean, that is, for a confidential discussion?'

'You've got the time, right?' said Chas.

'Erm…of course, of course', I replied, immediately forgetting the fact that my eight year old son in his magenta and black school cap had his own carol concert later that afternoon.

'So?'

'I'm a member of a lovely little club in Mayfair', I said in a whisper. 'Very discreet.'

'Oh? Me too', said Chas, angling me towards the door, followed by Martin Hotson. 'Lead the way.'

I took a quick look back at Georgina deep in discussion with Brenda and her glittering ring and walked quickly out of the door of the church, into the pouring rain and straight into the back of Martin Hotson's limousine.

'Where to, sport?, said Chas, opening up a drinks cabinet in front of him.

'Do you know a little club by the name of Velvet?' I asked the chauffeur. He nodded at me in his rear view mirror, Chas and Martin smiled and I suddenly felt very charming indeed.

***

'What do you know about murder, Jonathan?'

I looked at Martin Hotson through the bottom of my whisky tumbler in the Red Room at Velvet.

'I haven't done a murder yet', I answered truthfully.

'*Could* you do one, I mean, could you *defend* one?'

'Of course', I replied carefully.

Martin leaned so close to me that our cheeks were virtually touching.

'I have…a friend', he said slowly into my ear. 'A good friend. He is in a lot of trouble. He's just had some bad news from his solicitor.'

'Not a bill I hope?'

He looked at me stony-faced and I took another sip of the single malt lurking in the bottom of my enormous glass tumbler.

'Thirty years ago, roughly', he whispered, 'this…friend of mine was charged with murder.'

I nodded sagely.

'This friend of mine got a little drunk at a party. It was a wild time you know, drugs, drink, young girls in bikinis, that sort of thing.'

Chas looked away and took a big glug of *Jack Daniel's*. Martin's whisper became even softer.

'Anyhow', he continued, 'this friend of mine was meant to have strangled a girl and thrown her into a swimming pool. She died. Very unfortunate. He was charged with murder but then he was…'

Martin's eyes seemed to glaze over.

'He was…he was acquitted. Not guilty. But they got…they got him on a lesser charge of possession of an illegal substance. He spent two months inside and then they let him out. For good behaviour, you know?'

43

I nodded as best I could, difficult with Martin's head clamped so close to mine.

'After five years his...his crime was wiped from the records...'

'Under The Rehabilitation of Offenders Act', I whispered.

'Yes, that was it', replied Martin quickly. 'Anyhow, anyhow, anyhow...he...he was clean and free to...to get on with his life. He'd made a mistake, you see. But he'd paid for it. He'd paid all right.'

Martin paused for breath, loosened his collar and finished the remaining whisky in his tumbler.

'So what was the bad news from the solicitor?' I asked.

'I'm coming to that', he replied. 'I'm coming to that.'

I looked around quickly. No-one else in the Red Room was paying us any attention.

'The girl that died, the dead girl – she was eighteen I think – was from a well-known family. Well-to-do. They knew that...that my friend had served his time for the crime but they wouldn't let it rest. They bloody wouldn't!'

He squeezed his glass tightly.

'Anyhow, anyhow, anyhow. You see, the thing is, my friend's solicitor contacted him last week with some rather bad news. There's this change to the law see...'

His voice trailed off.

'Do you mean the new Criminal Justice Act?', I asked. 'The double jeopardy rule?'

Martin Hotson slumped in his chair and nodded slowly.

Chas looked at me quizzically.

'The *what*?', he asked.

'After eight hundred years Parliament decided to repeal the rule against being tried twice for the same crime. If new evidence comes to light then the State can decide to retry...Martin's friend for murder', I replied.

'That's a great comfort', said Martin gloomily. 'For my friend, I mean.'

'Who are your friend's solicitors?' I asked.

Martin looked at me.

'They haven't chosen a barrister yet', he said. 'But we...he'll need one, of course.'

'Of course', I replied.

'I got...I mean, my *friend's* got the best firm around.'

'Excellent. Then I'm sure your friend has nothing to worry about.'

'Right. That's what the solicitor said to him. Neat little chap, apparently. Name of Tarzi.' He looked up at me innocently. 'Do you know him, Jonathan?'

I pondered the bottom of my glass.

'Do I know him?', I said slowly.

When I opened the door to my room I noticed Jacob sitting in my chair looking at my laptop computer. I noticed someone had cleaned up my mess of papers, the mess in which I could find every single page. Someone had stacked my files neatly on a smart new set of modern shelving.

I noticed that the other desk in my room, the desk belonging to Archie Macdonald, a young lad of only six months' call, was gone. My room, for the first time in five years, actually looked presentable. Apart, that was, from the four hundred cartons of Marlboro lights stacked against a wall.

'Evidence', was the word Jacob used when he looked up at me from my own laptop computer. 'Evidence, Mr Berry sir.'

'Great', I groaned.

'Cleaned up fer you, sir.'

Martin Hotson was going to help me clean up. Customs paid me eighty an hour and he was going to pay me four hundred.

'Ee didn't do it, yer know, sir', said Jacob to me.

'What?'

'Hotson. Ee never done it.'

'How do you seem to know everything, Jacob?'

Jacob tapped his nose.

'Mr Tarzi's very pleased with you, Mr Berry sir. Very pleased. Ee's glad ee met yer. You should be glad 'n all.'

'I am, Jacob', I replied uneasily.

'Yer wife called', said Jacob. 'She said you missed yer son's carol concert. She said yer better 'ave a good reason.'

'Shit.'

Jacob pulled out a small light blue box and handed it to

me.

'This'll do the trick', he said.

I looked down and read the word *Tiffany* on the top.

'What's this?', I asked.

'A gift, sir. For yer wife. Lovely lady, deserves a nice gift.'

I opened up the little light-blue box and looked down at a sparkling eternity ring. There was a large diamond in the middle that looked a little like Brenda's glitterball of a rock.

'How much?' I asked.

'From Mr Tarzi, sir', he replied.

'How *much* Jacob? My wife is going to want to know how much of *our* money I spent on this. She's going to want to see a receipt. She's going to be suspicious.'

'All taken care of sir. I used your chambers account to buy it and Mr Tarzi will deposit the same amount into your account.'

'You arranged all this?'

Jacob nodded.

'How much?'

'Forty fousand pounds, sir.'

'*What?*'

'You love 'er, don't yer?'

'Oh God!'

'Well there you are then, sir.'

I was the one sweating now, not Martin Hotson, sizing up the massive diamond set into platinum and wondering what Jacob was doing with my laptop.

'Just givin' yer a new password, sir' he said. 'I fink yer might 'ave given yer uvver one away. To yer wife, maybe?'

'Yes', I replied, thinking of my new responsibilities, my two new cases, Kelsey and now Hotson. 'Yes Jacob. You're right. Thank you.'

'Thass alrigh' sir.'

'What is it, then?'

'It's V-5-L-V-5-T'.

'Velvet?'

'Thass righ' sir.'

Suddenly the telephone rang. Jacob picked it up, handed it to me and left me alone with the four hundred cartons of hooky fags and my shiny new filing system.

'Hallo?'

'It's Aziza, Mr Berry.'

'Who?'

'Mr Tarzi's assistant.'

'Oh. Hello Aziza.' She sounded pleasant enough, if a little tired. 'He's got you working late', I said.

'We have a lot of international cases, Mr Berry. Different time zones. Mr Tarzi wanted me to speak to you this evening.'

'Is he there?'

'Mr Tarzi has been called away on urgent business but he wanted me to clarify a few things with you.'

'Of course', I replied, turning the little light-blue Tiffany box over and over in my hand.

'We have instructions for you on two of our cases. The Nigerian arbitration and now the double-jeopardy murder.'

'Err...yes, that's right.'

'Mr Tarzi has asked, bearing in mind their importance, if you could refrain from taking on any further instructions.'

'Well of course I will need to discuss that with my clerk– '

'I understand from Jacob that you already have a rape and something to do with cigarette smuggling.'

'Yes.'

She cleared her throat.

'Mr Tarzi wanted me to ask you if any of your other instructing solicitors pay you in full in advance.'

'Oh?'

'Do they?'

'Errr...no.'

'Jacob sent us the tape of your conversation with Duncan Markson. Mr Tarzi has asked me to inform you, bearing in mind the financial arrangements, that he needs a little more effort from you.'

The tape? I didn't know Jacob had the tape. That meant

they'd heard Duncan laughing at me. It didn't sound very ethical somehow.

'Good. Good', I said uneasily.

'And the gift for your wife?'

'Sorry?'

'The ring for your wife?'

'Errm, it's beautiful', I said, flipping open the box in my hand. 'Thank you. I'm very grateful.'

'You should go home and give it to her. Good evening, Mr Berry.'

As I put down the phone I thought I heard a strange double click like a computer mouse.

I slipped the Tiffany box into my pocket and thought I'd better do what everyone kept telling me to do.

Go home to my wife.

CHAPTER FIVE

The situation was worsening. The hill tribes in Jadzikistan were dug into their positions and the combined NATO forces were finding penetration impossible. For each step forward, for the destruction of one cell with three grenade launchers, ammunition and fifteen-year-old guns, the NATO forces took five steps backwards. There were ambushes on steep mountain passes, retaliation exercises by those loyal to the new leader, Khaled Al-Khalim, which involved shooting whole villages. For every Jadzik killed by NATO, Khaled ordered the massacre of the non-racially-pure of his own people, of the villagers praying to a different God.

The destruction by Khaled Al-Khalim of his own people had brought in NATO nearly three years ago. He had taken over from his father, the notorious Sabbin Al-Khalim seventeen years before and appeared to be going down in history as the most wanted man in the world. The Jadzik programme of weapons of mass destruction had been halted, NATO was sure of that, or at least that was what Brigadier-General Mike Patton had told the Prime Minister of Great Britain in his last briefing via secure satellite link.

'Three months, Prime Minster', Patton told him, watching another mine explode in the distance. 'Three months and he'll be on his knees. We've cut off all UN aid, supply lines are down and his people all want him out. It's just the hill-tribesmen and the regular army.'

The Prime Minister had used this information at Question Time that Tuesday in the House of Commons to try to quell the minor revolt amongst his own back-benchers. An investment of three months to win back an important oil supplier was worth the penny hike in income tax that his Chancellor of the Exchequer had had to levy last year.

Meanwhile, Khaled Al-Khalim was, so the newspaper reports ran, in high-level talks with neighboring countries regarding his own escape and that of his family. The villa in the South of France, in *Cannes Californie*, had been seized by the French Government. The mansion on the shores of Lake Geneva had been boarded up and the duplex in Cadogan Square in London had been repossessed. Khaled's pre-planned escape valves had all been blown and he needed to get as far away from Jadzikistan as he could before NATO's tanks rolled into the capital, found his underground bunkers and carted him off.

Attempts to infiltrate Khaled's circle had failed miserably. Attempts to negotiate direct with him on humanitarian grounds had also failed.

Everything had failed.

There was no other option than to crush his country in order to remove the most evil despot since Attila the Hun, on whom, incidentally, Khaled modeled himself.

I asked Georgina to turn off the Ten O'Clock News when I got in. I got the tail-end of the Jadzikistan broadcast and I was glad I had missed the pictures of dying or dead children they normally showed. They reminded me of Sophie. Georgina switched it off with the remote control and stared at me.

'Are you having an affair?', she blurted out.

'What?'

'Are you having an affair?'

'Of course not.'

'You're never home before ten, Jonathan.'

'It's all this work.'

'Is it now? Is it really?'

She swiveled round on the large leather Knoll chair to face me, her hands grasping the arms tightly. I knelt down in front of her, still in my pinstripe suit and tie.

'Darling', I began, 'if I told you what happened to me today you wouldn't believe it.'

'Try me.'

'I got the biggest murder for years. It's Martin Hotson. Can you believe it?'

'No. no I can't. He doesn't need to murder anyone. He's rich, and anyway he's a friend of Chas and Brenda's.'

'It happened thirty years ago. At a party. With a swimming pool. He was acquitted. But now there's no more double jeopardy, you see and…'

'And they're going to try him again?' she asked wide-eyed. 'Really?'

'Really.'

I kissed her on the cheek and stroked her hair.

'Georgie? I felt so bad about missing Ben's carol concert and running out on the girls like that this afternoon. I've been a bad husband, I know I have. I got you a little something.'

I handed her the Tiffany box. She took it from me, opened it quickly and then shut it with a bang.

'How much?' she asked. 'How much did this cost, Jonathan?'

'I...I...'

'I can't be *bought*, you know.'

'It's to say sorry, Georgina.'

She took another look inside the box.

'It is rather lovely, though', she said after a long silence.

'I thought so, darling.'

'And you bought it for me?'

'Of course I did, darling.'

'Who's Kate Bowyer?'

'Who?'

What the hell was she talking about?

'She's another barrister', I replied calmly. 'She helped me on the Kelsey defence.'

'I see.'

Georgina stood up from the large leather swivel chair and walked over to the telephone answering machine.

'She left this at about nine', she said flatly and depressed the *Answer/Play* button. The answer-phone beeped and then burst into life.

'Hi Jonathan it's Kate', said Kate into the machine. 'I hope this is the right number. Just called to tell you that you really shouldn't have. It's so lovely! Anyhow I was thinking of getting one but it's a nice thought. I'll come round your chambers any time you like – after court - to look at any documents you like. You always were a charmer. Call me.'

The answer-phone beeped and Georgina turned it off.

'Well?', she asked.

'Well what?'

'What's all that about, Jonathan? She sounds like she knows you very well.'

'We went to law school together.'

'You never mentioned her to me. Have you been having an affair with her?'

I thought of that thing Kate did with her legs in my office.

'No', I replied.

'Have you ever slept with her?'

'No', I replied truthfully.

'Did you buy her a present too?'

'Darling, I – '

'What was it?'

Georgina slapped me hard round the face. I stood there and took it. My face had been going red before she'd even hit me.

'I didn't buy her anything', I replied truthfully.

'Then who did?', she shouted.

I shut my eyes in horror. Jacob Potts, Hussain Tarzi and the whole present business. It was getting out of hand.

'It must have been my clerk, Jacob. Or this new solicitor I told you about. You know. Tarzi.'

'*What?*'

'They knew she helped me and she didn't charge very much. Hundred and fifty I think. They're paying me a thousand times that, darling. Think about it.'

'Oh I am, Jonathan, believe me I am.'

She certainly looked like she was.

'I swear there's nothing going on', I said. 'I swear it.'

'You do, do you?'

'Yes.'

'Do you swear on your children's life that there's nothing going on with Kate Bowyer?'

I gulped.

'I swear on my children's life', I replied somberly. 'There's nothing. I swear it.'

Georgina opened the little blue box and stared at the ring. She looked up at me, smiling at her, her finger-marks still on my face.

'Well', she began, more softly, 'I suppose it is very beautiful.'

She took it out of the box and held it up under the light. It sparkled magnificently.

'You bought it specially for me, Jonathan?'

'Of course I did my love. You're the love of my life, the mother of my children. I'm sorry I'm working hard but if things continue then we'll be able to get the house we've always dreamed of – '

'Like Chas and Brenda's?'

'Maybe', I replied hesitantly. 'Maybe.'

'Jonathan?' she asked quietly.

'Yes my love', I replied.

'The ring you bought specially for me?'

'Yes, darling?'

'It doesn't fit.'

I knew I could trust the Middle Temple Treasurer, Sir Wilfred Lambert, my old senior tutor from Oxford. I'd known him since I was eighteen, seventeen whole years ago. He was utterly charming and had an equally charming wife Janice whose double-starred First had eclipsed even his own. He was an academic but he also understood the commercial world which is presumably why he was made treasurer.

'Well, well, well', he said after I'd explained my misgivings with H. Tarzi & Co. 'Well, well, well.'

'Well?', I asked. 'What's your view, Sir Wilfred?'

'My dear, dear boy. I'd just keep your mouth shut if I were you', he said. 'They pay you well and their actions, though a trifle eccentric, are not unusual.'

'No?'

'You see my dear boy, you've been acting for penniless crooks for a number of years and your fees have kept pace with the penury of your clients. That and the legal aid pay-scales, no doubt.'

'Yes, Sir Wilfred.'

'If you'd only have become a City solicitor like I advised you you'd be on half a million a year without all this shilly-shallying.'

Sir Wilfred had ulterior motives for everything but he was so transparent that it was really quite charming.

'Your old College fund', he continued, 'is looking dreadfully barren at present. Dreadfully barren indeed.'

He fixed me with a grin and a stare that heightened the veins in his cheeks.

'I don't suppose, my dear boy, that it would be too much to ask for you to distribute some of your largesse in the direction of the College? To give back to a worthy cause a small part of the fruits of your labours?'

'Well, of course not Sir Wilfred.'

I looked out at the view from his rooms, set on the top floor of an eighteenth-century building. You could just see the

River Thames. The heart of The Temple. The heart of London.

It made my room in Wessex Yard look like a prison cell in comparison.

'And we'll agree that you're doing absolutely the right thing with this, this Tarzi fellow. Absolutely the proper thing. What a gentleman would do. Take the bugger's money, keep your dignity, win a case and everyone comes up smiling.'

Just like Sir Wilfred was now.

'Would ten thousand be too much to ask?' he asked innocently.

If all my cases went the right way I'd make four times what I made last year. I could write off ten thousand against tax as a charitable contribution. I could earn that in one day on the Martin Hotson murder. I looked into Sir Wilfred's eyes and realized he'd already made the same calculation. After all, he'd always been one step ahead of me.

'I'd try and settle that arbitration, my dear boy', he said to me. 'Crime's your thing. I can see that now. Use your acting. I still remember you in that play...'

His eyes glazed over momentarily.

'You'll do your murder', he continued, 'and they'll be falling over themselves to get a little piece of you, mark my words.'

I nodded. He was probably right. I'd just scraped by with a Two-Two – a *Desmond* – and the intricacies of the Commercial Court were probably beyond me. Sir Wilfred was always right. He knew he was. That's why poor little barristers like me came to see him.

'Care for a sherry?' he asked, smiling beatifically.

'I'd love one', I replied, catching a glance at the morning papers on his desk. I wasn't on the front page with anything. It was just that bloody business in Jadzikistan, a full length picture of Khaled Al-Khalim in military uniform splashed all over *The Times*.

There was now only a week to go before Christmas and Georgina hadn't forgiven me. Ben, Mollie and Amy had already told Father Christmas what they wanted for their presents and the courts were now shut other than for emergency business. Chambers was emptying out and there was little incentive for me to work, seeing as there was no one else to talk to apart from Jacob, who didn't seem to celebrate Christmas. Tarzi was still away on business – he'd been gone for more than a week – and I'd heard nothing more from Martin Hotson or Chas Mullion since that evening at Velvet.

I didn't feel like visiting Desmond Lyons in jail – the thought was too depressing. Customs House had emptied out – civil servants' holidays started a week before everyone else's. I'd had a Christmas card from Kate Bowyer telling me she was off to Ireland for the holidays to see her sister but wishing me and my family a merry old time over the festive season. I burned the card, just in case Georgina came to visit. I wanted to surprise her and the kids, so I packed up my laptop and my leather document case and told Jacob that for once I would be taking a break from chambers over Christmas.

'Luvverly, sir', he said in his deadpan way. 'All the best for the season, sir.'

'No presents or cards for me, Jacob?'

'No sir. Just the one from Miss Bowyer, sir.'

'Oh. Yes. Nothing from Mr Tarzi?'

'Not a bean, sir.'

For once in my life I was elated *not* to have received a gift.

When I opened the door of our rented house in Holland Park an hour later, Georgina raced into my arms and kissed me full on the lips.

'I love you, Mr Berry', she said. 'You're so clever. And *I'm* the one who should be sorry.'

I smiled, not having the faintest idea what she was talking about. Maybe she'd got the ring to fit. Or maybe she was back on the tranquilisers.

'When were you going to tell me?', she asked.

'Tell you what?'

'Oh come off it, Jonathan. Shall we tell the kids together? I've kept your little secret.'

I still hadn't the faintest idea what she was talking about.

'Okay', I said hesitantly. 'Let's tell them. You can do the talking. I'm a little tired.'

My confusing wife, whom I noticed was finally wearing the Tiffany ring, dragged me upstairs to the children's playroom.

'Ben? Mollie? Amy? Mummy and daddy have got a surprise for you.'

I looked at their innocent faces, beautiful, staring up at us wide-eyed and expectantly.

'What is it mummy?', asked Ben, bouncing up and down on the lime-green sofa.

'What is it? What is it?', shouted Mollie. Amy just stood there sucking her thumb and watching me carefully with her big brown eyes. Georgina turned to them and grasped my hand.

'You know how cold and wet and miserable it is when England gets dark?', she said.

I was watching her just as eagerly as the kids were.

'Well', she continued, 'daddy has been very clever at work and has booked us…a holiday!'

I smiled, marveling at my own generosity and wondering where the hell I'd decided to take us all.

'Where, mummy?' asked Ben.

'Yes, tell them where', I said, giving Georgina a peck on the cheek.

'Mauritius', she said beaming, 'and we're going First Class!'

I gripped her hand tightly and tried to do the mental calculation. Five tickets, First Class…

'And what's more', Georgina continued, 'we're staying at one of those lovely big hotels where you can have your own room and they have special children's activities all day so mummy and daddy can do grown up things.'

'Wow!', said Ben.

'Wow!', said I.

'We're going on an aeroplane?', asked Mollie.

Georgina nodded.

'Where did you find the tickets?' I asked her.

'On your desk you silly fool. You must have forgotten to put them away. Unless you *wanted* me to find them. They're there now.'

'I'll just go and…errr…put them somewhere safe', I said, moving out of the room and crossing the corridor.

I popped into our bedroom and went to my desk over by the window. In the middle lay a velvet pouch stamped '*Royal Airways*' and inside were five tickets and a hotel reservation.

Perhaps I should have been delirious with excitement, but all I could think about was how someone must have broken into our house to deliver them.

CHAPTER SIX

It was all over. In a pre-Christmas offensive, the combined forces of NATO swept aside the last remaining vestiges of the Jadzik army and captured the bunkers that lay underneath the capital city, renamed *Khalim* in honour of its murderous leader. In front of me on my blue plastic tray, covering the whole front page of my complimentary copy of *The Times* was a picture of Khaled Al-Khalim in handcuffs, staring blankly at his military photographer.

'Thank God', said Georgina, looking over my shoulder. 'Thank God they stopped the bastard.'

'More champagne, madam?', asked the air stewardess.

'Lovely', said Georgina, holding out her glass. Behind us in row two the kids were fast asleep.

'I'll have some too', I said, looking up and smiling.

'Of course, sir.'

She poured me out a glass of Bollinger and handed me a menu.

'The chef's special today is grilled lobster with *Coquille St Jacques*'.

Georgina kissed me on the cheek.

'Oh God, not again', she said, smiling.

'Media circus', I said, looking down at *The Times* pull-out section entitled *The Final Days of Al-Khalim*.

'Disastrous dictatorship', she said to me, looking over my shoulder at the paper. 'Hope they can make something of it.'

'It's all about the oil, isn't it', I replied.

'Stop thinking about your arbitration', she said. 'It's all about *money*. It's all about greed.'

I raised my glass.

'To...'

'Be careful what you wish for', she replied. I took a long sip of Bollinger, looked again at the picture of Khaled Al-Khalim in handcuffs and felt, somehow, that the world was now a safer place.

'Isn't this your case?' said Georgina suddenly, holding another newspaper in front of me.

'Where?'

'Bottom left.'

I took the paper off her and looked down to the bottom left-hand corner on page five. There was a picture of Colleen Marden, the woman Desmond Lyons, my client, allegedly raped and then bludgeoned with a bicycle-pump. I scanned the accompanying article.   And then a second time, a little more slowly.

'Shit.'

'What is it Jonathan?'

'She committed suicide.'

'Oh no! Poor girl! Is that the one whose grandfather is…'

'Yes. Yes it is.'

I swigged my champagne quickly.

'No jury's going to acquit now', I said. 'Desmond's going down. I've never lost a rape before.'

'But if he did it…'

'It's not the point. I've never lost a rape.'

Georgina stroked my hand and stared at the black and white picture of Colleen Marden.

'I know how he must feel', she said slowly.

'Who? Lyons?'

'No! That judge. Lord Marden. Her grandfather. Like us. With Sophie. At least he's got someone to blame.'

'My client didn't kill her!'

'Jonathan! How can you say that? It's obvious why she did it!'

'You see? That's why I'm going to lose.'

I got up from my seat.

'Jonathan, where are you going?'

'I'm going to see if they've got a satellite phone on board.'

'Oh no you're not!'

Mauritius came and went. No satellite phone and no more surprises. We spent Christmas Day on the beach and instead of turkey we ate a giant swordfish, freshly-caught and roasted right in front of us. Work should have been the last thing on my mind but I'd brought my laptop with me. Jacob had scanned and uploaded all the old documents from the thirty-year-old swimming-pool murder and I read them all.

I was earning the five First Class tickets and the hotel bill. Every night, when the kids were in bed and we were sitting by the Indian Ocean feeling the cool breeze across the still water, Georgina toasted me and I silently toasted H. Tarzi & Co. for giving us our first proper holiday since our honeymoon in Italy.

We returned the day before New Year's Day. I called chambers to tell Jacob I was back. He picked up the phone on the second ring.

'Mr Berry?'

'Jacob. How are – '

'You better come over righ' now, Mr Berry.'

'Now?'

I looked at the clock. It was five minutes to five in the afternoon and I was still jet-lagged.

'I've got Mr Tarzi 'ere and 'ee wants a word.'

67

'Can't we speak on the phone?'

'Ee don't like phones, sir.'

I took the Volvo because it was the night before New Year's Eve and I'd never get a cab. I had left a message thanking Tarzi for Mauritius before we left but, as always, he'd been traveling. Now at least I'd be able to thank him in person, for the holiday and for Georgina's Tiffany ring.

The streets were misty and even though it wasn't raining I needed the windscreen-wipers to clear away the moisture which hung heavily in the air.

Sir Wilfred's words came back to me as I headed past Marble Arch. *Take the money. Keep your dignity. Keep your mouth shut.*

I cut right, down Park Lane and then left down Upper Brook Street. Claridges looked busy. I wiggled around the back roads and drove past Velvet. There was a long line of limousines with blacked-out windows all the way along the pavement on both sides of Mount Street, only leaving a gap right outside the Velvet front door. It looked like someone was having a party. A big party.

I'd put on one of the three new pinstripe suits I'd had made just down the road in Savile Row, tax deductible as I needed them for work. The tailor had let slip that all of Mr Tarzi's clients came there and received a ten percent discount. As I was a barrister, not a client, the tailor said he'd knock a little extra off.

I headed down to Holborn and then along Fleet Street. The porter was manning the security booth on Temple Avenue, sipping his hot chocolate and wiping the condensation off the windows with his sleeve. He waved at me when I pulled up and lifted the barrier instantly. I drove in and parked my reliable Volvo in between an Aston Martin and a Bentley. The commercial bar drove a better class of car than I did but then you couldn't get seven people in an Aston. I walked through the quadrangles and alleyways to 21 Wessex Yard where I found Jacob waiting for me.

'Ello sir', said Jacob as I walked through the door. 'Damp, ain't it?'

'Yes', I replied.

'Good 'oliday?'

'Lovely, thank you Jacob.'

'Read your murder documents, sir?'

'Yes thank you Jacob.'

'Eard abou' the Marden gel's suicide?'

'Yes, Jacob.'

I wondered if I should ask him how the plane tickets in their little velvet pouch got into my bedroom.

'Mr Tarzi's in yer room, sir, waitin' for yer.'

'Thank you, Jacob. Do you know what it's about?'

'Aven't the faintest, sir. I suggest you go in. Ee's in a funny mood.'

'Oh?'

I took off my coat and hung it on the peg next to Jacob's desk, smoothed down my lapels and walked into my room to find Hussain Tarzi holding one of the four hundred cartons of Russian cigarettes that Customs insisted I keep at chambers.

'May I take one?', he asked me, breaking open a carton and fishing out a packet.

'I think they're evidence, Mr Tarzi -'

'Believe me, it doesn't matter', he replied, lighting one of the hooky Russian cigarettes.

He exhaled deeply and I went over to the window to open it.

'Please don't', he said.

'You don't want me to open the window?'

'No, thank you.'

I shrugged and sat down. I couldn't see an ashtray anywhere so I buzzed Jacob. He brought one in almost immediately and left without saying a word.

Hussain Tarzi smoked the whole cigarette without saying a word either. I watched his delicate fingers as he held the fake Marlboro Light over the marble Art Deco ashtray and finally stubbed it out.

'I'm sorry', he said quietly, 'but it has been a long day. You have also been traveling?'

'Yes. We came back today. I'm probably still a little jet-lagged. Thank you for the –'

'Thanks are not necessary', said Tarzi. 'I hope you enjoyed your holiday. It has been a long time since I took one myself. All this work...all this traveling...I find it very stressful sometimes...very stressful indeed.'

'I know what you mean', I replied as sympathetically as I could.

'Do you?', Tarzi asked me, suddenly animated. 'Do you, Jonathan?'

'Well, I mean, the work, I enjoy it immensely. I like to think…I thrive on pressure', I said to him.

'There is pressure and then there is pressure', he replied. 'Do you work better under pressure, Jonathan?'

'I like to think I rise to the challenge.'

'We must all do that, Jonathan. All do our duty, whatever the risks.'

'Risks?'

'The risk of losing, Jonathan, hangs over all of us. It can eat a man up and swallow him whole, paralyse him with fear. It can stop him from doing his duty.'

I wondered who he was talking about.

'I think a positive outlook is best', I replied, 'negativity breeds negativity. I've never really worried about losing a case', I added, which wasn't quite true.

'Wisely said', said Tarzi. 'I'm glad we're working together, Jonathan. You positively fill me with confidence. I have no worries about the Kelsey arbitration and the Hotson murder. Jacob tells me you're well up to speed on both matters and that one of your other cases may soon fall apart due to the unfortunate demise of the prosecution's main witness.'

'I'm really not sure about that –'

'It will leave you more time. What are you doing this evening?'

'Well, I hadn't really – '

'Would you like to come to a party?' he asked, lighting another hooky cigarette.

I didn't need to ask him where it would be.

'Georgina?'

'Oh, Jonathan. I'd wondered where you'd gone. You took the car.'

'Yes. It's business I'm afraid. This chap Tarzi. Asked me to a party. Can't say no, really.'

'Darling…I was hoping we could have a quiet night in, put the kids to bed, open a bottle of bubbly…'

'I'd love to, but I think something big's happening.'

'Haven't you got enough on your plate? You're becoming a serial networker.'

'God I hope not. Isn't that what you and Chas used to do all the time at the bank?'

'Yup. That's one of the reasons I'm now a housewife.'

'I won't be late.'

'Look Jonathan, I'm jet-lagged and you must be too. I'll probably be asleep by ten. And remember you're driving.'

'I'll leave the car at the Temple overnight if I have to.'

'Bring in lots of work so you can buy me more presents like my beautiful ring.'

'I'll do my best', I replied, and hung up.

Velvet was extremely busy. Chas Mullion was there together with Martin Hotson, the man from Harbor Shipping and six others, all at Hussain Tarzi's table. It was funny us all being members of the same club.

'Always ten, you said Mr Tarzi?'

'Yes Jonathan.'

I nodded, counting only nine clients.

'We celebrate every year', said Chas Mullion, 'every year, the night before New Year's Eve.'

'Any reason?'

'Tradition', said Tarzi. 'Tradition. You know all about tradition, Jonathan, don't you? Your family has a wonderful history. I've read all about it. One of your ancestors was hanged, you know, by Oliver Cromwell.'

'Oh? Did Jacob tell you?'

'My assistant Googled you.'

'Ah.'

'Here he comes!', said Tarzi in hushed tones. 'The new President of the Club.'

All three hundred people in the enormous ballroom stood and clapped. They turned to the door and gazed at the man walking in, smiling and shaking the hands of the men in front of him, most of them in dinner suits. The applause was deafening and I strained to get a look at who it was. He was coming our way and another chair was whisked towards our table in readiness.

It was Lord Marden of Winchelsea.

'My dear Jonathan', he said to me as the sommelier brought another bottle of '82 Margaux to our table. 'I am very glad we're sitting next to each other.'

I watched as Tarzi removed another hooky cigarette from the packet he'd snaffled from my room and lit it, sending part of my Customs case evidence up in smoke.

'I am too, your Lordship', I replied warily.

'I've heard great things about you, my boy, great things indeed. I had dinner with Sir Wilfred Lambert only yesterday.'

'Oh?'

'He was very positive about you, very positive. I understand he is your, how shall I put it? Your mentor, I believe is the right term?'

'I'm very attached to Sir Wilfred, your Lordship.'

'Please, my boy. When we're here at the club you can call me Bill.'

'Alright. Thank you...Bill.'

'That's better.'

He took a long sip from his four hundred pound glass of wine.

'I can help you, Jonathan. If you like, I can *also* be your...mentor.'

'Err…thank you, Bill.'

'You can discuss anything with me here at the club and it will go no further.'

He tapped the side of his head with his forefinger.

'I keep a lot of stuff up here, Jonathan. And here is where it stays.'

I nodded sagely and took a gulp of the velvety red liquid in my glass.

'For example', he said casually, 'the Lyons trial. I am still in mourning for my grand-daughter so you must excuse me if I become emotional.'

I looked closely at his well-worn face, grooved deeply with a thousand cases, a thousand judgments, a face that had dealt with the death penalty in the Privy Council. He didn't look the least emotional. I wondered how many men and women he'd already sent to their deaths.

'Desmond Lyons is responsible for Colleen's death', he said in a whisper. He looked at me, waiting for a response. I looked down into my wine and took another sip.

'Cigarette, Jonathan?' asked Tarzi, holding out the packet to me.

I'd given up smoking years ago but I was a little unsettled and so I took one, letting Tarzi light it for me. I looked back at Lord Marden. He was still looking at me with those hooded eyes of his, waiting.

'Jonathan?', he said. 'What's your view?'

'I understand how you feel', I replied after taking a long drag from my own evidence. 'You know I do.'

'I wonder if you do', said Lord Marden. 'A successful attempt to discredit my dead grand-daughter would seem to be the only way your client can avoid paying for his crime.'

'How's it going, Jonathan?' asked Martin Hotson suddenly from across the table. 'All well?'

I gave him my most winning smile and nodded.

'It's going well', I said to him, catching another look at Tarzi, who was nervously lighting another cigarette from the still-burning embers of his last one.

'Do you understand what I'm saying to you, Jonathan?' whispered Lord Marden. 'As your mentor. As your *friend*, I hope.'

'I…I think so.'

'Lyons must pay for his crime.'

'I'm sure the jury will make the right decision', I replied carefully.

'As long as we understand each other. You have a bright future ahead of you', he said warmly. 'It would be such a shame for it to come grinding to a halt, all because of a simple misunderstanding.'

I took another cigarette from the pack on the table and lit it.

'It's fine…Bill', I replied. 'No misunderstandings.'

'Good boy', he said, patting me on the back.

'You settled yet?', the man from Harbor Shipping asked Tarzi loudly. Tarzi turned to me.

'Jonathan?', he asked. 'Would you like to tell our client

what progress has been made in the Nigerian arbitration?'

I suddenly wished I was at home with Georgina.

CHAPTER SEVEN

I got horribly drunk the night of the *Velvet* party, never before having been surrounded by so many of my cases in one place. I drove home that night and nearly crashed the Volvo, but I made it back to my bed, somehow. I spent the following day, New Year's Eve, with the kids and Georgina. We were all still suntanned from Mauritius. We went walking in Holland Park, watched the first snowflakes fall on the crisp ground and drank steaming hot mugs of tea in the park café. We laughed at the ducks scrabbling about on the ice and then we saw Chas and Brenda. Chas winked at me when he saw my bleary eyes.

'Been on the sauce, kiddo?' he said, elbowing me heartily.

'Ha ha', I replied with what I hoped was a convincing smile. 'Ha ha.'

'What you up to tonight?' he asked innocently.

'No parties', I replied. 'We're staying in.'

'Oh. Shame. We're having a big one round ours.'

'Thanks Chas. But I can only devote my attention to one

person tonight.'

That person kissed me on the cheek and I wrapped my arm round her. England was lovely when it was crisp and bright and clear.

England was even lovelier when you had a lot of money and I was feeling quite good because I'd billed more than a hundred hours on the murder trial, forty thousand pounds plus VAT, all in the space of two weeks. That night Georgina and I snuggled up to each other on the sofa watching men in kilts dance a reel on BBC2 and we counted down the New Year together before joining in with a chorus of *Auld Lang Syne*, just the two of us.

We spent the morning in bed, letting the kids run riot around the rest of the house. I read some papers in the afternoon, looked again at the Kelsey arbitration and had a quiet evening in, again. I tried not to think about work, but it was very difficult. All I could see swimming before my eyes was Lord Marden's face. All I could hear was Duncan Markson's laughter and all I could smell was the smell of my Customs evidence, my hooky cigarettes, chain-smoked by Tarzi and now me.

It was the night after New Year's Day. As I looked over at the red glow of the alarm clock – it was three in the morning and I couldn't sleep - I resolved to keep at least one of my resolutions.

***

It was pouring with rain as I stood outside the grim façade of the King Midas Kebab House in Tufnell Park, North London.

It was set in a small parade of shops which included a bookmakers', a boarded-up pub, an undertakers' and a Chinese restaurant. I looked up at the garish red sign with its gold lettering and the little picture of King Midas himself, holding a gold bar. *'From 11 til late,'* ran the little sign hanging by the door. My watch, my faithful old Rolex, told me I had five minutes to wait until the doors were thrown open and I could order from the long and uninviting menu that was plastered all over the window.

Apart from the small shopping parade the street was lined with good-looking but uncared-for semi-detached Victorian villas which had all been split into flats judging by the number of bells outside each front door. Five, I counted at one house. Eight at another. The sky was grey and the clouds moved across it quickly, hurrying to escape from the drabness of Tufnell Park on a wet Tuesday morning.

No-one had suggested to me that I come here. Tarzi had said nothing. The man from Harbor Shipping even less. No-one had discussed my defence, the one I'd drafted with the assistance of Kate Bowyer and served on Kelsey nearly a month ago. I'd tried to settle it three times now with Duncan Markson, counsel for Kelsey. The last offer was five hundred thousand but he'd turned it down.

I was thinking of writing off the record and without prejudice to the arbitrator to say that Harbor Shipping was prepared to fork out half a million dollars to settle.

It was called a *Calderbank* offer I think, although I wasn't exactly an expert, but I knew it would protect our position on costs if the claimants eventually won less than the amount offered.

Duncan had laughed at me for a third time, this time at the *Wig and Pen* over a beer. It was infuriating. He'd win nothing, I told him, and he said he knew. If Kelsey accepted half a million

I'd get half that from Tarzi and Harbor Shipping. I even considered offering Duncan a little something from my share but stopped myself. After all, I might not have been the only one wearing a wire.

On the basis that I needed to get to the bottom of the affair and on the basis that I wasn't about to go to Nigeria or Delaware, I'd decided to come to look at the one place referred to in my defence that was within spitting distance of my rented home in Holland Park. Someone had sent a telex to Kelsey from the King Midas Kebab House, Tufnell Park in the name of *Shell Nigeria* and I wanted to see the place.

The shutters went up, a key turned in a lock and the door swung open to the first customer of the day. Me. I'd dressed down, in my jeans and I hadn't shaved that morning on purpose. I'd decided to speak in *Sarf Larnden*.

'Mornin' guv', I said.

'Hello hello hello' said a fifty-year-old man wearing a turban with a long beard, ushering me inside. 'What's the poison today?'

'Huh?'

'Whayouwan'?' he asked. 'Kebab?'

'Oh, yeah, fanks mate. Wiv a bi' o' chilli sauce.'

'Doner?'

'Yeah, tha'll do.'

'You sit. You wait. Meat is cold.'

I sat. I waited. I watched the meat turning on the spit, warming up. It was obvious it had been there all night, for at least one night. The smell was not nice, a little like returning from holiday, turning on your fridge again and suddenly realizing you'd forgotten to clear out all the food before you left.

There certainly weren't any clues in the shop. The man serving looked a bit like Osama bin Laden but that wasn't uncommon in this part of London. He was actually rather personable and kept trying to amuse me as I waited for the meat to warm up.

'You live here?', he asked me.

'I live in Larnden, if thas' wo' yer mean', I replied.

'Is beautiful here, no?'

'Errr, yeah', I replied. 'Specially when the sarn's out.'

'The what?'

'The sun', I repeated, a little more clearly.

'No no no', he said. 'Sun too hot. Rain better. Cooling.'

'Where you from?' I asked him.

'Colindale', he replied. 'On the Northern Line', he added, proudly.

'Born there?', I asked nonchalantly.

'No', he replied. 'No, I was not born in Colindale. You drive taxi-cab?'

'Uuh? Naa', I replied, shaking my head. 'Why d'ya ask?'

'There is one on the other side of the street. It is illegally parked on the two yellow lines. The police will take it away.'

I peered out of the steamy window and saw the cab sitting

there. There was no driver, just a man sitting in the back with an earpiece, like the ones everyone uses for mobile phones.

'Not mine', I replied.

The meat was heating up on the large vertical spit and the rotten-fridge smell had given way to something a little more appealing.

'Smells luvverly.'

'I am a vegetarian', he said. 'Personally I not like the smell.'

'Ow can yer stand workin' 'ere then?', I asked him.

'Is job. You have job?'

'Oh, err, yeah, yeah I do. Err...work nights. Security.'

'You must be very brave man.'

'Err...naa, not really', I replied, wondering why I'd said I was in security.

'I am saving up', said the man with the beard and the turban. 'I am saving up to return to my homeland.'

I looked around the shop again as my kebab house chef started slicing the meat off the spit and laying it on a thick wooden block next to a packet of *pitta* bread.

He had delicate fingers, just like Tarzi's.

There was a telephone sitting behind the counter and what looked like an old fax machine, but I couldn't see a telex.

'You own upstairs 'n all?', I asked him.

He nodded and then I had a moment of inspiration.

'Ever 'ad a break-in?'

He looked up at me curiously.

'You mean, thievery?', he asked.

'Yeah. Ever 'ad a problem? See', I continued quickly, 'seein' as I gotta backgroun' in security I could check it 'ou for ya, give you a few tips, like.'

Osama scratched his turban.

'I had problem last year', he said. 'Would payment be involved?'

'Naaa. Maybe' – I looked quickly at the plastic menu behind him – 'maybe you could just throw in a bag o' onion rings.'

'You want eat first or after?', he asked me.

I looked at what I was going to get. I didn't want to eat at all. He grabbed an onion from a bag behind him and started chopping it quickly on the thick wooden board.

'After', I said.

'You not con-man?', he said suddenly, gazing hard at me.

I laughed.

There were only two rooms and they were both almost exactly the same. It looked like one person lived in each, Osama in one and the old man smoking a roll-up, also in a turban, in the other. He sat in a chair watching the BBC news on a black-and-white television set. He murmured something to me and I nodded deferentially to him. There were posters blu-tacked to the walls, pictures of a beautiful sunset over mountains, a vintage Ferrari and rather incongruously that famous poster of the girl in a tennis dress with racket and ball, baring her bottom. There were no papers, no filing cabinet, nothing out of the ordinary.

Apart from the television there was nothing remotely electronic. Not even a telephone. There were rugs on the floor, a single bed in each room and a small fridge on the landing. I looked inside the fridge and there were just bottles and bottles of Lipton's Iced Tea. I looked quickly at the locks on the windows and the skylight up to the roof, then headed back down again towards the smell of my kebab.

The first bite was good, the second fantastic. I hadn't had a kebab since university where Saturday nights involved getting drunk, eating a curry, getting a little more drunk, getting thrown out of the pub and then getting a kebab on the way home before throwing it all up again the next morning. I looked up at the clock. It was eleven-fifteen and I hadn't had any breakfast.

'Security's fine', I said between mouthfuls. 'Luvverly kebab, gov.'

'I take your word for it.'

'So where you from, before Colindale I mean?', I asked. 'Where's yer 'omeland?'

Osama's eyes glazed over.

'It is far away', he said. 'It is wild place. Beautiful mountains, people friendly but crazy government. You read newspaper?'

I nodded, taking another bite.

'Then you have wrong idea already', he said. 'You should go one day, go see why Jadzikistan is beautiful place.'

I looked outside. The black cab was still there on the

double yellow lines, the man in the back still on the telephone. Two builders came into the kebab house and asked for two doners. I finished my kebab quickly, paid Osama and left.

It was clearing up slightly and I walked round the corner to my Volvo. A parking ticket was stuffed under the windscreen-wiper. My year was not beginning that well. Whoever had sent the telex from The King Midas Kebab House had taken their machine with them. Either that or they hadn't sent it from the King Midas Kebab House at all.

I put the parking ticket on the seat next to me and set off for Middle Temple.

I passed a large sign advertising women's stockings and suddenly thought of Kate Bowyer. I hadn't responded to her answer-phone message, the one Georgina had found thanking me for a gift I'd never sent her.

She was all woman, was Kate, which also meant that there was no way she could be a member of Velvet. The least I could do would be to buy her a drink and find out exactly what gift I'd bought her. Unfortunately, before I could think of seeing Kate I had to pay another visit to my coke-dealing rapist to clear up any misunderstandings.

***

'Y'alrigh', *Janny*', drawled Desmond Lyons as I walked into his holding cell.

It wasn't a question.

'When did you hear about this, Desmond?'

'On telly, man. Two week ago, now.'

'How did you feel?'

'Bitch couldn' live wiv 'ersell, *Janny*. Shi' appens, like de number plate. I sorry for da woman.'

'This means the prosecution have lost their main witness, Desmond.'

He smiled, showing me dazzling white teeth and one large gold one near the centre.

'I knows, *Janny*.'

I shut my eyes and all I could see was Lord Marden's face warning me about misunderstandings.

'It doesn't mean the prosecution is dropping their case, Desmond. They've got the video tapes from the police station, the sixteen hours of interviews with Colleen Marden and they've still got all the forensic evidence.'

'When dey 'ears me speak, they knows I not dunn nothin', *Janny*. You tell me what to say and I say it, bro.'

'I think you should plead guilty.'

He stood up angrily and banged the desk with his fists.

'No way, man!'

The guard opened the door, electric stun-gun in hand but I waved him away.

'Sit down, Desmond', I said calmly.

'You fink I dunnit, don' ya? I tol' ya, *Janny*. I 'ad sex wi' 'er. That were all. I ne'er raped 'er. Der were consent.'

'But you did hit her with a bicycle pump?'

'Yeah.'

'That's assault and battery, Desmond. Two to five, just for that. No jury's going to believe you didn't rape her. Plead guilty, Desmond, for the love of God plead guilty.'

Desmond sat down and stared at the formica table-top.

'Fer da love a God', he said. 'Fer da love a God.'

'Is that a yes? If it goes to trial they could give you life or as good as.'

'You on my side, righ' *Janny*?'

'Yes Desmond. Of course I am.'

'You owes me – wha' was it now – a *dooty-a-care*.'

'Yes I do. Now who've you been speaking to, Desmond?'

'Dis bloke in 'ere, knows a little a da law, thas' wha' ee tol' me. Don' admit nuffin. Never.'

'Look, Desmond. I've been doing rapes for a long time and I can honestly say this case is unwinnable. Any other barrister would say the same.'

'*Janny*, da' ain't what me wanna hear.'

'But it's the truth.'

'Come closer, *Janny*.'

Despite the heavy odour I did as my client requested.

'You pu' me on de stand and I tell 'em the truth', he whispered.

'They won't believe you, Desmond.'

'Dey will. Dey giv da woman a blood test, righ'? I mean, after she go to da police station and tell 'em I rape her?'

I opened the file and checked. They'd taken hundreds of photographs, a semen sample and they'd found Desmond's DNA fingerprint. They'd found traces of her blood on Desmond too so they must have given Colleen Marden a blood-test to make the match. The trouble was I couldn't find the results in the file.

'I can't see them here, Desmond, but they must be somewhere.'

'You wan' me to tell you why I hi' er wid da bicycle pump?'

'Go ahead.'

'She cheat me.'

'What?'

'She cheat me da bitch! An' I taught 'er a good lesson in wha' 'appens to bitches tha' cheat me...'

'How did she cheat you, Desmond?'

'Is you writin' this down?'

I took my pad and pen out of my briefcase.

'Yes.'

Desmond cleared his throat and spat something disgusting out onto the floor next to him.

'Do you want a glass of water?', I asked.

'Alrigh', *Janny*.'

I poured him a paper cup-full from the plastic bottle on the table and handed it to him.

'I'm ready, Desmond.'

'Don' rush me now.'

'In your own time.'

He took a long gulp of water and leaned forward.

'She ask me if I wanna *do it* wiv a bit a Charlie', he said matter-of-factly. I stared at him for a moment and put down my pen.

'Can I record this?', I asked, taking my Dictaphone out of my pocket.

'No problem', replied Desmond. 'Keep i' fer posterior.'

'Posterity.'

'Yeah wha'ever.'

I turned on the Dictaphone.

'Can you say that again please Desmond?'

'Yeah. She ask me if I wanna do it when we's both high on Charlie.'

'Why would a total stranger ask you for sex and cocaine in the middle of Queen's Wood, Desmond?'

Desmond finished his water and smiled at me.

'Cos she weren't no stranger, *Janny*', he said in a whisper.

'Why haven't you told me this before?' I asked him.

'Ya never aksed, *Janny*. No-one ever aksed me if I *knew* da bitch.'

'How did you come to know Colleen Marden?' I said for the benefit of the Dictaphone.

'I me' 'er in a club in 'arlesden. Bout two year ago.'

'And?'

'An' wha'?'

'What happened next, Desmond? After you met her in a club in Harlesden about two years ago.'

'She became one of me bitches.'

'For the record, what do you mean by that exactly?'

'We be seein' each other.'

'For what, exactly?'

'Wha' you fink? You seen da pictures. She were *fine*.'

Desmond stretched out the word *fine*.

'You were having sexual intercourse with her?', I asked.

'Thas' right.'

I poured myself a cup of water from the plastic bottle and took a sip. I had a packet of hooky Customs cigarettes in my jacket from the second carton I'd opened.

I took out two cigarettes, lit them and passed one to Desmond who took a deep drag.

'How long were you having sexual intercourse with her, Desmond?'

'Bout a year.'

'A *year*?'

'Thas wha' I say.'

'Why did you and Colleen Marden *stop* seeing each other?'

'She were usin' too much of ma product.'

'Can you be more specific, Desmond?'

'She were a coke-'ead and kept stealing all me deliveries.'

I took out another cigarette.

'Did her family know about you?', I asked.

'Dunno.'

'So what were you both doing in Queen's Wood the day she said you raped her?'

'I didn't know she were *gonna* be there. I 'ad a delivery to make, see, fifty gram bag fer tree grand.'

'So can I just clarify that', I said into my Dictaphone. 'You went to Queen's Wood that day because you'd arranged to sell someone fifty grams of cocaine in exchange for three thousand pounds? Is that correct?'

'Thas correct.'

'And did you know who you would be meeting?'

'No. It were wha' it is call a *blind drop*. Can I 'ave anudder ciggy, *Janny*?'

I passed him one. The packet was nearly empty but I had another one in my other pocket.

'Da *drop* were Colleen', he said, exhaling deeply into my face, making me cough. 'I please to see 'er, she please to see me.'

'That's when you had consensual sexual intercourse with her?'

'Thas correct, *Janny*. It were totally natural-like.'

'I see.'

'Like I say, she were *fit*.'

'Then why did you beat her with the bicycle pump?'

Desmond gritted his teeth.

'Cos after, like, when we do the deal, da bitch only give me *two* grand, not tree', he replied. 'She try to trick me.'

'So?'

'So I gives her only 'alf da coke, takes all da money and beats her wid da pump to make her boss show more ri-spec next time 'ce do business wid me.'

'If this is true then why would Colleen go to the police and say you raped her?'

'She go' nuffin to lose, man. She know I been inside 'er, she know I bea' er. Bet she didn't tell da cops about da coke, huh *Janny*?', he said, laughing. 'Thas why I aks you if she 'ad a blood test. It'd be sky-high fer coke. She doin' it all day every day. Takes seven days to ge' out a da bloodstream.'

I switched off the Dictaphone and held my head in my hands.

'*Janny?*', asked Desmond, looking concerned. '*Janny?* Y'alrigh' *Janny?*'

I didn't reply. All I could see was Lord Marden breathing down on me, his nostrils flared, warning me about misunderstandings.

***

I was late for Kate. She'd said to meet at the *Wig & Pen* but I didn't want to be around a bunch of lawyers or run the risk of seeing Duncan Markson or Hussain Tarzi. We couldn't go to *Velvet* because Kate was a woman and so we found a little Italian-run bar near St Paul's which was empty apart from us and the bar-man.

'I didn't know you smoked', she said to me over a glass of chianti.

'I didn't', I replied. 'I'm just a bit flat-out at present.'

'So what's on your plate, Jonathan?' she asked me, crossing her legs and leaning forwards so that my eyes were drawn inexorably to the top of her breasts.

I looked down at my little plate of olives and *foccacia* and then up at Kate, watching me with those wide brown eyes, her black plastic glasses sitting on the table, her legs crossed, her breasts inches from my hands.

'I know what you're thinking', she said slowly.

'No', I replied, 'you don't.'

'Things are going well for you, aren't they?', she asked me, crossing her legs the other way now. 'I've heard you've got

94

some big things in the pipeline. Some great new cases.'

'It's certainly got busier', I replied.

'And the money?' she asked.

'It's very good', I said proudly. 'Can't complain.'

Kate elbowed me affectionately.

'You lucky bugger', she said. 'I bet you're billing way more than me. You know what my hourly rate is, don't you?'

I did because I'd paid it for help drafting the Kelsey defence. One hundred and fifty pounds, plus VAT.

'So what's yours?', she asked.

'Four hundred', I said, lighting another cigarette from the embers of my last one.

'You can get a nice room at Claridge's for that', she countered.

I took another sip of my Chianti.

Making love to Kate Bowyer was *worth* four hundred an hour, maybe more. I didn't *need* her. Of course I didn't *need* her. I had a lovely wife, lovely children, a career going places, at last. No. I didn't need Kate.

We left the Italian bar at six thirty and made it to Claridge's by seven in a cab. It was still early in the New Year and the traffic was light. I stopped at a cashpoint on the way to take out a round thousand pounds. Georgina always checked my credit-card bills and I didn't want this showing up.

We took the lift up to the fourth floor – I'd asked for a

smoking room – and the concierge hadn't raised an eyebrow when we'd checked in as Mr and Mrs Johnson, with no luggage. I turned off my mobile phone and Kate turned off hers.

'Why are we here, Kate?'

She sat down on the large double bed, crossed her legs and started unbuttoning her jacket.

'I think we both know why we're here, Jonny.'

I watched her.

'I've never done this before', I blurted out. 'Not since I've been married.'

'Flattering for me, then.'

'Have you?', I asked.

'Have I what?'

'You know…done this before?'

She removed her jacket and started unbuttoning her blouse.

'Will my reply have any bearing on what we're *about* to do?', she answered, removing her glasses.

'Er…no. I suppose not.'

'Then shut up and kiss me.'

I did.

'That's nice', she said. 'Very nice. I'm wearing your present.'

'Oh. Good. Glad you like it.'

I realized I didn't know what Tarzi had actually got her.

'You were sending me a message, weren't you, Jonny?'

'Err..'

'I was going to get one but they're very expensive.'

She held up the Cartier bangle to my face.

'Thank you.'

She kissed me again and took off my jacket.

CHAPTER EIGHT

I got back home just after ten and started on the whisky. Georgina was already asleep. I couldn't believe I'd just done what I'd just done. Ten years – ten whole years with one woman and then... I drank the single malt like it was water. It had been a mistake. Kate was a mistake. I crawled up the stairs at about two and saw Georgina sleeping soundly. She was still sun-tanned from our holiday. I think she'd topped it up with some *St Tropez*. I pulled off my smoky clothes and tossed them on the floor, crawled in next to her and shut my eyes.

The next morning, for the first time, our Volvo didn't start.

'Jonathan?', asked Georgina, coming out in her dressing-gown and my slippers. I peered under the bonnet.

'What's wrong, Jonathan?'

'It won't start.'

'No. What's *wrong?*'

I looked up at her.

'What do you mean?'

'You came back in a bit of a state last night, judging by the amount of whisky you left in the bottle.'

'It was a long day.'

'Shall I order you a cab?'

'I suppose so. Thanks.'

'What happened to your mobile?'

'Sorry?'

'I tried to call you last night. Where were you?'

'Out with Tarzi', I replied instantly. 'At that club. They make you turn off your mobiles.'

'How convenient.'

I laughed.

'Why don't we get a *new* car?', she said suddenly. 'In fact, why don't we get two new cars? A big family one for me and something a little racier for you?'

I thought about it. Why not?

'I'll talk to Jacob', I replied. 'He's good on cars.'

She kissed me.

'You smell nice', she said. 'What's that?'

'One of those fragrances they hand out in the loos at the club', I lied.

'It suits you', she said. 'I'll just get the phone.'

I watched as she walked back into the house, leaving me outside in my suit and coat with the dead Volvo and my thoughts.

So much for bloody reliability.

I had to talk to Kate and the minute I walked into my room at chambers the telephone rang.

'It's me', said Georgina icily.

'Hello, darling', I replied, a little surprised. 'Everything alright? Has the tow-truck arrived yet?'

'I'm watching television, Jonathan.'

'Oh?'

'Do you have a television there, Jonathan?'

'Er, yes, Jacob's got one.'

'I suggest you put on CNN. Now.'

I walked out to Jacob's desk with the portable telephone handset from my room switched to mute. The television was already on CNN and Jacob was staring at the screen.

'What's happened, Jacob?', I asked him. 'My wife's just told me to watch.'

'You better 'ave a look then, sir', he replied, drawing me up another chair.

On screen there were pictures of Jadzikistan, of people cheering in the streets and firing off rounds from pistols in celebration of the downfall of Khaled Al-Khalim. I pressed the mute button again.

'I'm watching it, darling. Lots of men firing rifles and shouting.'

'Keep watching', she replied stonily.

A presenter's face filled the screen and he started speaking in a throaty American accent.

Jubilation in the streets of Jadzikistan's capital as Khaled Al-Khalim, the toppled leader, is led to the Jadzik Court of Justice under heavy armed guard.'

I stared at the screen, trying to see Khaled's face. There he was now, the most wanted man in the world, walking impassively up the steps of the pillared building, manacled and surrounded by burly armed guards.

'As Khaled Al-Khalim prepares to face charges of genocide and other crimes against humanity he gives us no clue as to what he is thinking.'

CNN showed a close up of Khaled's face, cold and emotionless.

'His team of lawyers, led by his fellow countryman Hussain Tarzi, has been with him for the last forty-eight hours, desperately trying no doubt to piece together a defence. A defence that...'

'Jonathan?'

'Yes darling?'

'Did you just hear that?'

'Yes darling.'

Hussain Tarzi's familiar face now filled the screen, speaking into a barrage of microphones in front of the court-house.

'It is a question of doing the right thing', he said. *'We are all*

innocent until proven guilty. My client is no different to any other.'

'And you believe him to be innocent, Mr Tarzi?' asked a reporter.

'I do not believe it is right to comment on this before we have seen what charges Mr Al-Khalim has to face. Good day.'

CNN switched back to the studio and I walked back into my room with the phone clamped to my ear.

'Well?', asked Georgina coldly.

'I don't know what to say', I replied. 'I didn't know he was acting for Khaled Al-Khalim.'

'No. I bet you didn't.'

'No really I didn't, Georgina.'

'I believe you Jonathan.'

'What do you think I should do?', I asked her. 'I've got two cases with him.'

'Look for a good divorce lawyer', came her reply.

'What?'

'You heard me.'

'What are you talking about, Georgina?'

'You said you spent last night with Tarzi. Last night Tarzi was in Jadzikistan with that maniac Khaled.'

I shut my eyes.

'Where were you Jonathan?', she shouted down the phone at me. 'Where were you? That was perfume I could smell, wasn't it? Who were you with, you bastard?'

'I…I…'

For once I couldn't think of anything to say and the phone went dead.

'Kate Bowyer, please.'

'I'm sorry, sir. Miss Bowyer's unavailable at the present time.'

'I need to speak to her urgently. It's Jonathan Berry, 21 Wessex Yard.'

'Uh, hello Mr Berry. I'll see that Miss Bowyer calls you immediately on her return.'

'Do you know when that'll be, roughly?'

'Haven't the faintest, sir but I'll get her to call as soon as she's back.'

'Fine. Fine. Thanks.'

'Thank you, sir.'

Just then, Jacob Potts poked his head round my door to see me sitting at my desk staring blankly out of the window.

'Alrigh' sir?'

'Can I have a TV set in here, please Jacob?'

'Of course, sir. I'll see what I – '

'It's very important.'

'Yes sir. I'll get on to it right away, sir. By the way, sir, I've got Lord Marden on the line fer you.'

I shut my eyes. My head was about to explode.

'OK', I said as calmly as I could. 'Put him on.'

'Right you are, sir.'

I grabbed another carton of my hooky Russian cigarettes, took out a packet and ripped it open. The cigarettes flew out all over my desk. I picked one up and lit it just as the red light on my phone started to flash, telling me his Lordship was waiting for me to pick it up.

'Hello?'

'Bill, here. How are you, Berry?'

'I'm very well, sir. A little snowed under at present', I replied as Jacob walked in with a flatscreen TV and set it up in the corner of my room.

'I understand you visited Desmond Lyons yesterday', he said lightly.

'Yes sir, that's right.'

'Any…developments?'

'Developments, sir?'

My mind was racing. How could Lord Marden know I'd been to see Lyons yesterday? Why was he asking me this *now*? Did he know about Colleen's history?

'Yes, my boy. Developments. Anything interesting?'

I bit my lip. I'd just lied to my wife and been caught out. I couldn't lie to a Lord of Appeal in Ordinary.

'Is this in confidence, sir?'

'You know it is, my boy. Everything you say will remain with me up here.'

I could see him tapping his head now, just like he'd done at *Velvet*.

'Well sir. Off the record, it appears that your grand-daughter may have been acquainted with Mr Lyons before the attack.'

'Really, Berry?' replied His Lordship incredulously. 'Really? You must tell me what Mr Lyons said to you.'

'I really can't, sir. It would be breaching my client's confidence.'

'Meet me tonight at the club', he said. 'Eight o'clock.'

'But – '

'I'll see you there at eight. Goodbye.'

I heard a strange double-click and the phone went dead. *I'll see you there at eight.* It wasn't an invitation. It was an order.

***

'Jonathan?'

'Kate?'

'Yes. Is something wrong? My clerk said you needed to get hold of me urgently.'

'It's Georgina.'

'Oh, you're – '

'She knows.'

'About last night?'

'She knows I lied about where I was last night.'

'So she doesn't know about me?'

'No. No I don't think so.'

'Good. So we're alright then.'

'I'm not sure, Kate.'

'In what way not sure, Jonathan?'

'She smelt your perfume on me.'

'Oh for God's – '

'Georgina's smart, Kate. She's smarter than I am.'

'Obviously.'

'Are you upset with me?', I asked.

'I'm married too, Jonathan, remember that.'

'Yes I know. I thought we agreed…a level playing field…isn't that what you said?'

'I said a lot of things, Jonathan. She doesn't know it's me, does she?'

'No, but she will suspect you. The answerphone message you left – '

'Oh Christ! That was your *home* number?'

'Yes.'

'But your clerk Jacob forwarded it to your office voicemail. I swear, Jonathan. I swear.'

I put the phone down and marched towards the door. Then I stopped. There was no point alerting Jacob to the fact that something was very wrong. I walked back slowly to the phone and picked it up again.

'You've got to help me, Kate. What do I say to my wife?'

'Lie to her.'

'Again?'

'Call yourself a lawyer? I have to do it all the time. Don't tell me you've never done it.'

'Alright', I replied, after a long crackling silence.

As I put down the phone, Jacob walked into my room.

'What do you know about cars, Jacob?', I asked him.

'Lovely deals at the moment, sir', he replied.

'I need two', I said. 'A big family one for my wife and something a little racier for me.'

'Cash or HP, sir?'

'Which is faster?'

'Got a lovely deal at the moment, sir, flyin' aroun' the Temple. Dealer in Manchester. Get you an Aston for seven 'undred a month. An yer wife a Range Rover. Any particular colour?'

'Black. She likes her cars black.'

'Black it is sir. Bout five 'undred a month.'

Jacob got out a calculator and tapped in a few numbers.

'I'll need a deposit, sir. Bout forty fousand.'

'No problem.'

'I'll debit your chambers account, sir?'

'When can I have them by, Jacob?' I looked at him earnestly. 'I'm in a bit of a fix.'

Jacob looked away for a moment, almost embarrassed.

'I'll have 'em delivered by the end o' the week', he said slowly. 'Both automatic?'

I nodded.

'And yer Aston? Wot colour?'

'Erm…I don't really care. Black, too?'

Jacob scratched the side of his face.

'Y'alright, sir?'

'Why do you ask?'

Jacob looked over towards the Customs evidence that I was depleting rapidly.

'No reason', sir. 'Everyfink alrigh' wiv 'is Lordship?'

'Yes, thank you.'

'Funny abou' Mr Tarzi, ain't it?'

'Hilarious.'

'Ee's gonna be very 'igh profile, sir, now, ain't he? Can't do yer any harm, neither.'

'No', I replied. 'None at all.'

I couldn't get hold of Georgina all morning. The telephone rang and rang but it always clicked through to the answerphone. I didn't leave a message. I tried her mobile but it was continually engaged.

I smoked a few more hooky cigarettes and watched some more of Tarzi on CNN. At noon I went to *Hallmark* near St Paul's and bought Georgina a card, got on the tube and got out at Holland Park to deliver it personally. I walked up Abbotsbury Road, the park to my left, passed a stationary taxi and stopped. In the back was a man talking on a mobile phone earpiece. I couldn't be sure, but he looked suspiciously like the man sitting on double yellow lines outside the King Midas Kebab House in Tufnell Park.

I was becoming paranoid. Where was the *Berrie* charm? I'd used it, I must have, on Kate Bowyer. Everything had been so wonderful with Georgina even though I missed the carol concert. Bloody Tarzi, sending Kate that bangle. But then the holiday had been fantastic and Georgina loved her ring. At least, she had before this morning.

It was cold and breezy but the birds were still singing. The sun was out. I had two arms and two legs and lots of money sitting in the bank.

If work carried on like this I'd make nearly four hundred thousand this year. As I walked quickly up our front drive it occurred to me that I couldn't *afford* to get divorced now and I wouldn't need to anyway when Georgina looked out at the front drive at the end of the week and saw her brand new Range Rover sitting there in black, her favourite colour.

I put the key in the lock but I couldn't open the door.

'Georgina?'

Nothing.

'*Georgina*?', I shouted though the letter box.

I tried the key again. I looked hard at the lock. It was silver, not brass like before.

'Georgina!'

I shoved the card through the letter box and climbed over the fence to the back garden, snagging my trousers and getting a splinter in my thumb in the process. The patio doors at the back of the house were locked. There were no lights on inside. The security grille was down and I had nothing to force it open with. I was stuck in my own back garden with the bloody birds tweeting at me.

'Fuck off!' I shouted at them.

They took no notice.

***

Chas Mullion's house was literally a thirty second walk and when I arrived there, a little muddy and with a small hole in my trousers, the butler gave me a snooty look.

'Mr Berry?', he enquired, raising an eyebrow.

'I don't suppose my wife's here, is she?'

He faced me sternly.

'They're in the middle of luncheon', he said.

'I must see her', I said as I barged past him.

I headed through the enormous entrance hall, gilded and grand with a massive portrait of Chas and Brenda and through to the even more enormous dining room where at an enormous table sat Brenda and Georgina, looking out over the park with half-finished glasses of wine in their hands and grilled salmon in front of them.

'*Jonathan?*', said plastic Brenda, turning to see me. Georgina stood up and glared at me.

'What are you doing here?', she asked.

'I was looking for you', I replied. 'I wanted to explain about last night but you wouldn't let me.'

'This I *have* to hear', said Brenda.

'This is between me and Georgina.'

'You're in *my* house.'

'Yes. I couldn't get into mine.'

'I told Georgina to get the locks changed.'

'*What?*'

'Everyone does it in America.'

'We're not in America, Brenda, we're in London and I want to talk to my wife to explain where I was last night and why I had to lie to her about who I was with.'

'Alright, Jonathan', said Georgina. 'I want Brenda to hear

this too.'

'I'm a great bullshit detector', said Brenda.

I stared at my jury of two.

'I came here to give you a card, darling – '

'Don't call me darling!'

'Please let me finish! I came here to give you a card. I posted it through the letter box.'

'You shouldn't have bothered. It's that Kate woman, isn't it? The one who left the message?'

I shook my head.

'Darling, I swear it isn't.'

'On our children's lives?'

'Yes.'

'Then who were you with?'

'Jacob.'

'Your *clerk*? He wears perfume does he?'

'It must have been his aftershave. It's very strong. But they really do have those little perfume things in the loos at Velvet.' I turned to Brenda. 'You can ask Chas if you don't believe me. I'm sure he can get you a sample.'

'What were you doing with your clerk?'

'We were talking about cars.'

'Cars?'

'That's how I knew Jacob was good on them. Remember what you suggested to me this morning, when the Volvo died?'

'I remember.'

'Well I…I didn't want to spoil the surprise…'

I could feel tears building in my eyes. This was working.

'Well?'

'But there's a surprise coming on Friday.'

'What surprise?'

'I've bought you a Range Rover?'

'Colour?'

'Black.'

'Oh.'

'Brand new.'

'I see.'

'And Jacob said I needed to up my image – you were right darling, you're always right – so I ordered an Aston, same colour.'

'This is all a bit coincidental, isn't it?' she asked, sipping her wine.

'Not really', I replied and fixed Brenda with a withering stare. 'But it seems to have been taken out of all proportion.'

Brenda gazed down at her plate of salmon. Georgina looked out towards the park through the enormous windows. I looked down at my muddy shoes.

'Sorry if I've said anything stupid', said Brenda quietly.

I shook my head.

'It's perfectly alright Brenda', I replied, looking at my wife gazing out at the trees and bushes.

'Georgina?

'Yes.'

'I'm sorry I lied to you.'

Georgina finished her wine slowly and turned to face me. She gazed at me as if analyzing a spreadsheet, something she used to do at Silverman Bach all the time.

'Black, you said?', she asked finally, handing me a set of silvery house-keys.

I walked back to the house with Georgina and made her a cup of coffee. It was going to take more than a Range Rover to crack her. I told her that I would have to be at the club tonight because his Lordship demanded it but that we could spend the afternoon together if she wanted.

'You better be home before ten', she said.

We did the afternoon school run together for the first time. Little Ben, Molly and Amy were ecstatic to see their daddy picking them up.

'Where's the car?', Ben asked. Georgina glared at me. Neither of us answered his question.

We stopped at *Tootsies* and we all had a burger and chips and drank apple juice. Even me. I was a good daddy today. A better one than I'd been last night anyway. We walked through the park as the sun was setting and we let the kids have a go in the adventure playground. It was a perfect evening other than the fact that Georgina wasn't talking to me.

We got the kids back by six and shared bath-time duty. I left Georgina to read them a story as I freshened up and got myself ready for my evening date at *Velvet*. The cab – on the chambers account - arrived early and I blew kisses to Georgina and the kids as they stood in the window on the first floor with all the lights on, waving at me. Georgina didn't wave.

Once the cab turned onto Holland Park Avenue and we were heading towards the West End I got out my mobile and called Jacob and Chas Mullion to sort out my alibi for last night and the perfume thing. They were fine about it. We were all members of the same club now.

I got to *Velvet* by half seven. His Lordship had said eight o'clock and I didn't want to keep him waiting. I didn't know exactly what he wanted to say to me but I think I knew exactly what he wanted me to say to him. Everything. He would want to know everything Desmond Lyons, North London coke addict and alleged rapist had said to me the previous day.

'Ethically there's nothing wrong in telling me everything', his Lordship said to me smoothly after he'd removed his cloak and greeted me at the bar. 'You said Lyons knew my grand-daughter?'

'Err…yes.' We hadn't even sat down yet. 'Did you see Hussain Tarzi on television, Bill?'

'You're not changing the subject are you, Jonathan?'

'No no. It's just I thought it was interesting.'

'Hmmm?'

'Maybe not *that* interesting, then.'

115

His Lordship ordered us a bottle of Puligny-Montrachet. We sat down at a table well away from anyone else. I watched a couple of members eye me up and down, the young buck with the ear of the president of the club.

'Hussain Tarzi is one of the best solicitors in England', said Lord Marden. 'I'm not surprised he got the case. He's well known for handling difficult situations.'

'And?'

'And that's all there is to know. I'm sure CNN will help you fill in the blanks. Now…tell me what Lyons told you.'

'Off the record?'

'But of course my dear chap. Everything stays in here.'

I thought for a second and then I told him everything. After all, I didn't want to harm my career. When I'd finished his Lordship pursed his lips.

'This can never come out', he said to me. 'Never.'

'I see.'

'The family would not be able to deal with such revelations.'

'Of course, Bill, they are difficult - '

'There can be no trial, Jonathan.'

'I'm only defending him, Bill. I can't stop the prosecution.'

'You do not understand what I'm saying, Jonathan.'

I looked up. Lord Marden's voice had dropped to a whisper and it had the desired effect of making me pay even more attention to what was coming out of his mouth.

'There can be no trial', he repeated, getting up from his chair and putting his arm round my shoulder. 'See to it, will you?'

'I don't understand, Bill. I can't stop the trial.'

Lord Marden signaled for his cloak and a waiter brought it over swiftly.

'For a trial to take place', he said as if addressing a lecture-hall, 'there needs to be a defendant.'

'Err…of course.'

He put his head right next to mine.

'Dangerous places, prisons', he said softly. 'Terrible things can happen.'

'I'm still not with you.'

'You will be', he replied. 'As I've said before, I know I can count on you.'

He left me on my own with the bottle of Puligny Montrachet.

And the bill.

CHAPTER NINE

I didn't sleep that night. Neither, I think, did Georgina. We both lay awake on opposite sides of our large double bed, staring at the ceiling. I knew what was keeping both of us awake. Georgina was wondering whether to believe me or not. I was wondering whether or not I'd understood Lord Marden correctly. *'Misunderstandings can wreck a career'*, he'd said to me. Well they could also wreck a marriage. I wondered if Hussain Tarzi was married and, if he was, what his wife thought about him representing a butchering murderer like Khaled Al-Khalim. Sir Wilfred's words came back to me yet again: *'Take the money. Keep your mouth shut.'* Maybe that's what Tarzi was doing. But what was *I* doing?

I dredged myself up from bed at five in the morning and stood in the garden smoking one of my hooky cigarettes in my dressing gown and furry slippers. I went back inside and turned on the television set to CNN. There was more footage of Hussain Tarzi standing outside the Jadzik court-house, surrounded by hordes of cameras. He said something about a preliminary hearing scheduled for later that week when full charges against the deposed dictator would be read out in open court.

'*Only at that time*', said Tarzi on-screen, '*only when faced with the accusations can we deal with them logically, methodically and exhaustively.*'

God the man was right. That's what I had to do with *my* cases. Deal with them logically, methodically and exhaustively. I needed to prioritise. The cartons of hooky cigarettes in my room - the Customs evidence - decreased in number every morning but the case behind them wasn't urgent. Martin Hotson had called to set up a meeting for me to take a statement from him but that wasn't until three o'clock. As for Desmond Lyons and Lord Marden…I just couldn't deal with that right now, I really couldn't. That left the arbitration, the one Tarzi had already paid me for and the one I was meant to settle.

They brought the Aston in through the Temple Avenue gate and parked it in my normal chambers' spot, the one usually reserved for my Volvo, now up for sale on Ebay. It was Jacob who handed me the keys.

'Lovely motor', he said, grinning at me as I opened the morning's newspapers.

'I'm going to settle that bloody arbitration today, Jacob.'

'Shall I ge' Mr Markson on the line fer you, sir?'

'No, no. That won't be necessary.' I slipped two cigarette packets into my pocket.

'I think I'll go and see him personally.'

I arranged a meeting with Duncan Markson on the Kelsey arbitration, our fourth. I offered to take him to *Velvet* for lunch and he agreed. I said I'd pick him up and I couldn't wait to see the look on his face.

'My dear fellow', he said, eyebrows raised, 'this is a corker of a motor car.'

'Isn't it?' I replied casually.

'Things going well, then?' he asked me as we sped down Embankment, attracting admiring glances at each traffic light.

'Not bad', I said, 'but I've decided to concentrate on crime.'

'Very wise', said Duncan as I burned rubber around Trafalgar Square, scattering a few pigeons in the wake of my twin exhaust pipes.

Duncan looked down at the dashboard, the aluminum and the leather and pressed the little switch on the seat to make it slide backwards electrically.

'How's Georgina?', he asked brightly, peering at the SatNav.

We got to *Velvet* and sat at a small dining table. Duncan helped me empty a bottle of '95 Leoville Poyferre.

'Nice place', he said, looking up at the gilded ceiling with its intricate frescos.

'Yes', I replied, 'yes it is. Would you like to become a member?'

Duncan looked at me and took another drink from the velvety red liquid in his glass.

'That why we're here, old chap?' he asked.

'No', I replied. 'Not really. I wanted to discuss the Kelsey arbitration with you somewhere private.'

'Again?'

'There have been a few interesting developments.'

'Such as?'

'Such as, Duncan, how is your year going?'

Duncan didn't catch my eye.

'I don't see that that has anything to do with it.'

'Oh but it does', I countered.

'I don't drive an Aston, if that's what you mean old chap.'

'Would you *like* to, though? Drive an Aston I mean? Or a Bentley?'

'Errm...well, I suppose I wouldn't say no. Apart from Kelsey my pot's a bit dry at present, old chap.'

The waiter filled our glasses from the bottle.

'How much you getting?' I asked him.

'What?'

'For Kelsey. What's your brief fee?'

'My dear fellow, I never discuss money. It's not proper, somehow. That's what clerks are for.'

'Come off it Duncan. What's your brief fee?'

'Well. If you must know, and strictly between us, it's twenty thousand plus a thousand a day for the arbitration itself. Should come to a round thirty-five.'

'I see', I replied, deliberately not catching his eye.

'Why d'you want to know?' he asked.

'Curiosity.'

'I told you mine, you tell me yours.'

'Hundred and fifty thousand.'

He spluttered on his wine.

'*What?*'

'Hundred and fifty thousand', I repeated.

I leaned forward. I had his attention now.

'How would you like to earn another fifty thousand, on top of what they're paying you?' I asked, watching his pupils closely, something I always did with my criminal clients. They widened.

'Say that again', he said.

'You heard me the first time.'

'Yes, yes I did but I wanted to hear it from you again my dear chap. You're not drunk are you?'

'No.'

'Hmmm. How would I earn this additional fifty thousand, Jonathan?'

I noted he wasn't laughing now.

'We need the Kelsey arbitration to settle', I replied.

'We do?'

'We do.'

'I see.'

'I need you to persuade Mr Kelsey to settle his claim with my client for one hundred thousand dollars.'

I did the maths. That would give me four hundred and fifty thousand dollars less the fifty thousand pound bung to Duncan.

'But you've already offered my client five hundred thousand.'

'I know. But this time, I'm offering *you* fifty thousand pounds *cash*, no questions asked.'

'Cash?'

'That's right.'

'And my client - let me get this right Jonathan – my client has to agree to accept one hundred thousand dollars and go away?'

'Nail on the head.'

Duncan Markson peered into his glass of Leoville Poyferre. His lips moved but no words came out. After a few moments he raised his head.

'This isn't ethical, is it, Jonathan?'

'Your client doesn't stand a chance. You're only telling him the truth.'

'Cash?'

'Yes, cash.'

'Why?'

'Don't ask why. Just do it, take the money and keep your mouth shut. It's not illegal.'

'No?'

'It's not illegal to advise your client to settle when he's going to lose.'

'Off the record Jonathan I've already advised him to settle.'

'And?'

'He said no.'

'I think you can try a little harder, can't you?'

Duncan Markson scratched the back of his neck and then his nose. I watched his lips move again as though he were talking to himself, but nothing was coming out.

'Duncan?'

'Alright', he said finally. 'I'll do it for sixty thousand.'

***

When I got back from the club, Martin Hotson's limousine was waiting in Wessex Yard to take me to his offices in the City. I thought it prudent not to take the Aston.

We headed up towards St Paul's and cut through the back of the Barbican to Ropemaker Place where I was greeted by a huge glass structure not unlike the Lloyd's Building. The limousine stopped outside and the driver opened the door for me.

'Thirty-seventh floor', he said to me.

I nodded, straightened my tie and walked across the smooth, expensive-looking flagstones towards the revolving door, my documents case grasped firmly in my hand. It wasn't a no-smoking building because I couldn't see any people lingering sheepishly outside. Through the door I went and into the atrium, a soaring marble-floored cathedral of a place with jazzy lighting and black-clad security personnel. I turned to look at the huge silver board to my left, almost fifteen feet high, which listed all of the businesses that operated from the building. There must have been a thousand and even though the wall-space was enormous the lettering was very small indeed. I moved closer and closer still and looked for Martin Hotson's holding company, Halcyon, named after an old hotel in Holland Park that was going to be turned into expensive apartments.

Halcyon had the thirty-sixth and thirty-seventh floors of the building, which, according to the sign, included the roof gardens. Only the very top floors would do for Martin Hotson but then he was a billionaire. I quickly scanned the names. Across the five floors immediately below Halcyon was one of the many offices of Silverman Bach. No wonder he and Chas Mullion knew each other so well. They could visit each other's offices and count their money together.

Below them was a jumble of companies called 'Oligarch 1333 plc' or 'Ropemaker Place 2226 Ltd', dummy off-the-shelf companies whose names had been chosen by bunches of unimaginative lawyers.

There was Yukon Blues, Inc., Money for Nothing Limited, Socrates plc and Genevieve International SA. Were all of these Martin Hotson's? Gin Palace (Cayman Islands) Inc, Borry Cove Holdings, Dungeoneer 5 Ltd and Harbor Shipping (Delaware), Inc. Harbor Shipping? My client in the Nigerian flake arbitration had an office here? Why didn't Tarzi tell me?

The address for service was listed in Delaware, not Ropemaker Place, London EC2. And what was 'Prune Tree Holdings' all about?

I shifted my documents case from my right to my left hand. It was a little heavy because when I came back from Mauritius thinking I'd read all the documents, Jacob had presented me with another stack of files all about Martin Hotson and the murder of which he was acquitted more than thirty years before.

'Can I help you, sir?', asked a very pretty girl in a tight-fitting grey skirt.

I turned on the *Berrie* charm and smiled.

'I'm here for Martin Hotson', I said. 'It's Jonathan Berry and he's expecting me.'

'He'll be waiting for you on the top floor, sir. High-speed lift's to the right.'

'Thank you.'

The lift had only one button and as I pushed it the doors whisked shut very quickly. The lift climbed almost instantly, smoothly but so fast that I could feel my stomach hovering somewhere between Prune Tree Holdings and Dungeoneer 5 Ltd.

The doors whisked open as quickly as they'd shut leaving me staring at a wide reception desk with three of the most Barbie-doll receptionists I'd ever seen, all no doubt with the same hairdresser as plastic Brenda.

'Good morning Mr Berry', said the one in the middle in a posh English accent. 'My name's Lucinda and I'll take you to Mr Hotson.' She sounded like an air-hostess and then I remembered that amongst other things Martin Hotson owned three airlines.

I walked past a poster of 10cc's '*I'm Mandy, Fly Me*' signed by the band. There was a life-sized model of a man dressed up as Elvis Presley to the right of the foyer and next to it was a shark sitting in a glass box swimming in formaldehyde.

'Hirst?', I asked Lucinda.

'I wouldn't know', she replied. 'He's in there.'

'Thank you.'

The inner sanctum of the Hotson empire, Halcyon, had a spectacular view of the City of London. Manhattan had lots of skyscrapers and thirty-seven floors was nothing to a New Yorker but in London thirty-seven floors was higher than Mount Everest.

The sun flooded through the windows. It was bright and airy and designed by Italians. I had an Aston Martin but this man's office was like a spaceship. There was a helipad on the roof, a massive roof-garden in front of us and even a hot-tub. I watched as he strode towards me purposefully in a cream linen suit, grinning broadly.

'Thanks for coming', he said.

'My pleasure.'

At four hundred an hour I don't know many people who wouldn't have.

'Drink? I'm having a Scotch.'

'Just some fizzy water if you have it.'

'Sure.'

He poured it out himself. The room was huge and we were the only ones in it.

'Funny about Tarzi, isn't it?', he said to me.

'Yes, yes it is', I replied.

'I didn't know he was Jadzik.'

'Me neither.'

'He's good, though, isn't he?' said Martin.

I nodded in agreement.

'If anyone can get Khaled off, Tarzi can', he added hopefully. 'And if he can defend a butchering psychopath, there's hope for me yet, isn't there Jonathan?'

I looked down into my Perrier.

'It feels good to talk about it now', he said nervously, turning his glass round and round in his hand. 'The documents don't give you the full story.'

'They never do', I replied.

***

Thirty years and six months ago, a young man by the name of Martin Winters was invited to a party in a house in Berkshire. It was a country house belonging to the parents of a beautiful young girl, a debutante by the name of Elspeth Huntingford-Smith. It was 1975 and glam rock had arrived with punk just around the corner. The sixties and flower-power had receded a little but the weird clothes had got even weirder. The first picture I saw was that of Martin Winters aged twenty-one in a pair of flared jeans, a brown and pink kaleidoscopic shirt with an enormous collar and a medallion round his neck.

'When did you change your name?', I asked him.

'Afterwards.'

'Sorry Martin, but you'll have to be more specific.'

'In 1977. I've got the deed poll somewhere.'

'And presumably you changed it – '

'Because of this? Yes. You don't know what it's like.'

'A lot of my clients change their names', I replied. 'It's very common.'

'So nothing to worry about?'

'Nothing at all.'

Elspeth Huntingford-Smith's parents were Roger and Willa and their respective family trees stretched back nearly as far as mine. The house in Berkshire had a hundred and seventy acres of land, paddocks, tennis courts, a bothy and a swimming pool modeled on the one up the road at *Cliveden* where Christine Keeler had flirted with John Profumo not so many years before.

In August 1975 Roger and Willa were on holiday in Italy. It was summer. The sun shone in England's royal county, dogs lazed in the heat and Elspeth was planning a party. Martin Winters was a young man about town, a playboy. He never seemed to have much money but he was exceptionally good-looking and well-mannered. He'd done the London season, a mixture of tennis balls, horses and boats and he was ready for the house parties that were to follow.

'I think we met in Chelsea in '73. Saw each other on and off after that.'

'How often?'

'Once every couple of weeks. We'd go out somewhere. She was very good, you know. She always paid for me. She was very liberated, was Elspeth.'

'Did you love her?'

'Did I *love* her?'

I fixed him with the resigned look of a man who is simply doing his duty.

'Yes', he replied, looking right into my eyes. 'I did love her. And that is why I could never harm a hair on her head.'

In my experience, most murders happened between people who loved each other. I looked at the clock. Including traveling time I'd already billed one hour. Four hundred quid. Money for Nothing Ltd.

'Go on', I said to him. 'Let's go through exactly what happened the day of the party.'

Martin poured himself another Scotch and I looked out at the men cleaning the windows of the building opposite. Their metal carriage hovered above the abyss, suspended by two ropes. Their large rubber wipers were hypnotic. I watched them as I listened to Martin.

About twenty of them got to the house by lunchtime, including Martin. He had managed to get his small rucksack into Elspeth's room before anyone else. He'd laid out his toiletries in her ensuite bathroom and even hung up his party clothes in one of her many built-in wardrobes. He always slept on the left and so he'd put the book he was reading, *The Collector* by John Fowles, on the left-hand bed-side table. The view out of the first floor window was beautiful. Landscaped gardens led down to a pond, the heated swimming pool with its various terraces and a barbecue area. This area, which he could see clearly from the first floor window, was to be the focus of that night's celebrations. He hadn't brought a swimming costume because he wouldn't be needing one.

Elspeth walked into her bedroom and stopped by the door.

'Martin?'

'Yes, Ellie?'

She looked at his things arranged in her room and smiled.

'Do you want one of these?' she asked, holding out a small, tightly-folded piece of paper. 'For later?'

It was LSD and he said yes.

Martin was tripping by nine o'clock when the bulk of the guests started to arrive. He was stuck by the barbecue watching little elves dance sideways from the flames and huge mushroom clouds erupt from a packet of lamb chops. Ellie was dressed in a flowing kaftan with nothing underneath. The night was warm and a couple of guests were already in the pool, flooded with underwater lights. They weren't wearing any clothes. The music belting out was Pink Floyd. There were no neighbours to complain because the closest house was nearly a mile away and tall trees cushioned it from the sound.

Martin watched the elves and the mushroom clouds and then a vision swam before his eyes, the lovely Elspeth. She was removing her kaftan over her head and jumping into the swimming pool. He watched her splash about with two naked men and suddenly felt very ill. He wobbled back to the house and threw up in a toilet. When he came back outside again he felt fabulous. No paranoia. He didn't have the shakes or anything. It was only ten o'clock and he felt fabulous.

By midnight Martin was lying on a sun-lounger naked, kissing another girl. All the other loungers were similarly occupied and some of the occupants had got a lot further than the kissing stage. Ellie was back in her kaftan, dancing around the pool to '*All the Young Dudes*'.

'It must have been two o'clock in the morning. The music was going strong. There were girls all over the place, most of them naked. A lot of the blokes were naked too. We were all drunk, or high or both. I'd been high but now I was just a little tipsy, nothing more.'

'Okay.'

'Someone had brought some fireworks with them and they set up a display in a field near the tennis court.' 'Everyone went to watch the fireworks. Everyone that is, apart from Elspeth and me.'

'Why didn't you go?'

'I've never followed the herd, Jonathan.'

I nodded sagely.

'She was in her kaftan, I was in some weird trousers.'

'Where were you both?'

'On sun-loungers. She was on one and I was on the one next to it.'

'And?'

'We started talking.'

'What did you say?'

'She…she told me that she was having a lovely time. I said…I said I was too.'

'Go on.'

'And then…and I don't know why, Jonathan, or how…but my hands were suddenly round her neck.'

'Riiight…'

His voice was very low, very calm and very matter-of-fact.

'I squeezed her neck tightly. Very tightly. She couldn't make a noise. I remember watching the veins stand out on her neck. She didn't look so pretty then. Not as pretty as she'd looked before. Not nearly as pretty as she'd looked before. She was gasping, trying to tell me something but I couldn't hear her so I squeezed some more. And then she stopped moving, so I threw her in the swimming pool.'

He looked out of the window, a tear in his eye.

'I'll never know why I did it', he said shakily, 'but I really, really didn't mean to. I regretted it almost as soon as I'd done it, you see. I knew it wasn't me doing it. It was someone else.'

'Someone else?'

'Yes. It wasn't me. I could see the hands tightening around her neck and I could see her face but it wasn't me doing it, you know, Jonathan, it was someone else. I had no reason to do anything to her. It couldn't have been me. I loved her. Despite the way we both lived, despite the fact we were both very young, I loved her. I think I'll always love her.'

I listened to the hiss of my Dictaphone which was now the

loudest thing in the room and wondered how he'd got off the first time.

'There were no witnesses', he said. 'So they couldn't pin anything on me. But that's changed, now, hasn't it?'

I opened the folder.

'If...if Tarzi can defend that Khaled Al-Khalim, you can defend me, can't you Jonathan?'

I pulled out the copy of the diary that Elspeth's elderly parents had managed to obtain from a girl that had witnessed what Martin did. She'd been too scared to testify back in 1976 but now, for some reason, she'd changed her mind.

'This woman wants to wreck me', said Martin, slamming his glass down on the table. 'After all this time. You'll get me off, won't you? Tell me what to say? Think of a way out?'

My throat was dry so I took a sip from my fizzy water.

'I didn't do it, you see', he said. 'I loved her. It must have been someone else.'

I nodded, watching his pupils closely.

CHAPTER TEN

They delivered the Range Rover to Holland Park and Georgina signed for it. There was a bunch of flowers in the driver's seat. Trust Jacob, I thought. It was a nice touch. She called me to tell me that the car had arrived and that the kids would love it because it had little DVD screens in the back of the front seats. But, she added, she still wasn't sure if she could believe what I'd said about where I was that night.

Jacob told me someone from Harbor Shipping of Delaware had called to ask me where I wanted them to pay my four hundred and fifty thousand dollars, half the money I'd supposedly saved them by settling the case. Jacob told me Harbor was very, very happy with me. Not half as happy as I was with them. I asked Jacob to get them to pay the money straight into my chambers account and then I asked him if he could take out sixty thousand pounds in cash for me today.

'Expenses, is it, sir?' he asked, staring at me.

'That's right, Jacob.'

At lunchtime I bought a small briefcase on Chancery Lane, put the money in it and delivered it to Duncan Markson in my

Aston Martin.

'Everybody wins', I said.

'My client's still down twenty-two million', Duncan replied.

I shrugged, got in my car and drove back to chambers.

When I got home that night I found Georgina flicking through a property brochure from Knight Frank. I sat next to her and she let me peck her on the cheek. The houses inside were wonderful. They even had one in there like Chas Mullion's, but it was fourteen million pounds.

'I like that one', said Georgina, pointing to the picture of a house on a quiet street just round the corner from where we were renting.

'Hmm', I mused, 'not bad is it?'

'Shall we take a look?'

'It's two and half million, Georgie.'

'So?'

Bedford Gardens was one of the pretty cross streets that ran between Kensington Church Street, full of antique shops that never seemed to be open, and Campden Hill Road, site of a great pub and the old Thames Water Reservoir. It was only a ten minute walk from our rented house on Abbotsbury Road. The rooms were grand but not as grand as Chas Mullion's wedding cake of a mansion a few streets away.

'Five bedrooms', said our estate agent Clarissa, smiling warmly. 'And they'll take an offer.'

We'd brought the kids with us and they were roaming around upstairs, already picking their bedrooms. From the street the house looked typically mid-Victorian.

Wisteria climbed up the tall flat-fronted façade, only the ground and basement floors stucco, the other three floors stock London brick. There was a small front garden and a sixty-five foot rear garden.

'Lovely for the children', said Clarissa, looking out towards it.

'We can afford this, can't we?' Georgina asked me flatly.

'They want two and half for it?' I asked Clarissa.

'Yeees', she said hesitantly, 'but they'll look at all offers. Can I ask what you do, Mr Berry?'

'I'm a barrister', I replied.

'Lovely!'

'Have there been any offers on it?'

'Truthfully', said Clarissa, screwing up her nose, 'no.'

'And how long has it been on the market?'

'About six months', she replied. 'Do you have anywhere to sell?'

'No. We're renting. Just round the corner, Abbotsbury Road.'

'Lovely!' said Clarissa. 'The vendor would find that very attractive. No chain, I mean.'

'We haven't made an offer yet', said Georgina.

'Go on', urged Clarissa. 'The market's picking up. Good idea to get in before everyone else does.'

'They've had no offers in six months', I replied.

'It doesn't show well', countered Clarissa. 'No furniture you see. People have no imagination, do they really? I mean, these days they want to see Plasma screen televisions and Wifi and underfloor heating and all the furniture perfectly arranged.'

'Ben! Molly! Amy! Come down here will you?' shouted Georgina.

We heard the clatter of feet on the stairs.

I walked through the double reception on the first floor, high-ceilinged, corniced and with French windows at both ends. I unlocked one of the doors and stepped out onto an ornamental balcony. Clarissa was locked in conversation with Georgina behind me. I stood at the door and looked up and down the street. It was very pretty and quiet. Five bedrooms. Three for the children, one for us and a guest room. Or maybe an office. This house would make my wife happy.

Sophie's little beaming smile came to me suddenly from nowhere and I gripped the handrail firmly as tears welled up in my eyes.

'I love you Sophie', I whispered, looking up at the sun peeking through a gap in the clouds. 'Daddy's been naughty but now he's going to be good.'

'Jonathan?'

'Yes, Georgina?'

I turned round, wiping my face on my sleeve.

'What do you think?' she asked me.

'It's nice but it's expensive.'

Clarissa stood right behind Georgina, sticking to her like her shadow. The kids ran in.

'What do you think, guys?' she asked them. 'Is this a nice house?'

'It's cool', said Ben.

'I think so', said Clarissa.

'Yeah!' said Ben.

'Jonathan?' asked Georgina. I looked into her eyes. They were boring into mine. 'We'll never need to move again', she added, suddenly slipping her arm into mine.

'It's a lot of money, Georgina.'

Had she forgiven me?

'Everything's relative. We can't rent forever. No-one rented for long at Silverman Bach...'

If Georgina were still at Silverman Bach she could have bought this house with just one of her annual bonuses.

'We'll think about it', I said to the agent.

***

'Jonathan?'

'Kate? Er...how are you?'

'Your clerk called. He calls me more than you do.'

'Ha!'

'He called me to tell me you settled the Kelsey arbitration.'

'Yes', I replied, thinking of the look on Duncan Markson's face and the money sitting in my chambers account.

'Calls for a celebration, don't you think?'

'Kate. Listen. That night - '

'He's asked me to put in for five thousand, as a thank you.'

'Oh?'

'So it's on *me* this time.'

'What's on you?' I asked.

'Claridges.'

'*What?*'

'You lied, didn't you?'

'Sorry?'

'To your wife. You lied?'

I didn't answer her because I couldn't take my eyes off what was unfolding on the flat-screen television in the corner of my room.

'Hold on a sec', I said, 'I've got another call coming through.'

I pressed the mute button and turned to CNN. Live from the court-house in the capital in Jadzikistan, Khaled Al-Khalim was being led out onto the stand under armed guard and in handcuffs. Behind him, impassive, was Hussain Tarzi. Al-Khalim stared straight ahead of him, his eyes drilling into those of the judge who looked away, obviously petrified.

'*Coming to you live from Jadzikistan*', intoned an American TV reporter, '*we are about to hear what charges the people of Jadzikistan are bringing against deposed dictator Khaled Al-Khalim.*'

I pressed the mute button again to find Kate still waiting for me.

'You're back.'

'Can I call you later, Kate? Something important's just come up.'

'Don't be saucy.'

'Speak to you later – bye.'

I put down the phone and lit another cigarette.

It was late January and judging by the number of overcoats they had cold winters in Jadzikistan. The court-room was packed and very noisy. The judge held up a thick wad of papers and began reading them in *Jadzik*. The camera closed in on Khaled's face. The CNN translator's voice cut in after a few seconds and I turned up the volume so I wouldn't miss anything.

'*The newly-formed people's republic of Jadzikistan under the interim constitution drawn up under the power of the United Nations hereby brings charges of murder, genocide, rape and treason against the accused, Khaled Al-Khalim and calls for a full trial in accordance with the laws of the state.*'

The judge cleared his throat and as he did so Hussain Tarzi rose to his feet.

'*Your Honour*', he said in English, '*we would like to challenge the jurisdiction and impartiality of the Jadzik court to try this case.*'

The judge looked up at Tarzi in amazement.

Khaled Al-Khalim blinked, but kept his eyes trained firmly on the judge.

'*Yes?*', said the judge in English, peering towards the gallery where a number of Western observers sat grimly.

'*I would like to submit an application to the court for this matter to be tried in an impartial state, in a place where the venom of the Jadzik people will not find as easy a channel as my client's blood.*'

Tarzi passed the judge five sets of papers and the judge, rather than reading them, looked up again at the Western observers sitting in the gallery. They all nodded their heads.

'*I…will need time to consider this application Mr Tarzi.*'

The split-second that the judge banged his gavel onto his large wooden desk the court erupted in shouting and chanting.

'*Death to Khaled! Death to Khaled and his evil lawyer!*', said the CNN reporter, '*that's what they're saying. In a daring move by Hussain Tarzi, Khaled's lawyer –*'

I turned down the volume but kept watching as Khaled and Tarzi filed out of the courtroom. The cameras followed Tarzi out into the street and into his car. As he was whisked away through a cordon of military personnel I could swear I saw Hussain Tarzi take out his mobile phone and dial. Just then my telephone rang. It was Brixham Prison. Desmond Lyons was dead.

CHAPTER ELEVEN

The funeral was on a Thursday and, unlike Brian Dunne's funeral, I felt obliged to go. It was held at a cemetery in Archway, close to Desmond's flat on St John's Villas, North London.

'Desmond was a difficult man, but, in his heart, he was a good man', said the Irish priest, unconvinced, to the congregation of five, including me. 'Would anyone else like to say a few words?'

For once, I kept my mouth shut. I just kept thinking about what his Lordship had said to me on the phone that morning:

'Justice has been done, my boy.'

'Err...'

'No need to say any more. I don't know how you did it so quickly, but that's even more impressive.'

'Done what?'

'Come come, Jonathan. No need to be modest. I must go now. Lord Willoughby wants to see me about something. Tell me when you're next at the club. We must talk some more about your future.'

'Thank you…errr…Bill.'

So here I was standing at the funeral of the man I was meant to have had killed. I wondered if there was a section on *that* in my Professional Ethics handbook.

'We come from nothing', the priest said, 'and it is to nothing that we return, with only our souls to live on eternally in the kingdom of heaven.'

He threw a clod of earth into the grave.

'Ashes to ashes, dust to dust.'

I blew my nose. It was freezing. My cases were disappearing as quickly as my clients. I only had two left – Hotson and Customs – and soon I might have a large mortgage to service. The papers said Desmond Lyons had been garroted with a three-foot section of fuse-wire.

I'd left the Aston at home. Not a good idea to leave it lying around on a street somewhere in Archway. I walked across the cemetery away from the other mourners. I had one of the most senior judges in the land believing I'd managed to bump off Desmond Lyons. If it were true – which it wasn't – then he would be guilty of procuring the commission of a murder, as would I. Life. That would be our sentence. Just like Martin Hotson's. It was interesting to think about. An unfortunate coincidence, but, like his Lordship had said, prisons were very dangerous places. I put another hooky Russian cigarette between my lips and lit it, trying to work out how to get back to the tube station. No money for cabs today.

I walked out onto the main street and found myself just up the road from the King Midas Kebab House in Tufnell Park.

It was nearly one o'clock and I was feeling hungry. I wondered if Osama would recognise me in my smart suit.

'Whayyouwan'?' he asked me as I walked in through the open door. 'Doner? Do you nice doner?'

'Do you remember me?' I asked him in my cut-glass *Berrie* accent.

He squinted at my face.

'No', he replied.

I didn't think he would. I ordered a doner with chili sauce and watched the spit turn. At least it was warm in here. I remembered the smell and that it tasted much better than it looked.

Osama sliced off the meat from the spit and gathered it together with some lettuce leaves into a fresh piece of pitta bread straight out of an Asda wrapper. His delicate hands worked quickly.

'Best kebab in London!' he said. 'Two pound, please sir.'

I handed over the coins and grabbed a couple of napkins from a dispenser on the counter.

'Can I eat it over here?' I asked, motioning to a small white formica-topped table. He nodded.

I sat on a rickety wooden chair and took a big mouthful of kebab. Osama had a television set in a metal cage above the counter and he flipped it on with a remote control that he kept in the front pocket of the spattered apron he wore. It was a satellite channel in Jadzik, a fast-moving guttural language.

Behind the presenter was a large picture of Khaled Al-Khalim. The picture dissolved to the front of the courthouse and the arrival of Khaled's legal team.

I couldn't understand a word anyone was saying so I just looked at the pictures. Hussain Tarzi was there on television flanked by a number of other lawyers. The presenter's voice was blaring out something or other.

'You want I translate?' said Osama, looking at me proudly. 'I from Jadzikistan. Before Colindale.'

I smiled and nodded.

'They say these are lawyers for' – he spat the words – 'Khaled Al-Khalim.'

On screen the cameras milled about outside the large pillared court-house. A hundred microphones strained to reach the team of lawyers addressing the world's press. I tuned out Osama's voice. It was pretty clear what the lawyers - but not Tarzi, who I couldn't see - were saying. One by one they were protesting their client's innocence, and every time any of them spoke the crowd around them surged forward, nearly breaking through the cordon of UN peacekeepers.

'Death to the lawyers', Osama said.

'Halleluyah!' I murmured.

'You lawyer?' he asked me, looking at me carefully in my thousand pound suit. I nodded. No point lying now.

'They want trial come to England. To London', he added. 'Best city in world.'

I nodded in agreement.

'Justice for all!' he cried.

I looked back to the screen.

A man had broken through the cordon of Al-Khalim's lawyers and was ranting at the camera, his face right up against the lens. I could see UN soldiers' arms trying to pull him away but he was helped by the surging crowd who were converging quickly on the group of legal brains standing like turkeys in front of the world's press.

Suddenly there was a loud bang and the camera angle changed dramatically. The camera was lying on the ground, the picture was jumping fuzzily and the presenter's voice in the studio went up an octave. There was another bang, then three more in quick succession and then a burst of machine gun fire. A cloud of smoke drifted across the lens and the studio presenter was screaming something that must have been unintelligible even to a Jadzik. I turned quickly to Osama.

'What's he saying?' I asked, mouth full of kebab.

'This man shoot someone', he replied.

'Who?'

'I dunno. He screaming.'

'Can you get CNN on this?'

'This is American channel?'

'Yes. A news-channel. In English.'

Osama pushed a few buttons on the remote-control and quickly found it.

'*We bring you breaking news*', said a harsh American voice, '*from the capital of Jadzikistan where the court was today due to hear an application to transfer the trial of Khaled Al-Khalim to the United Kingdom on the basis that there could be no fair trial of the deposed dictator in his own country.*'

The screen cut to the court-house in the Jadzik capital. On the ground lay three bodies with bloody sheets tossed over their faces. A Chieftain tank had drawn up outside and its turret was trained on the crowd facing the cameras.

'In a surprising and shocking development, it seems that a lone gunman first attacked a local Jadzik camera unit and then turned his gun on the lawyers for Al-Khalim. Eyewitness reports say one cameraman and three lawyers are dead, with another lawyer seriously injured...'

I put down my kebab and suddenly felt rather ill. I pulled on my coat and wobbled over to the door. I crashed against it, making Osama turn. He looked at me strangely and then turned back to the television sitting in its little metal cage. I made it out into the street. I felt sick. I was going to vomit. I reached for the shop window and used it to stop myself from falling over. I edged across the outside of the shop and round the side, into a filthy alleyway. There was a skip in front of me and a set of metal doors along the right hand side. I headed over to a large upturned metal barrel, grasped the sides and vomited into it. The stench of the rubbish inside made me vomit again, and again. I stood up, weakly. At least I hadn't got any of it on my coat.

I looked back towards the end of the alleyway, towards the street. The metal doors, now on my left, were all numbered. They were in the same building as the kebab house but the sign above them read '224-A.' The street number for the kebab house, I remembered from the Kelsey documents, was 224. I took a few deep breaths, trying to draw fresh air into my lungs and leaned against a door. Just above it, next to a large number '4' were four little screw-holes, as though a tiny brass plate had been removed. I brushed my fingers against the holes. They were fresh.

I walked down the alleyway in the other direction until it came to a dead end. Dirty washing hung outside grimy windows and there was rubbish piled up in heaps on the ground. An old fridge lay on its side next to a large pile of ashes. I knelt down and sifted through them. Someone had burnt a huge quantity of documents, bank statements or computer print-outs. Or hundreds of sheets from a telex machine.

The ground wasn't clean but I got down on my hands and knees, sifting through the muck. A gust of wind took some of the ash and blew it over my coat. I had bits in my eyes and bits coated to my face. I rubbed my eyes with my sleeve and then, when I looked down, I saw a tiny warped piece of plastic with the letters 'NASON' barely legible.

I picked it up and popped it into one of my jacket pockets. My old metal Rolex told me it was nearly half past one.

I had a whole afternoon ahead of me and I realized I'd run out of cigarettes. Outside on the street there was a cab parked on double yellow lines with no-one in it. That was a shame. I needed a cab.

I got back to chambers at two thirty, went straight for the cigarettes and turned on my computer. I flipped open the case of the Sony Vaio and watched the little icon flash green to show me I was ready to surf. I went to the Companies House website and searched for companies registered either to the address of the King Midas Kebab House or to 224A just behind it. I was looking for the name that might have been on the little brass plaque that someone had removed.

Nothing. I went to the Land Registry website and tapped in both addresses - 224 and 224A - to call up the details of who owned the kebab house and the building behind it. A little white and orange screen told me the charge was two pounds for each search. I tapped in my credit card details and got out my Dictaphone to record what I was doing. I didn't have a printer in my room – we all shared Jacob's – and I didn't want to share my findings with anyone. The results pinged back instantly. Number 224 was owned by the local council – Osama was probably getting a good deal on rent. The results for number 224A, though, the doors in the alleyway behind the kebab shop, made me put down my Dictaphone and stare at the screen.

At the top of the PDF document generated by the Land Registry of England and Wales was a space for the registered owner. For 224A the registered owner was a company called Prune Tree Holdings Ltd.

I went back to the Companies House website and did a search for the registered office of Prune Tree. It pinged back the answer straight away. Prune Tree's registered office was in Ropemaker Street, London EC2. It was the same company name I'd seen at Martin Hotson and Chas Mullion's offices, one of the hundreds listed in tiny little type on the large silver board on one of the walls of the gigantic atrium, along with that of Harbor Shipping Inc of Delaware. I quickly looked up the shareholders of Prune Tree, paying another five pounds on my credit card for the privilege. There was only one shareholder, Genevieve International, SA of Switzerland. Another name from the silver board. I lit another fake Marlboro light and inhaled deeply.

I picked up my Dictaphone, pressed the record button and then I heard a click. I'd finished the tape. I looked for the eject button so I could put in another one. Bloody machines. And suddenly I couldn't take my eyes off the Dictaphone. I quickly fished out the little warped piece of plastic I'd picked up in the yard which said 'NASON'.

I'd done a Google search on 'NASON' but Google just came up with history professors at colleges in Utah and a brand of Australian nasal spray.

I placed the piece of plastic next to my Dictaphone. The font was the same, the lettering a similar colour. 'NASON' was part of the word 'PANASONIC', a large Japanese company that made Dictaphones, stereos and, last but not least, telex machines.

***

I didn't need to think very hard of an excuse to go round to Ropemaker Place and have another good look at all the names on the silver board. Prune Tree Holdings and Genevieve International S.A. of Switzerland were up there. I'd got Jacob to set up another meeting with Martin Hotson and, as I was a few minutes early, I wandered into the offices of Silverman Bach on the thirty-second floor and asked if I could say a quick hello to Chas Mullion. Thirty seconds later he was gripping my hand.

'Welcome to hell!' said Chas, grinning. 'Good to see you Jonny.'

'And you Chas.'

'Passin' through?'

'That's right. Meeting with Martin. Handy you being in the same building.'

'Yeah, ain't it just.'

'Are those all *your* companies, Chas? All those little names downstairs?'

'Huh?'

'You know, on the silver board.'

'Awwh, they're just, ya know, they're…why ya wanna

151

know?'

'Lawyer's curiosity.'

He frowned.

'That's not why ya came here is it, Jonny?'

'No', I replied. 'Of course it's not.' I turned around three hundred and sixty degrees approvingly. 'What fantastic offices', I said. 'I think Georgina would love it here.'

'You mean…?'

'I could try and persuade her to come back. We could always use the money.'

'Now you're talkin', Jonny! Seein' sense.'

'Just you and Martin in the building?'

'Yup. We own the whole shebang between us.'

'Fantastic.'

'Yeah.'

'So all those names on the board downstairs are yours?'

'Yeah…a few. His are all called Halcyon something or other, ours either Silverman something or something Bach. Hey Jonathan, does it matter?'

'Oh gosh, so sorry, Chas.' I made a big thing of checking my watch, the reliable metal Rolex. 'Oh dear. Is that the time? Look Chas - I've got to go and I'm sure you're busy. I'll make sure I tell Georgina I popped round.'

'Well, yeah, good to see you, Jonathan. Kiss your gorgeous wife for me, will ya?'

Chas opened the door for me and I turned to him, beaming.

'Just one last thing Chas… those other companies in your building…if they ever need the services of a barrister –'

'I'll be sure to tell 'em, Jonny. Anyhow, they're all Tarzi's. I'd talk to *him* if I were you.'

'All the company's are *Tarzi's*?'

'I guess. His or his clients.'

'It's a small world.'

We shook hands, said our goodbyes and I headed out to the lifts.

***

Martin Hotson sat for an hour reading the statement I'd typed out for him while I sipped a *Perrier*. He rubbed his nose, he scratched his head and he kept nodding quickly as he read. Finally he put the statement down and gazed up at me, smiling.

'I'm fucked, aren't I Jonathan?'

'It's your word against hers.'

'So I'm fucked.'

'No. No. I can make a big thing of how she failed to come forward with this evidence thirty years ago, I can question her motives in coming out with it now, I can rubbish her character, dredge things up that'll hurt her, that sort of thing.'

'Do we know her name?' he asked me.

'Only her maiden name', I said. 'But I can easily find out what she's called now.'

'Can you? Can you, Jonathan? I think that would be most helpful.'

He came and sat next to me on the calf-skin sofa.

'I had a drink with Lord Marden last night', he said in a whisper.

I watched his pupils very closely.

'Oh, really?' I said as nonchalantly as I could.

'Yes, yes it was most enlightening, most enlightening. We talked about you. He told me – in complete confidence of course – what a fantastic job you did on that rape case. Making sure it didn't get to trial, I mean.'

'What exactly did he say, Martin?' I asked, my voice wavering slightly.

'I think you know *exactly* what he said, Jonathan.'

The word *'fuck'* escaped from my mouth before I had a chance to close it.

'Exactly', said Martin.

We sat in silence.

'I had nothing to do with Desmond Lyons' death', I whispered.

'Of course you didn't', said Martin flatly. 'Now. This woman. How much will it take?'

'What do you mean *how much will it take?*'

'To make the problem go away.'

I watched as Martin took a company chequebook out of his pocket.

'My company makes high value payments all the time', he said. 'Nearly every day.'

'But —'

He waved me away and smoothed out the chequebook on the table.

'Do you have a favoured currency, Jonathan?'

I thought for a second of the companies on the silver board downstairs. Genevieve was a nice name. It had a tax-efficient ring to it. I took another sip of *Perrier*.

'Swiss Francs', I replied.

He smiled at me and I watched carefully as he wrote out the amount, signed the cheque and left the rest blank.

CHAPTER TWELVE

I got back to chambers to see Hussain Tarzi's face filling the screen on CNN, looking bullish. Four out of five of Khaled's legal team had been shot and only Tarzi - who happened to be inside the court-house at the time - had escaped a bullet. A number of groups all over Jadzikistan proclaimed death to Khaled and his supporters. Tarzi – the only lawyer left - was under heavy military protection. Thank God he paid in advance.

'Justice must not just be done', said Tarzi, his face beaming live across the world on CNN, *'it must be seen to be done.'*

The six members of the UN Council nodded.

'Khaled Al-Khalim must be tried in England, the fount of all justice. All we seek is a fair trial', continued Tarzi.

The UN Council members conferred for a few minutes and then turned to the giant screen behind them, filled with the face of Hussain Tarzi in his secure location.

'We will need to prepare the exact wording of the UN Resolution', said the British representative, Mark Jennings, CMG, a career

diplomat, *'but I can confirm on behalf of the Committee and Her Majesty's Government that in this instance we are prepared in principle to accede to your request, in the interests of natural justice.'*

Tarzi smiled and then the giant screen went black. Khaled Al-Khalim had instructed him to find a jurisdiction where there was no death penalty and that is just what he'd done. CNN switched instantly back to another studio where a pundit called Gareth Morgan faced a grizzled presenter by the name of Donald Donald.

'Gareth - can you tell us something about the likely procedure if the Khaled trial goes to England?' asked Donald Donald.

'Sure', said Gareth. 'The prosecution will be brought by the combined states of the UN – '

'And the judge?'

'Someone very senior, I should imagine.'

'And what about Khaled Al-Khalim's lawyers? He had five but now he has only one. Can Hussain Tarzi defend Khaled Al-Khalim all by himself?'

'Yes and no, Donald.'

'Gareth?'

'The English system, Donald, is different to, say, the American model.'

'And can you explain that difference to us, Gareth?'

'Of course. Tarzi is a solicitor. He deals direct with the client but may not have a right of audience – the right to appear before a judge - in the higher courts.'

'Who does then?'

'Barristers', replied Gareth. 'The ones in wigs and gowns. Like John Cleese in *A Fish Called Wanda.*'

Donald and the others in the studio smiled.

I turned off the television and got up quickly from my desk. Jacob had his own television on outside and he was also on the phone. When he saw me he muttered something into it and put it down quickly.

'Jacob?'

'Sir?'

'Who was that?'

'No-one, sir.'

'You watching this, Jacob?'

'Yes sir. Rivetin' stuff, sir.'

'You're not thinking what I'm thinking, are you Jacob?'

'Well sir...you 'ave settled the Kelsey arbitration and what with the rape gone now, sir, you 'ave what we in the trade like to call *capacity.*'

'Capacity?'

'That's right, sir.'

'I'm flat out, Jacob. Has Tarzi called?'

'No sir.'

'Good. Good. If he does, please tell him...tell him I'm unavailable for further cases. That I'm busy with the Hotson

158

murder. And Customs – I've ignored all those cigarettes and caravans for too long now, Jacob.'

I thought of the cheque in my pocket.

'And I have to go away somewhere on family business', I added.

Three million Swiss francs - about two and a half million dollars - but no account to pay them into. Tarzi wasn't the only one who paid in advance. Jacob gave me a puzzled look.

'I've never turned daan an instruction, Mr Berry, sir. It's not ethical.'

'Well there's a first time for everything. Like I said. I've got too much on my plate right now.'

'Very good, sir.'

I walked quickly back to my room and looked at my Customs evidence. The four hundred cartons were now three hundred and fifty. I ripped open another one and fished out a pack of twenty. I felt as if someone was boiling water inside my head and that steam was about to come out of my ears. I needed something to help me depressurize.

Kate Bowyer was a very understanding woman. Even though it was six o'clock and she'd just come back from court she agreed to meet me at Claridge's. We booked the same room again in the name of Mr and Mrs Johnson.

'You seem very stressed, Jonny' she said to me as she lay in my arms, naked apart from the stockings that I liked her to keep on. 'Is it work – or is it something else?'

'It's everything.'

'Is it me?'

'No. It's not you.'

'Is it *her*?'

'No. No, it's not Georgina. It's…I've…I've got an awful feeling I'm being asked to do something – some *things* – I don't want to do. And I think…I think…I may have already agreed to do them. Sort of.'

'You *think*? *Sort* of? What *are* you talking about?'

'I suppose it'll all come down to money.'

'You seem very distant, Jonny.'

I turned to her suddenly and angled her face towards me gently.

'Money isn't everything, is it Kate?'

'Well…it all depends how *much* money we're talking about and what you're being asked to do.'

'Kate!'

'What?'

'It's just…that's a little…*mercenary*, isn't it?'

'You telling me you don't do any of this for the money, Jonathan?'

She looked at me unblinkingly.

'I used to think like that', I replied. 'But now…'

'How much would it take?' she asked me, stroking my hair away from my face. 'How much would it take to make you do something you *really* didn't want to do?'

I thought of the portrait in Dorian Gray's attic. I was tired of talking. It was nearly eight o'clock and I turned on the television set.

'Oh good!', said Kate, 'A comedy. That'll cheer you up.'

I looked up at the television screen to see the opening credits of *A Fish Called Wanda*.

'I think I'll have a bath', I said, rolling off the bed and onto the floor.

***

I got back home at ten to find Georgina watching the end of the film, the part where John Cleese and Jamie Lee Curtis are sitting on the aeroplane with the stolen diamonds and flying off into the sunset, leaving behind *his* family and *her* brother.

'Good film?', I asked, flopping down next to her on the sofa.

'Don't get any ideas', she said, staring at the screen.

I turned to look at her, her tired face, her lined forehead, the stretchmarks just above the top of her tracksuit-bottoms. She wasn't looking good tonight, nothing like Jamie Lee Curtis. We sat in silence watching Newsnight on BBC2, the whole programme dedicated to Jadzikistan and the prospective trial in London. It was grimly fascinating, like watching someone preparing your own funeral.

'Chas called', said Georgina. 'Wants me back at Silvermans. Said he saw you earlier.'

'Hmm?'

'We could afford the house, Jonathan…'

'Shhh.'

Tarzi was saying something on BBC2 and I was missing it.

'Did you hear me, Jonathan?'

I nodded, my ears only for Kirsty Wark.

'I'm tired, Jonathan', she said abruptly, standing up. 'I'm tired of staying at home all day and I'm tired of talking to a brick wall. I'm going to bed.'

'Er…OK.'

'Do you really love me Jonathan?'

I was concentrating on Tarzi's face, filling the widescreen television. He was saying something about justice.

'I SAID do you love me?' she shouted.

I turned towards her.

'You're asking me if I love you?'

'Twice.'

'What do you think, Georgina? Of course I –'

'If you loved me you'd buy that bloody house!'

'Not *now*, Georgina…'

'Fine', she said coldly. 'Just fine. You seem rather odd tonight and you smell lovely again. Another visit to the club, was it?' She leant closer and whispered into my ear. 'Or were you just fucking *her*?'

'What?'

I knew I looked startled.

'You're all the same.'

'What? Georgina? I've been -'

'I'm going back to work for Chas and I won't need you or your precious money. I don't want you here any more. You can just take your clothes and your precious Tarzi and fuck off. Call it a trial separation. Call it what you want. You're the lawyer. *Do we understand each other, Jonathan?*'

I nodded. Perfectly.

I woke at five, shaky. I'd slept maybe an hour in my study because Georgina had locked the bedroom door. I loaded what I could into the Aston and got to Heathrow airport by seven. I parked the car with all my stuff in the boot and walked into the terminal with two thousand pounds in fifties, Martin Hotson's cheque and my Dictaphone. British Airways had a flight leaving for Zurich at seven forty-five and they had three seats remaining in business class. I paid for my ticket in cash and walked quickly through passport control and baggage check. I bought a brown leather briefcase from a shop in Duty Free and headed straight to the gate via one of those interminable travelators.

Three hours later I was standing in the snow on *Banhofstrasse*, the heart of the Zurich banking district and also the location of Genevieve International SA's registered office. I pulled the lapels of my coat around my face and bought a pair of gloves. The Berrie charm needed to be kept above freezing point for it to function properly, if it was capable of functioning at all today.

'It's a zero-sum game', Chas Mullion said to me once. *'If someone wins, someone else has to lose.'* Desmond Lyons and Colleen Marden had lost. And who was the winner? The bloke wearing a new pair of gloves on Banhofstrasse, that's who. *'Keep your mouth shut. Take the money'*, Sir Wilfred had said. Well I had the money from Martin Hotson in my pocket. All because of a misunderstanding. Paid in advance by negotiable instrument. For Christ's sake, I was a pillar of the Establishment - as everyone kept reminding me – with a provenance stretching back hundreds of years. I was good old Jonathan Berry of the Norman *Berries*. Someone you could trust. I wasn't a criminal. I just worked with them.

Banhofstrasse is a long street of expensive boutiques and financial institutions. I had a huge selection of banks from which to choose and as I had no way of distinguishing one from another I pressed the buzzer of the most nondescript frontage I could find. It was for a Swiss bank called *JP Chartrier & Freres*. The frontage was blacked out, the windows heavily tinted and the pavement outside had been swept clean of snow. I heard a camera whir above me and I turned to it, flashing a bit of the *Berrie* charm. A light flashed green, one door slid open and I walked into a small cubicle. The door behind me slid shut quickly and I had to press another button. The second door had a handle and as another light flashed green I heard a click and I pushed it open.

'Guten Morgen', said a pleasant-looking girl sitting at a reception desk. *'Kann ich Ihnen helfen?'*

'I'd like to open an account.'

Just then my mobile telephone rang. I saw the number flashing up on the screen. It was Tarzi. Would he be able to tell I was in Switzerland? I let the call go through to voicemail. I looked up at a tall bald man with square wire-framed glasses standing in front of me. He bowed.

'Daniel Wesselman at your service, sir.'

He led me over to another door behind the reception area and pressed in a six digit code. 'Please follow me, sir.'

I noticed he hadn't asked me for my name.

We walked through the open door and it swung shut behind us, leaving us in an internal corridor with a number of meeting rooms off.

'We'll take *Eiger*', said Wesselman, nodding to the shiny name-plate above the door.

There was coffee steaming in a silver pot and two cups and saucers. There were fresh croissants and slices of ham and cheese. There were no windows.

'How would you like me to address you, sir?' he asked.

'Mr Desmond', I replied, thinking of the name I'd written onto Martin Hotson's blank cheque.

'Daniel Wesselman at your service, Mr Desmond. And how can I be of service?'

'I'd like to open an account today.'

'Of course, sir.'

'I'd like it to be a numbered account if possible.'

'Of course sir. How will you be making a deposit?'

I took out the Halcyon Enterprises cheque for three million Swiss francs in the name of *Mr Desmond*. Wesselman studied it and nodded.

'Very good, sir.'

He turned to a computer on the desk and typed in a few numbers. A few seconds later the printer next to him spat out a single sheet of paper.

'I can allocate you a number this morning, sir, and I will need a six digit password from you. Your cheque will clear five working days from today.'

Wesselman wrote out a ten digit number on a cream-coloured card and handed it to me.

'This is your account number, sir. I will need one signature here.'

He pushed the single sheet of paper towards me and I signed where indicated on the dotted line as *Mr Desmond*. God rest his soul. Wesselman opened a drawer and removed a credit-card-sized object that looked like a miniature calculator. It had a tiny little keyboard with twenty six letters and ten numbers.

'First you type in your ten digit account number', he said. 'And then you will be prompted for your password, which must be a minimum of six characters, ideally a mixture of letters and numbers. The first time an account number is typed in the password will be set. You will be the only person who knows the password.'

He handed me the little calculator.

'It is yours to keep.'

'How kind.'

'Most of the banks use these now', he said. 'It is another layer of security. May I ask you to type in your ten digit number in order to set your password?'

I did as he asked and the machine prompted me for a

password. I typed in V-5-L-V-5-T. The machine then spat out a four digit number.

'To make deposits, withdrawals or transfers from your account you will need to give the cashier your ten digit account number and the four digit number, which changes every fifteen minutes. You never tell anyone your password.'

'So I only use this machine when I'm in the bank about to make a withdrawal?'

'Or just before. Some of our customers prefer to perform this exercise just *before* they enter the bank's premises.'

'I see.'

Wesselman picked up my cheque and placed it inside his jacket.

'Is there anything else, Mr Desmond?'

I turned the little calculator over and over in my hand. No documents, no folders, no wallets, no promotional material. No free holiday insurance and no-one trying to sell me a loan. Just a little thing the size of a credit card and a cream business card with my account number written on the reverse.

'What happens if I forget my account number or my password?'

'You must *not* forget them', replied Wesselman. 'As you have requested a numbered account you must be aware that anyone with your account number and password and that machine will be able to access the money in the account. We do not ask questions, Mr Desmond. We simply serve validated clients. Do *you* have any more questions, Mr Desmond?'

'Five days?' I asked.

'The cheque will clear in five days', he replied.

I stood up and Wesselman led me to the door. I had no more questions.

Six doors down the street I found the little brass plaque announcing Genevieve International SA. The address matched the one I'd read into my Dictaphone. The stone-fronted building was nondescript but there was only one button to press and I couldn't press it. What would I say? And even if I got inside, I could see two little cameras whirring around the entrance lobby. I wasn't meant to know anything about Genevieve. I moved away from the window and thought about curiosity and cats.

I sat inside a small café on a side-street, sheltering from the cold with a large cappuccino, Tarzi's message burning a hole into my mobile phone. I didn't want to listen to it. I'd just paid in a cheque for three million Swiss francs or nearly two and a half million dollars. No more joint accounts. No more tax. I lit one of my hooky Marlboro lights and stared out of the window.

'*Ten mill*', Chas had said to us round his Holland Park Mansion. '*Ten mill is fuck off money. But REAL fuck off money is a hundred mill. Then you can go anywhere and do anything.*'

My telephone vibrated again. I wasn't yet in a position to say fuck off to anyone so I took out my phone and listened to Tarzi's message.

CHAPTER THIRTEEN

I got back late and spent the night at Claridges on my own. The next morning was cold and bright. Georgina didn't speak to me when I came to collect my tennis clothes and my racket. I noticed she hadn't changed the locks this time. Just after eight I walked down Abbotsbury Road – out of the house I used to live in - and into the park, past a string of empty cabs parked on double yellow lines. I was early – Tarzi had said eight-thirty - and so I warmed up on court, practicing my serve. I was getting a sweat going when at twenty past I saw a group of five men walking towards me, all in tennis clothes. Tarzi walked in the middle, easily the shortest, with his distinctive wooden rackets in their presses. The men surrounding him were burly, with earpieces and bulging pockets. They hung back slightly as he shook my hand.

'You must excuse the company, Jonathan, but it's necessary.'

The four security guards walked onto court behind us. Two of them carried rackets.

'Perhaps a doubles?' I asked.

'I don't think they play, Jonathan. *We're* not playing either.'

'Oh?'

'The trial', he replied. 'I came to talk to you about Khaled Al-Khalim. He's a very charming man. You'll meet him soon. You'll be representing him in court.'

I stood holding my racket in the morning sun, surrounded by four bodyguards and my instructing solicitor and I suddenly wished I was somebody else. Perhaps the man in green overalls by the Orangery picking up leaves with a metal stick. Birds singing, sky blue, fresh air all day and no dictators.

'Jonathan?'

'Yes?'

'You seem distracted.'

'Err…I am a little.'

'I've discussed the fee with Jacob. You are happy to take the case?'

'Errr…'

'I have been very good to you, Jonathan. You cannot say no. Not now.'

'I can't?'

'No.'

He said it very emphatically.

'What if – for the sake of argument only you understand – I *did* say no?'

Tarzi looked down at his wooden rackets.

'Your clerk has already accepted the case on your behalf, Jonathan.'

'But I told him – '

'To say no?'

'Not to accept any big instructions just now because I'm…I'm very busy.'

'You only have one important case which if I understand correctly from Jacob might never come to trial. I am also the instructing solicitor on that case and I do not think you will have any problems with *capacity*.'

'Surely I'm not senior enough?'

'Of course you are. Lord Marden has no problem at all with you appearing before him. In fact he *wants* you to appear before him.'

'What's he got to do with it?'

'He has everything to do with it. He has been chosen as the judge before a jury of twelve.'

'How convenient.'

'Yes, isn't it?'

'*All members of the same club*', I murmured under my breath.

All five of them stared at me, waiting for a response. I saw the top of a pistol butt poking out of one of the bodyguard's trousers. He started bouncing a ball on his tennis racket, counting 'one thousand, two thousand, three thousand…'

'They killed the others', I said. 'They said *death to the lawyers*.'

'England is not Jadzikistan', replied Tarzi. 'You are safe here.'

I looked behind him at the four burly men with earpieces and pistols. I didn't feel very safe.

'Khaled has been granted legal aid to fight the case. All of his accounts have been frozen and the money confiscated', said Tarzi.

'He's on legal aid?'

'If...*money* is an issue, I can make you a top-up payment from my own funds. To help with the school fees, perhaps? You have three children don't you Jonathan?'

I couldn't remember telling him I did but maybe Jacob had. Maybe Aziza had Googled me again, found the piece we put in *The Times* when Sophie died. I didn't like him talking about my kids when we were having a conversation about defending a genocidal maniac.

Tarzi moved closer to me. I could smell his aftershave. It was strong and flowery. Exotic. A little gold necklace was hanging out of his tennis shirt and I could read the legend because he was standing close enough to kiss me.

It said *Genevieve*.

***

When I parked the Aston in my spot in the Temple I received admiring glances from a gaggle of clerks standing on King's Bench Walk having a fag. I made it into chambers for ten thirty and changed into my suit in my room. Jacob came in with a cup of Earl Gray.

'Proud a yer, sir', he said.

If I died, I thought as I pulled on my jacket, my three million Swiss francs would accrue interest at one per cent per annum in perpetuity or until *JP Chartrier & Freres* shut its doors for the last time.

'Thank you, Jacob', I replied.

Jacob sloped out and I lit another hooky cigarette. I was the only paid hit-man in 21 Wessex Yard. I could only think about one death at a time and it was best not to think about my own. Maybe Martin Hotson's murder witness had a weak heart. I still didn't know her name or her address. Maybe I could ask Jacob to make her go away for me? And then again, maybe not.

I had lunch in Middle Temple Hall. Lasagne with green beans and parsnips followed by bread and butter pudding, which was my favourite. I had two portions and topped it off with a glass of *Chateauneuf du Pape*. I looked around at the chattering barristers, stuffing their faces with bread and butter pudding. They were an ugly lot. Not quite as ugly as Brian Dunne, but in general not much better. Maybe they were looking at me, pointing out to their friends the barrister who could make defendants and witnesses go away. Maybe a change of career was in order. Maybe I should buy a yacht.

It was at that glorious moment, the moment when I could feel the sun shafting through to the colour portrait in my black and white attic that a hand rested on my shoulder. It was his Lordship, resplendent in black gown.

'Glad you're on the team', he whispered into my ear. 'I hope you've had media training. We're all in for a rough ride.'

'We are?'

'Of course. But it'll be worth it, my dear boy, it'll be worth it.'

I turned to watch him walk down through the gap in the benches, gladhanding as he went.

***

'Penny for your thoughts?'

'It's going to take a bit more than a penny, Kate.'

'You've just had an hour of my time, Jonny. That's a hundred and fifty and I'll let you off the VAT.'

'How long are we going to keep doing this, Kate?'

'Doing what?'

'Come off it!'

She swung her legs off the bed and sat on the edge.

'Until we get tired of each other,' she replied.

'And how long will that be?'

'It depends.'

'On?'

'Shut up, Jonathan.'

I sat holding my head in my hands and staring at the checked bed-spread.

'I'm weak, Kate. I'm as weak as water. It's a family trait.'

'It's called being human, darling.'

It was the first time she'd ever called me darling.

'Do you love me?', I asked her.

'Do I love you?   I don't know you well enough to love you, Jonathan.'

'Not yet, maybe.'

We sat for a moment, staring at the Pugin-papered walls.

***

The Aston purred like a giant tiger, the twin exhausts marking my territory as I weaved through the streets of Mayfair and towards Hussain Tarzi's offices on Mount Street. I'd never been inside before and I wasn't sure if I was looking forward to it. In fact, apart from the car I was driving I was feeling neither dynamic nor purposeful. I felt all eight hundred years of *Berrie* charm dissolve slowly inside me and seep out of my exhaust pipes.

There didn't appear to be any security on the street. No Jadzik banners outside the offices. No anti-Khaled demonstrations. Not yet, at any rate. In fact, it was very quiet and the weather was warm and sunny. Tarzi would be up there somewhere in the brick-fronted office, probably staying away from the windows, waiting for me with the file. The Khaled file. Maybe I would finally meet Aziza, his assistant.

I used the parking sensors – there were five on the rear bumper – to let me know when I was getting close to the taxi-cab parked behind me.

I had money for the meter in the glove compartment and I took out two pound coins. I opened the door of the Aston and stepped out, avoiding the gutter, when suddenly an arm gripped my own and, before I could do anything, pulled me into the taxi-cab parked behind my Aston. The door slammed and I was dumped on the back seat as the central locking clicked shut.

'Good morning', said an American voice next to me. 'I don't believe we've met before. My name is Jim Kelsey and I believe you know where to find my twenty-two million dollars. Fancy a ride?'

'But – '

The man who'd thrown me in the cab jumped into the driver's seat, started the engine and pulled away. He was wearing an earpiece and I realized now, as I saw his face in the rear-view mirror, why he looked familiar. As we turned the corner I realized I hadn't had a chance to put any money in the meter for the Aston.

'Where are we going?'

'You like the countryside?', replied Kelsey, poker-faced.

We drove up the Marylebone Road – the A40 – out of London and into the green belt. The meter was running and I made a mental note of the cab number.

'He'll wonder where I am', I blurted out. 'I'd arranged a meeting -'

'He'll have to wait.'

'He'll be suspicious. My car's outside his office.'

'You'll think of a good excuse. You lawyers are full of excuses. Just like the FBI.'

'What are you going to do with me?'

'I'm going to talk to you.'

'We can talk here.'

'You wearing a wire, Mr Berry?'

I shook my head.

'You surprise me.'

The house was behind a line of tall cypress trees and the electric gates swung open for us as we approached. Up the graveled driveway we went and towards a large modern house built of steel and glass and wood. The cab swept up in front of the house and stopped. The meter read thirty-seven pounds sixty pence.

'You can pay me later', said Kelsey as the central locking clicked open. 'Now get out.'

The driver with the earpiece, the man I'd seen outside the King Midas Kebab House and near my house in Holland Park held the door open for me. I stepped out onto the gravel and brushed myself down.

'It's this way, Mr Berry', said Kelsey, motioning towards the large black main door. The driver was staring at me. He pointed towards the door and I followed Kelsey inside. In the entrance hall a man in a black suit and tie swept me with a metal detector just like the ones they use in airports. He also made me turn out my pockets.

'He's clean', he said.

'We'll see', said Kelsey. 'Follow me, Mr Berry. Drink?'

'Scotch.'

'Get us two Scotches would you William?'

'Very good, sir', said the man with the metal detector.

We walked into a huge open-plan living area, multi-leveled and with a soaring twenty-five foot glass ceiling. I couldn't help looking up at it, watching the clouds fly across the sky and thinking about death.

'I'm not going to hurt you, Mr Berry', said Kelsey, handing me a Scotch from William's tray. I hadn't even noticed him come in. 'I take it you know why you're here?'

'You said it was something to do with your twenty-two million dollars.'

'You have a good memory. Now sit down.'

He motioned to a large sofa not unlike the ones Martin Hotson had in his spaceship of an office. I sat, but Kelsey didn't.

'I'm very pissed-off', he said. 'Very pissed-off indeed.'

'But —'

'What were you doing at the King Midas Kebab House, Mr Berry? Dressed in jeans and then a second time in a black suit?'

'I was…curious the first time. I was on the case and it was a legitimate visit. And the second…I'd just been to a funeral down the road. You can check. That was the black suit. It was a client. Desmond Lyons.'

'Curious to see where my twenty-two million two hundred and fifty-seven thou plus change had got to?'

'Yes.'

'And did you find anything?'

'Not much.'

He stared at me over a fat glass of Scotch. I was guessing he couldn't make the connection between the giant silver board in Ropemaker Place, Tarzi, Genevieve and his money. I was guessing, and it was only a guess, that Kelsey had unwittingly paid for my wife's Tiffany ring and my holiday in Mauritius.

'I tell you what, Mr Berry, he said measuredly. 'I've got a proposition for you.'

I turned the large tumbler round and round in my hand, looking up at my new benefactor.

Kelsey's man dropped me off in his cab a few streets away and I walked the last few hundred yards. Tarzi had seen my car outside his offices, a parking ticket shoved under the windscreen-wiper and had assumed someone had either kidnapped or assassinated me. So when I finally turned up four hours later than planned, he hugged me like a brother.

'This is Aziza', he said, introducing me to a short, slightly dumpy-looking woman in her early thirties wearing a head-scarf.

'Hello Aziza. Good to meet you at last.'

From the pallid tone of her skin I don't think Tarzi let her out much.

'I will take you to meet Khaled Al-Khalim tonight', said Tarzi.

'He's in England?'

'Of course. He must face trial here next month.'

'That's quite soon, Hussain. Will it give us enough time to prepare a case?'

'Ample', he replied, grinning at me. 'I'm so glad you're not dead', he added.

'Me too.'

'What happened to you?'

'Bloody Customs and Excise – you remember, all those cigarettes? They demanded a meeting, which they never do. I just had to go.'

'It is wise that you did.'

'Oh. I'm glad you agree, Hussain.'

'I find it is best to treat all tax authorities with the utmost of respect. Better to pay the tax', he lectured, 'than to get caught.'

He was a much better liar than I was.

'Absolutely', I replied, marveling at the size of his pupils.

'Could you leave us Aziza?' he asked. Aziza smiled at me and did as Tarzi requested. He shut the door behind her and locked it.

'Where are the bodyguards?' I asked him.

'Two downstairs, two on the roof.'

'Very sensible. Will they be with us when we go to see Khaled?'

'Two of them will. Two will stay here.'

'I can't get more than two in my car.'

'Don't worry, Jonathan. No-one's going to put a bomb under your Aston Martin. We have our own special car, anyway. Just a thought, but why don't you work from here until the trial is over? It might be safer than Wessex Yard and we can easily clear some desk-space for you. I'm sure Jacob would have no objections seeing as this case is going to take up all of your time.'

'Yes', I mused, thinking how close Claridge's was – where I had all my clothes now. A five minute walk. I had my laptop with me, in the boot of the car, passworded V-5-L-V-5-T. Customs and Martin Hotson had my mobile number and Jacob would always be able to get hold of me. I'd always preferred the West End to Temple. More real, somehow. And the club was only just around the corner. Plus I remembered what Kelsey had proposed to me. It would do me no harm to be in close proximity to Hussain Tarzi's filing cabinets.

'This case means a *lot* to me, Jonathan', said Tarzi. 'Let me tell you how much it's going to mean to you.'

I leaned forward, catching another whiff of Tarzi's expensive aftershave.

My list of benefactors was growing.

CHAPTER FOURTEEN

The engine-noise was so well dampened that it felt like we were gliding rather than driving through the streets of London, Hussain Tarzi and I, sitting in the back of the black Mercedes S500 behind our two bodyguards, cocooned by the retro-fitted security options and bullet-proof windows. I wondered where they were keeping Khaled Al-Khalim. I used to see them take all the IRA terrorists to the Old Bailey in a convoy of large white police trucks and squad cars every morning at about nine-thirty or so, ready for the off at ten or ten thirty depending on the court and the judge. Khaled wasn't IRA though. If there were terrorist threats then the Old Bailey, the country's top criminal court, was an obvious target.

Maybe he had been taken to the Houses of Parliament, already high-security, to one of the secret vaults underneath the building sunk far lower than the River Thames. We seemed to be heading for the river now, so maybe that was where he was. We reached the river and we crossed to the other side, the south side. We drove along the South Bank and then cut north again. The car drove quickly through the London streets. The S500 had diplomatic plates and the driver, one of the bodyguards, paid no attention whatsoever to bus-lanes, traffic lights, pedestrians or other motorists.

'He is Jadzik', said Tarzi as we sped down another bus lane and straight through another red light. We were now in King's Cross, passing a string of drug dealers and prostitutes and police cars that did nothing to stop us flouting all the traffic regulations right before their eyes. The driver swung the car round north again and we headed up towards Camden Town, Kentish Town and suddenly we were driving past the King Midas Kebab House. I tried to act as nonchalantly as I could. I watched Tarzi. He barely gave it a second glance as we whizzed along, borne up by the Merc's powerful air suspension.

The prison gates were familiar. This is where I'd come to visit Desmond Lyons, my dead client, in his holding cell. Brixham was a high-security prison but not an obvious choice for the world's most wanted man. Perhaps that was a good thing. There was a solitary wing and Tarzi told me that no-one in the prison knew Khaled Al-Khalim was there. He had been brought in with a bag over his head under a different name and dumped straight into solitary confinement. Tarzi had requested a few little extras for him – after all, Khaled was used to life's little luxuries – and so he had a small television set, DVD player and radio, two packs of playing cards and the bible.

'He is a religious man', said Tarzi, walking quickly down the corridor.

I couldn't think of anything to say in reply. The man who had garroted Desmond Lyons was being held in the same part of the prison. Dangerous places, prisons, and even with the bodyguards and Tarzi's confidence I felt like I always did when *inside*: paranoid.

'We've come to see number sixteen', said Tarzi to the prison guard. 'Mr Wazeem.'

The guard looked blankly at Tarzi. He didn't recognize him. They didn't watch CNN in this prison. No-one watched *Newsnight* either. No-one in here cared about reality unless it was reality TV. All the inmates wanted was mindless escapism. They preferred *The X Factor* and *I'm a Celebrity, Get me out of Here.*

Khaled Al-Khalim was very tall and extremely good-looking. He was manacled with his hands in front of him. His legs were also chained together with about a foot of give. He had a charming smile and his teeth were very white, as white as Brenda Mullion's. His fingers were long and delicate just like Tarzi's and just like the man in the kebab house. One bodyguard was in the cell with us whilst the other was waiting outside with six armed SAS or MI6 tasked with stopping anyone getting to Khaled.

'Jonathan Berry. Khaled Al-Khalim.'

'Hello Mr Berry. Delighted to meet you.'

Khaled shook my hand, rattling his chains as he did so. He was as calm as if he were at a tea-party handing out cucumber sandwiches. 'Tarzi tells me you're an Oxford man.'

'Yes, that's right.'

'I am as well.'

'Oh? I didn't know.'

'I didn't actually attend the university, Mr Berry, but I endowed one of the colleges with a fellowship for Jadzik Studies.'

'Very commendable.'

'We're very similar you see. You and I can both trace our family trees back hundreds of years, in my case to Attila the

Hun.'

I thought it prudent not to doubt his lineage.

'My grandfather was hanged for treason. Hussain tells me you lost a relative in the same manner. I feel we both understand loss. I was very close to my grandfather.'

'Mine was hanged in 1649', I said, 'so we weren't that close.'

Khaled looked at me sadly.

'No. No, I suppose you can't have been.'

I stared at his pupils. They were heavily dilated. Either he was on heavy medication or he was completely insane. Or both.

'Do you like to play Monopoly?' he asked.

'Sometimes.'

'Excellent. We might have a game sometime. You can be my *get out of jail free* card. Ha ha ha! I always have the little silver hat, you understand? Maybe you can have the car or the dog.'

I nodded. The man was barking mad.

'He'll do' he said to Tarzi.

'Splendid', Tarzi replied.

I obviously had no say in the matter.

'Is there anything else?' asked Khaled, 'because there's rather an important TV programme at eight.' He looked at his watch. 'Which is in one minute.'

I looked at Tarzi. He shook his head and quickly ushered

me out of the door. I stood in the corridor and watched the guards lock up as the unmistakable opening strains of the theme from *The Bill* percolated through the metal grille in Khaled's cell door. Tarzi led me down the corridor again and out of the solitary wing.

'He likes you', said Tarzi as we got into the S500.

'Is that good?'

'It all depends on *why* he likes you.'

'And *why* do you think he likes me, Hussain?'

Tarzi shrugged. Probably because he was getting me a lot cheaper than Lord Marden.

I moved into H Tarzi & Co.'s offices the next morning and was given a desk next to Aziza which meant she could keep an eye on me. A whole wall of the room was dedicated to the charges and evidence in the Khaled case. A lot of it was photographic and a lot of it was in Jadzik, which Aziza was tasked with translating.

I flicked through the pile of photographs in front of me, all numbered and glued onto white paper. They were horrible, just like the pictures they showed on television that made me want to look away.

Children burnt, fathers decapitated, houses destroyed, mothers raped. However, the photographs, although disgusting, did not necessarily prove anything. They were circumstantial evidence. It could not be proved how a man's head came to be separated from his body or who had done it or who had ordered it or why. None of these things were clear from the photographs. The pleadings, at least the ones I read in English, were not quite so unclear. They detailed more than six hundred and fifty individual charges against Khaled Al-Khalim, sometimes one charge dealing with thousands of deaths.

In many cases there were hundreds of signed statements, including some from Khaled's own soldiers detailing the horrors which he had ordered. Ethnic cleansing on a grand scale, petty jealousies worked out via murder and rape and a plundering of the Jadzik Treasury's coffers. I scratched my head. There were three hundred files, each one about five hundred pages. I had to start somewhere. I picked up the first file in a series of fifteen and turned to the first page.

In the years since his father died Khaled Al-Khalim – on behalf of the people of Jadzikistan - received nearly seventeen billion dollars in foreign aid. Only five billion was ever spent. The other twelve billion vanished.

It made Martin Hotson and Chas Mullion's wealth pale into insignificance. You could buy a whole country for twelve billion and that's exactly what Khaled Al-Khalim had done. It was very difficult to tell where the money had gone because it had been removed in cash, sometimes more than ten million dollars a day, over a number of years.

'Aziza?' She looked up. 'How long has Mr Tarzi acted for Khaled?'

'Many years. He used to act for his father.'

'Has he ever been under suspicion? I mean, he is his lawyer. He won't be arrested will he?'

'Oh no. Mr Tarzi was investigated some years ago by a Foreign Office Committee in conjunction with the Law Society. They found nothing because he is a very honourable man.'

'Of course. I was just…wondering.'

I was wondering if Lord Marden had been on that committee.

***

I wasn't missing Georgina much. Apparently she'd started work at Silverman Bach and had a nanny to look after the kids in the day and to do the school run. Chas called me up and said she and I should get back together. I lied and told him that I'd be happy to. I missed the kids but I spoke to them every evening in between dealing with Khaled, Kelsey and Hotson and I'd go and see them at the weekend.

Jacob sent round a couple of cartons of my hooky cigarettes to Claridge's for me which was rather nice of him. He knew – my mind-reading clerk knew – that I was on the verge of something special, that my career in one way or another was going to take off big-time, that I'd soon be one of the hottest properties around. As Jacob received a percentage of everything I made he was willing me success from the very bottom of the purple lining of his checked *Paul Smith* suit.

Aziza didn't talk much. She worked twelve hour days translating documents from Jadzik into English. We had three weeks to prepare for the trial, which in the real world wasn't enough time but Tarzi kept telling me it was. One of the four bodyguards sat outside his office twenty-four hours a day. Tarzi must have had an ensuite toilet and coffee-making facilities because I didn't see him come out much.

I put my fingers round the tiny little calculator in my trouser pocket, the one Daniel Wesselman gave me in Zurich, the one controlling the destiny of my three million Swiss francs. Maybe Tarzi had another little calculator for Genevieve International SA, the company whose office was only six doors from Daniel Wesselman's? Maybe, maybe if I could find his little calculator and the account number I could guess the password, the one that would spit out four little numbers that unlocked all funds, all twenty-two million less *expenses* from which Kelsey would give me a cut. Maybe if I swapped my little calculator with Tarzi's he'd never know. I'd be taking an awful risk.

'Does Mr Tarzi have a safe?' I asked suddenly. Aziza looked at me with the bleary eyes of someone who had slept in the office the previous night and needed a shower.

'Why do you want to know?'

'I have some valuables. I was wondering if I could put them in his safe. I don't trust the one at Claridge's.'

'Ask him yourself', she replied. 'He's in there now.'

I got up and walked across to the corridor. One of the bodyguards was gazing ahead of him, side-pocket bulging. His eyes were open but there was no-one home. I walked straight past him and into the office. He didn't even turn. The door was unlocked.

'Jonathan?' said Tarzi, looking up from his desk.

'I need to put something in your safe, Hussain. I'm walking around with it and I don't feel…comfortable.'

His eyes lit up.

'Is it valuable?'

'It is to *me*.'

'Of course I'll put it in for you. Just leave it here and I'll do it in a moment.'

'Thanks Hussain.'

I took off my wedding ring and handed it to him. He stared at it for a moment and then shook his head sadly.

'Sit down, Jonathan', he said paternally.

I sat and he stood, walking over to the portrait of the Queen hanging behind his desk. He took it down to reveal a small metal safe about twelve inches by eight in the wall.

'I can't help thinking about the children when a marriage breaks down', he said, twisting the combination lock a few times and making sure he blocked my line of sight. 'Sometimes a gift...'

'She's had enough of those', I replied.

Tarzi opened the safe quickly, popped my ring in and closed it again swiftly. He twisted the combination lock a few times and then replaced the painting of the Queen.

'All done.'

'Thank you Hussain. That's a weight off my mind.'

He sat down opposite me and folded his arms.

'Three weeks to go, Jonathan until we begin. The press want me to give an interview but I have refused. Please tell the reporters that you have no comment if they try to get you to say anything.'

'I will.'

'What's happening on our *other* case together?'

'You mean the Martin Hotson double-jeopardy thing?'

'Yes. He told me he's asked you to do some special research for him. He didn't say what, exactly. I hope it's going well.'

'I...I...it's a bit of a dead-end at present', I replied.

I'd nearly forgotten I was meant to be tracing Martin Hotson's witness and disposing of her. I'm sure I could find someone to do the disposal for less than fifty thousand quid – perhaps one of my old clients - but I wasn't sure I could find the target.

The prosecution, understandably, was being very secretive. The witness's maiden name was Diane Yarrow but no-one was releasing details of her married name. All I could find was a birth certificate and the old police records for her from thirty-odd years ago. It all seemed to stop after 1976. She must be about fifty now, probably with a couple of grown up children.

Tarzi shrugged.

'Never mind', he said, 'I think you really must concentrate everything on Khaled Al-Khalim, don't you? At least for the next few weeks.'

'Yes Hussain. You're right.'

'You're happy with your fee?'

'Yes it's very generous.'

My official fee was about ten thousand. My unofficial fee, so Tarzi had told me, was three hundred thousand pounds. Jacob would receive an additional hundred thousand on top. No wonder Jacob was being so nice to me. I stood up and headed out of the door. It was time to call on one of my old clients.

The advantage of being a criminal barrister is that you always knew where to go to find a safe-cracker. I'd got off Bobby Thornton about two years ago and we'd got on very well. Of course, I must admit, he'd been guilty. Bobby Thornton lived in a tiny studio flat in Chelsea – *Sloane* something or other - that wasn't much bigger than some of the safes he'd broken into.

Chelsea was only fifteen minutes in the car and the Aston didn't look out of place amongst the four-by-fours and sporty Audis belonging to the other residents.

Bobby had had a privileged upbringing, private school, university and some money and after all of that his chosen career was safe-cracking.

'Why?' I remember asking him the first time I interviewed him about three years before.

'For the big one', he replied. 'That's why we all do it, Jon. All you need is one big one and you never know, not til you crack it and get in, how big it's going to be.'

'How big does the big one have to be?'

'You'll only know when you get it', he replied, smiling and tapping his nose.

Everyone's definition of fuck-off money was different and Bobby agreed to help me stage a break-in for five thousand in cash no questions asked.

'I'll be there with you. We just need to get Tarzi out and keep Aziza and the bodyguard distracted.'

'How we gonna do that, me ole' china?'

'It's OK Bobby. I've got an idea.'

The good thing about driving an Aston Martin is that you drew covetous glances from men and lascivious ones from women.

It was a pulling machine and swift lunchtime drives around the block yielded pleasant results.

I reckoned I could have bedded a different woman at Claridge's every day that week and probably twice-over at weekends. I didn't however put it to the test. I contented myself with the lovely Kate. She was very supple and slender and sexy and I never got tired of the way she crossed and uncrossed her legs or the way she took off her black-plastic-framed glasses or the way she smiled and the tiny wrinkles around her eyes made her look even sexier.

'Do you love me?' I asked her one night at Claridge's.

'Don't ask me that.'

'We've seen each other nearly every day this week.'

'I know we have.'

'Doesn't your husband notice anything?'

'No. He's not the jealous sort. Actually he's a police officer. Scotland Yard.'

'Does he have big feet?'

'Enormous', she replied, and we both collapsed in laughter on the bed.

CHAPTER FIFTEEN

Faster, faster down the stairs, breathing noiselessly they came. Down from the roof, across the stairwells, guns in hand, Glock pistols with silencers, black jackets hanging open, trousers baggy and loose. Silent in black and grey *Nike Air* trainers, Tommy Hilfiger jumpers and black baseball caps.

'I saw them out there', I said, trembling behind a desk. 'Three of them. Maybe more. They...they threw something into my car.'

One of the black baseball caps nodded at me. I held Bobby Thornton's hand. He was shaking but his disguise was perfect. Officially Bobby was helping me today with my research on the Hotson murder. He wore large metal-rimmed spectacles and a geeky suit. He looked like a nerd, which is how I introduced him *sotto voce* to Tarzi. I knew Tarzi had to leave early, that he had a meeting at Velvet that evening, probably with Lord Marden. They weren't meant to speak to each other, certainly not about Khaled Al-Khalim, but then anything that went on inside the club was sacrosanct.

Tarzi locked his door and took the two-person lift with

Aziza to the basement.

'I need a couple of hours', I said to them as the doors were shutting. 'And I need to calm down.'

'Take your time', said Tarzi. 'But do whatever the security guards say.'

I gave him a flash of Berrie charm as his face vanished behind the old sheet-metal door. We were meant to stay away from the windows in case there were snipers – as if there could be snipers in Mayfair – and I was pleased to see the guards were taking the whole thing seriously. One of them was stationed on the roof with night-vision binoculars whilst the other three were skirting around my car, my lovely Aston. I'd thrown a piece of rock wrapped in cloth through the windscreen of my own pride and joy. The car alarm had been really impressive.

'How long do you need?' I asked Bobby but he was already fiddling with the lock on Tarzi's door and opened it as I turned to him.

'Not long.'

We both kept low because the curtains were open and the guards might have been able to see us if we stood. There was enough light from the streetlamp for Bobby to see what he was doing and for me to see what Bobby was doing. He wore gloves, as did I, clear plastic ones from the garage round the corner. He was tapping the area around the combination dial of the safe. I looked down at the portrait of the Queen resting against the wall.

'Evening ma'am', I said and turned the picture over so she couldn't see what we were doing.

Thirty seconds was not a very long time but it felt like a very long time when you were a criminal.

'That'll do it', said Bobby as the safe-door swung open.

'Move away please Bobby', I said, handing him an envelope with five thousand pounds inside. 'I'll take it from here.'

'How are you going to lock Tarzi's door, Jon? And what about the safe. Do you know how he left it?'

I shook my head.

'Then, Jon, I suggest that I stay.'

I couldn't risk using a torch so I peered into the corners, letting my eyes adjust to the dim light. My wedding ring was still in there, untouched. It lay in a little plastic tray with a few other bits of jewellery and a gold cigarette lighter. Under it were some personal papers including Tarzi's passport. No bank statements. No mini calculator from *JP Chartrier et Freres*. I looked again into the little plastic tray of jewellery. I could see Tarzi's gold pendant, the one that said *Genevieve*. I picked it up and turned it over. Etched onto the back was a ten digit number.

'Where are they, Bobby?'

Bobby crept out into the corridor.

'Still downstairs. You've got one minute, Jon and then I reckon they'll be up here.'

I keyed the ten digits carefully into my telephone.

'Jon – they're coming inside!' hissed Bobby.

I replaced the gold pendant carefully back in its tray, next to my wedding ring. Bobby shut the safe carefully and then we headed quickly out of the door. Bobby locked it behind us and suddenly we were back at my desk, sweating lightly. I started writing feverishly as one of the guards ran up the stairs. Neither of us looked up as he checked Tarzi's door. Satisfied it was locked he headed back downstairs. Just as he left my phone beeped with the text message I'd just sent myself with the ten digit account number for Genevieve.

'It's addictive, ain't it Jonathan?' said Bobby with the faintest of smiles. 'Crime, I mean?'

I just stared at my text message, oblivious to everything else.

***

There were just so many of them that it had to happen sooner or later. They must have followed me back that night after the men came to repair my windscreen. I drove the Aston back to the underground car-park near Claridges as I didn't want to leave it outside Tarzi's office all night. The next morning, when I drove past Velvet on my way to Mount Street I saw them in their droves, holding their large Nikons and Canons, zooming in on my face as I sat behind the wheel of the Aston, taking digital photo after digital photo. A television crew was on the pavement outside Tarzi's front door.

There was a private basement entry round the back but it only took one car and I knew the S500 would be in there.

It was almost eight in the morning and there was a meter free almost right outside. I used the parking sensors and zoomed quickly into the space. I checked my face in the mirror. I had a few more grey hairs and the crow's feet around my eyes seemed a little more pronounced.

I slotted four coins in the meter and strode towards the

main door of the building amidst a flurry of flashguns.

'What's your defence Mr Berry?' someone shouted. 'Does your client admit to ordering the deaths of three hundred women and children in the village of *Raddo* in 2002?'

I stopped for a moment.

'Is it true no-one else would take the case Mr Berry?' shouted someone else. 'Can we ask why *you've* taken it?'

I was paralysed on the doorstep, listening at first hand to what the world thought of me and my client.

'How much money are you getting, Mr Berry? Isn't your client legally-aided?'

'Have you had death threats?'

'Where's yer wedding ring, Mr Berry?'

'Is it true you've separated from your wife?'

I ran inside and slammed the door.

No-one had mentioned Kate Bowyer yet or her policeman husband.

He'd probably break me in two if he found out I was banging his wife and then Georgina would run me over in her black Range Rover.

'I said it wouldn't be easy, Jonathan.'

'You did, Hussain. So did Lord Marden.'

'You mustn't take any notice of what the press say.'

'How do they know I've separated from my wife?'

'They've probably been following you all week.'

'*What?*'

'Jonathan, Jonathan I need you to be *calm*', said Tarzi. 'You really must learn to relax. There's absolutely nothing to worry about.'

'There isn't?'

Tarzi smiled and shook his head.

'I'm with you all the way', he said as he walked past the bodyguard, into his office and locked the door.

I looked up at the clock. It was eight thirty. Would Tarzi notice anything? Had Bobby set the combination lock back to its original position? Had I remembered to replace all the jewellery in the little plastic tray? I stood and knocked on Tarzi's door.

'*Yes?*' he asked.

'It's me.'

I heard him unlock the door and then it opened.

'Yes, Jonathan?'

'I think I better take my wedding ring back. The press are going to have a field day.'

'Of course, my boy. If it makes you feel better.'

He removed the picture of the Queen from the wall, quickly opened the safe and handed me my wedding ring.

'Thanks Hussain. Last question. Do you have a

calculator?'

'A *calculator?*'

'I need to work something out and I've left mine at the house.'

He sighed, unlocked the middle drawer of his desk and looked inside. Suddenly an old Texas Instruments LED calculator in black plastic flew across the room and I caught it.

'Keep it', he said.

'Thanks.'

I watched as he re-locked the desk-drawer. It had been a long-shot.

'Is there something else Jonathan?'

I shook my head, aware of the fact I was beginning to irritate him. I headed quickly out of the door of his room and into my own.

'Good morning Aziza', I said brightly as she walked in wearing a blue headscarf that completely covered her face.

'Don't joke, Mr Berry', she replied in a monotone.

At eleven o'clock I received my first death-threat. The call came through to the H Tarzi & Co. reception, someone asking to speak urgently with Jonathan Berry, counsel for Khaled Al-Khalim.

They told the receptionist that they had some sensitive information. I picked up the telephone wondering who it could be.

'Is that Mr Berry?'

'Yes. Who's this?'

'I am the man tasked with killing you and your family.'

'*What?*' My voice dropped to a whisper. 'Who are you? What do you want?'

'The death of Khaled Al-Khalim and all those who seek to defend him.'

'But…but I'm just a lawyer. If you kill me they'll just appoint another one.'

'Then someone else will be tasked with killing your replacement.'

'Who are you? WHO ARE YOU?' said Tarzi into my ear, suddenly on the line.

The phone went dead and Aziza looked at me sympathetically.

'You got one too?' she asked.

Tarzi stormed out of his room.

'No more calls!' he bellowed. 'No-one takes any more calls. Is that understood? They're trying to intimidate us. But it's not going to work. This sort of thing never works.'

Aziza and I nodded. I didn't know about *her* but the intimidation was working with *me*. It was little comfort to know that Hussain Tarzi was fighting my corner, protecting me from harm and listening to all of my telephone calls.

I rang Georgina and told her about the death threat. Tarzi said he'd have someone protect her and the kids, but what were they going to do? Hang around the school playground with a Glock automatic and walkie-talkies? This wasn't Streatham, it was Kensington. Men in hoods and sneakers with thick necks and bulging pockets were thin on the ground on Campden Hill Road.

'Resign from the case', said Georgina, cutting straight through my bullshit. 'Think of the children if not me.'

'I don't think I *can* resign, Georgina.'

'Why not? Has Tarzi threatened you? Has Al-Khalim threatened you? Has anyone else threatened you?'

'Not as such…'

'Well then. Do it tomorrow. You could even quit being a barrister, Jonathan. I can make enough for both of us at Silverman Bach. Chas says there's a big deal round the corner and he's getting me in on it as his right-hand woman.'

I hadn't told her about the Swiss francs and I hadn't told her about the money from the split settlement on the Kelsey arbitration. In total it was not far off three million dollars or four million Swiss francs. Not *fuck-off* money. In fact it wasn't even enough to buy the house on Bedford Gardens or even one floor of Chas and Brenda Mullion's Holland Park wedding cake mansion.

I wasn't counting the money in the joint account because Georgina had access to that.

No, I was just counting the money that only *I* had access to. If I let Georgina earn the money I'd lose control. I still had my pride and I now had the account number for Genevieve International S.A. of Zurich.

'You mean, you want me back?' I asked.

202

'I don't know. We'd have to take it one day at a time but if it gets us all out of this horrible mess…'

'Do the kids miss me?'

'I'd be lying if I said they didn't.'

'OK. I'll speak to Tarzi when the moment's right.'

I put down the phone and closed the file I was looking at, the one filled with pictures of starving and emaciated children from Jadzikistan. I'd brought it back to my hotel room at Claridges. The management had agreed a rate of fifteen hundred pounds a week which Tarzi had agreed to pay for the duration of the Khaled trial. He also said he'd cover anything from room service and it was amazing what you could order if you knew the right people. I slipped on my dressing gown and waited for the knock on the door that signified my five o'clock was ready for me.

***

Silverman Bach was founded in 1948 in the years just after the end of the Second World War. Aloysius Silverman and Johann Sebastian Bach the Sixth, Junior (it was no joke) agreed to create a partnership whose sole aim was to make money. Silverman Bach became one of the most successful New York stockbrokers and corporate financiers. They were big in bonds, derivatives, fixed income, equities, raw materials, mergers and acquisitions and general corporate advice. They had nearly four thousand employees, average earnings a hundred and seventy thousand dollars – which included the secretaries - and two hundred partners of whom Chas Mullion was one, guys who were worth for the most part in the hundreds of millions.

Silverman Bach's balance sheet had grown from less than a hundred thousand to more than eight billion dollars. It was an astonishing success story and the partners had decided to keep it a private partnership rather than floating the business on a stock exchange, purely for the reason that that was how most of their clients liked things. But times were changing and Chas Mullion was one of the crew keen for the business to float. He would make nearly three hundred million dollars from the float on day one, plus another couple of hundred in carried interest. Why *wouldn't* he be keen? '*Fuck the clients, think of the poor bankers*', Chas would say in partnership meetings and most of the heads round the table would nod in agreement.

'You know', said Chas to my wife at nine o'clock that evening on one of Silverman Bach's many gargantuan trading floors, 'as a senior VP you'd make five mill – dollars – from a float.'

Georgina smiled, sat down on the edge of Chas's desk and crossed her legs.

'But as an associate partner, you could double that', he added.

'Associate partner?'

'You heard.'

Georgina's skirt seemed to creep up ever so slightly and her smile seemed to widen.

'And how, Chas my dear, does a woman at Silverman Bach make it to associate?'

'By making a partner, of course.'

'Any partner, Chas? Because you know there's always Don Fardle. I've always gone for short fat bald men with big cigars.'

'You crack me up, Georgie.'

Chas and my wife held each other's gaze across his desk. Georgina put on some lip gloss whilst Chas watched her.

'Where can we go?' said Georgina. 'I assume home's out of the question?'

'You bet - Brenda's got radar. No. I know where we'll go.' Chas picked out about five thousand pounds in fifties from his drawer and stuffed them into his pocket.

'They do the *best* room service…'

I let a couple of days go by before I decided to try and have another look for the little calculator for Genevieve's account at *JP Chartrier et Freres*. I knew it wasn't in Tarzi's safe. I discovered from Aziza that Hussain Tarzi lived at a succession of hotels ranging from Le Meridien on Piccadilly to the Lanesborough to the Savoy. He didn't have a fixed English address other than the office. I couldn't believe he would trust the little calculator – if he had it of course – to one of the hotels. Perhaps he carried it with him but I couldn't believe, for example, that he had it with him when we first met on a tennis court in Holland Park. No. It had to be somewhere in the office. Somewhere safer and less obvious than the safe.

The car that Tarzi used was registered to H Tarzi & Co and as Hussain Tarzi was the only partner he was effectively the registered owner. It was kept in a high-security underground car-park, a top of the range Mercedes S500 in which I had traveled on that first visit to Khaled Al-Khalim in Brixham prison.

I got in early and took the elevator down to the basement level but when the door opened I came face to face with one of the bodyguards.

'Excuse me', I said. 'I think I left something in Mr Tarzi's car.'

He just stared at me, thick-faced and cold-eyed.

'Sorry, do you speak English?'

The man nodded.

'Would it be possible to look in Mr Tarzi's car?'

Another stare and I saw the bulge of a gun in his jacket.

'Maybe I should ask Mr Tarzi first?'

The man nodded again and I got back in the elevator.

'Sorry to have troubled you', I said as the steel-plated door slid shut in front of me and a little voice announced we were going up.

I walked out of the elevator and towards my desk where I could see a stack of that morning's newspapers. I sat down as Aziza walked in, this time in a brown head-scarf. *'Bring back hanging!'* was the front-page headline of one of the red–tops. *'Where are they keeping Khaled?'*, the headline of another, offering a hundred thousand pounds for his whereabouts. But the one that made my flesh creep was on page five of a far more sober newspaper.

'Legal aid barrister Berry drives an Aston' ran the heading, beneath it a picture of me getting out of my car in front of Tarzi's office, harassed and grim-faced, my jacket flapping in the breeze. Even worse, underneath someone had snapped Georgina putting the children in the Range Rover, their little faces blanked out but Georgina's and that of our expensive four-by-four very visible.

'Barrister Jonathan Berry, 35, specializes in rape, robbery and

cigarette smuggling but he's never done a murder. Married to Silverman Bach banker Georgina, 34, he is best-known as one-time defence lawyer for Desmond Lyons, the man accused of raping Colleen Marden, granddaughter of Lord Marden of Winchelsea. Berry didn't have to prove himself in court, however, as Miss Marden committed suicide and Lyons was mysteriously garroted in prison.'

'Not yet Queen's counsel, Berry seems an unusual choice to defend the most evil dictator ever to stand trial in England, neither senior nor high-profile enough. He is up against Nicholas Furniss QC, 55, a top barrister in the million pound club with a spectacular record. Berry's instructing solicitor, Hussain Tarzi of H Tarzi & Co, declined to make any comment as to the choice of Mr Berry as Khaled's counsel. Incidentally, Lord Marden is the judge appointed to the Khaled trial.'

'Jonathan?'

I looked up to see Hussain Tarzi and his bodyguard.

'Have you thought again about having one of these?' he asked, pointing to the bodyguard.

'A bodyguard?' I asked.

'Perhaps one for you and another for your wife.'

'Err…'

'If you change your mind, Jonathan, just let me know.'

He turned to go back into his room and I looked down at the newspapers, the picture of me, the picture of Georgina, the picture of my children and I took a deep breath.

'Hussain?'

'Yes Jonathan?'

'I'm having…doubts.'

Hussain Tarzi stopped and walked slowly back towards me, a concerned look on his face.

'Doubts? What sort of doubts my boy?'

'The press are raising a number of questions about me and my wife and children and...and I'm not used to receiving death threats. Neither are they.'

'Do you know how many times my life has been threatened, Jonathan?'

I stared at him blankly. He looked so calm.

'No', I replied, hesitantly.

'Hundreds. And yet I'm still here, aren't I? If a man bows to terrorism he shrivels and dies. He becomes frightened of his own shadow. We have to go and see Mr Al-Khalim this evening and I don't want to hear about doubts. Mr Al-Khalim will not want to hear about doubts. He will want to know how we are going to defend him. He will want to know our strategy. He will want to know *your* strategy.'

'But I don't have a - '

'Enough', he said firmly. 'Enough. Why do you think you are paid so well, Jonathan? You are happy to take the money, but you are not happy with the responsibility that comes with it. Just do your best and stop having doubts.'

He headed in the direction of his office and before I could say anything he'd gone inside and locked the door.

I turned back to the newspapers. Suddenly 21 Wessex Yard and seven-seat Volvo estates were looking very inviting.

I made it out of the basement exit of Tarzi's office and walked quickly around a few blocks before jumping in a black cab. I think I managed to get to 21 Wessex Yard without being followed by either the paparazzi or anyone trying to kill me. Jacob wasn't sitting at his desk when I walked through the door. He was sitting at mine and in front of him on the desk was something that made me catch my breath. It was a tiny calculator. I stopped dead and Jacob slipped it quickly into one of the pockets of his Paul Smith jacket when he saw me.

'Morning sir', he said rather hurriedly.

My mind was whirring so fast I felt like vomiting. I'd come here to escape from the West End, to check up on messages and to see if Customs or Martin Hotson had called – Kelsey certainly wouldn't - but now all I could think of was the little machine in Jacob's jacket pocket and whether or not it could possibly – somehow – be what I was hoping it might be.

'Morning Jacob', I replied as casually as I could. 'What's up?'

Jacob stood abruptly.

'I was just leaving, sir.'

'Oh? Where are you off to?'

I was praying it wouldn't be Zurich and I couldn't help noticing that Jacob's voice seemed to have lost some of its cockney twang.

'Back to me desk, sir.'

And now the twang was back again.

'You couldn't get me a cup of Earl Gray could you Jacob?'

'Yessir. Nice to 'ave you back sir.'

I went straight over to my hooky cigarettes and pulled open another carton. I had to be quick but Jacob always took off his jacket when he made me a cup of tea and the kitchen was all the way down the hallway.

I waited a moment and then poked my head out of my door. There was Jacob's jacket, resting on his chair, St Paul's cathedral and the Tower of London etched into the purple lining. He had no reason to be suspicious of me. I had a *Desmond* after all. I quickly took out my mobile phone to check on the account number that I'd copied into the memory from the reverse of Tarzi's gold necklace. I reached into the purple jacket pocket and found the little calculator. I looked up again. I could hear the kettle boiling. I didn't have much time at all. Just a drop of the tea-bag into the cup, a dash of milk and he'd be off. How did I know this was Tarzi's, anyhow? Perhaps lots of banks gave these out. Perhaps it was Jacob's own account containing all the commissions that weren't paid in the usual way, in which case it wouldn't accept Genevieve's ten digit account number. Perhaps it was just a calculator.

I tapped in the ten numbers. The machine thought about it for a split second and then came up with the magic letters I had been hoping for: PASSWORD.

I already knew what I was going to tap into the tiny keyboard: V-5-L-V-5-T. The little grey screen went blank. I could hear Jacob walking down the corridor, his steps coming closer and closer. In a minute he'd turn the corner and see me standing there with it. *Come on, come on…* It was like watching the lottery with five balls in the bag and waiting for the sixth. The china cup rattled against the saucer only a few feet away and suddenly the grey screen spat out a four digit number.

'Your tea, sir', said Jacob, rounding the corner and handing me a china cup.

'Thank you, Jacob', I replied, feeling the little calculator now sitting in my trouser pocket. I hoped that in my haste I'd put the right one in there.

I walked back into my room, drank my tea so quickly that I scalded my tongue, stuffed two packets of hooky Marlboro lights into my pockets and headed out the door.

'Must get back', I said with a flash of Berrie charm.

Twenty-two million was a lot more than three. No-one would know I'd switched machines unless they went to the bank in Zurich. I couldn't go right then because Tarzi had told me that we had to meet Khaled that evening and I didn't want to make him suspicious by not turning up. Maybe, maybe if I took a night flight then I could be back before lunchtime the next day. Twenty-two million was *fuck-off money* by anyone's standards and no-one, I mean no-one, would ever know who'd done it. Not if I was careful. I could always tell Jim Kelsey I'd been unsuccessful and Tarzi would never suspect me. After all, *I* was the one having doubts. *I* was weak and *he* was strong. I'd never be capable of pulling off anything even remotely clever. I just had to make sure I wasn't followed.

As I walked down Wessex Yard towards the Royal Courts of Justice I lit a cigarette. Jacob had set me up. He'd set me up with Tarzi and they were all members of the same club, the one of which Lord Marden was president and I was now a member. Maybe they'd all been in the Nigerian scam together – the flake deal – Harbor Shipping, Jacob and Tarzi.

In every game there's a fool and if you can't spot him then it's you. Or me, the malleable criminal barrister exhibiting all of the *Berrie* traits that had gradually eroded our fortune over the centuries. I was respectable. I was reliable. I wasn't very clever. I used to drive a Volvo and I was still pining over my little Sophie. I was perfect.

I passed by the grand gothic building that housed the Royal Courts of Justice, the barristers in their wigs and gowns milling around the imposing entrance with their instructing solicitors and their clients. They all looked so engrossed in their own affairs, not in the least interested in mine. I thought about the Bar Ethics Code. I thought about the statute book. Maybe I should go to the authorities and tell them what I knew? Perhaps I should stop the whole thing getting out of hand before the portrait of Jonathan Berry started to ooze blood?

And then I thought about twenty two million two hundred and fifty seven thousand reasons not to.

CHAPTER SIXTEEN

Night fell and the large Mercedes whisked us on another circuitous route through the London streets, weaving in and out of traffic at high speed with the diplomatic plates acting as a deterrent to the Metropolitan Police Force and anyone else trying to follow us.

Hussain Tarzi and I sat on the heated leather seats, bundles of documents on our knees. One of the documents Tarzi had received that afternoon was the full schedule of the forthcoming trial and the exact charges which Khaled Al-Khalim was going to face. In order to expedite matters - and no doubt on Nicholas Furniss QC's advice – the prosecution had decided to focus on one horrifying incident that it felt would prove Khaled's guilt beyond all reasonable doubt. It was the butchering of three hundred women and children in the village of Raddo in Southern Jadzikistan in 2002.

By way of evidence, the prosecution would be producing forty-four separate witnesses to Khaled's involvement including three Generals, Khaled's former Minister of Defence and his third wife. There was also the signed order which in translation read as brutally as the transcripts at the Nuremberg

Trials after World War Two.

It would be impossible for me to destroy the credibility of every witness and it would be impossible to claim that the signed order was a forgery because Khaled signed each of his orders in his own blood. I quickly studied the DNA sheet before me. A perfect match.

The eight hundred and seventy photographs spoke for themselves. Some of the witnesses had admitted to taking part in the atrocity and to make matters worse they were receiving no special plea-bargains for doing so. They were testifying out of remorse or possibly even a belated sense of justice. Just like the Nazis, they pleaded *Befehl ist Befehl* – orders are orders - and everyone knew what Khaled did to soldiers who disobeyed orders. The severed heads of army deserters jammed onto the iron spikes outside the Jadzik Royal Palace served their purpose very effectively.

'What do you think, Jonathan?' asked Tarzi as he lit one of my cigarettes. 'Can you get him off?'

I had more chance of becoming Queen and Tarzi knew it. I checked my watch. It was nearly eight o'clock. I hoped this wasn't going to go on because I needed an early night and I was worrying about the little calculator sitting in the room-safe at Claridges.

Khaled's eyes were large and very dark, almost black. Only after Fawzi showed him the charge he was to face did he turn off the television set. He fixed me with the same gaze that the Jadzik population used to fear, beamed to them time and again across the State-run television network. I still couldn't quite believe I was in the same room as him.

'I cannot win, can I Mr Berry?' he said quietly.

Fawzi looked away, leaving me on my own.

'It will be difficult', I replied, choosing my words carefully despite the fact that Khaled was handcuffed and manacled at the ankles.

'So what do you estimate my chances at, Mr Berry? In percentage terms?'

'I think, sir, that Mr Tarzi has saved your life by getting the case transferred to the United Kingdom. To be brutally honest, I am not sure, in the face of this overwhelming evidence, what more I can do, although I will do my best at the trial. You see, no jury will acquit under these circumstances.'

Khaled nodded.

'Then I must look at my position from a question of *status*, Mr Berry. I use the word *status* in the same way mission control uses it on a space mission. We are where we are, no?'

I nodded, warily.

'If no jury will acquit, then we must take the jury out of the equation and plead guilty', said Khaled, 'and you must beg for the judge's mercy.'

'You want to plead guilty?'

'I do.'

'He does', said Tarzi firmly.

'And I wish to make restitution to the people of Jadzikistan, to the thousands of fatherless families. This would have a bearing on the court's leniency, would it not?'

'It might', I responded.

'Do you think a billion dollars might do it?' he asked

innocently, eyebrows raised.

Tarzi dropped me back at Claridge's at ten. The second I got up to my room I checked the safe in the cupboard next to the mini-bar. The *JP Chartrier et Freres* security device – the one I'd switched with Jacob's - was still in there and he presumably still had mine. I'd called him three times during the day to ask if there were any messages and to make sure he hadn't got on a plane. He'd answered the phone on the second ring each time without a hint that anything was amiss and he was even there at half-nine when I called him from the Mercedes on the way back from Brixham prison.

I went over to the desk by the window and opened the big hotel folder filled with London travel information including a list of British Airways flights out of Heathrow. I quickly checked for any flights that evening to Zurich but the last one was at ten-thirty.

I'd never make it. The first one tomorrow morning was at ten to six. That was a possibility.

I'd pay cash again and come back on the eleven o'clock. With a following wind I'd be at my desk just after lunch.

Suddenly I noticed that the phone next to my bed was flashing red. Someone had left a message for me and only three people knew I was staying here – Jacob, Tarzi and Kate. I flicked the play button.

'Jonathan? Jonathan are you there? Bugger it...'

I heard the beep – beep – beep of a public call-box and then the sound of Kate dropping another coin into the slot.

'Jonathan? Listen. It's me. I've had a terrible row with Mark. I'm in Islington and I'm coming over. You'll be there won't you? Jonny?'

I could hear the desperation in her voice. Mark was her husband and tonight was the one night I didn't want her to come over.

'OK...I've seen a cab. See you later.'

The phone went dead and I checked the message time. Nine-forty-five. She'd be here soon and there was nothing I could do to stop her. I was still booked in as *Mr Johnson* and presumably they would simply let *Mrs Johnson* – i.e. Kate – straight upstairs to see me. The trouble was, *Mr Johnson* needed to sleep. Tomorrow was going to be a big day. I needed a clear head. And then...and then there was Kate. I leaned over, pressed the button for room-service and ordered a bottle of Bollinger.

I jumped in and out of the shower and when she knocked on the door I suddenly realized that today was the first day I'd forgotten to ring my children. I looked across to the ice-bucket and the two glasses, slipped on a thick toweling dressing-gown and switched on the television. A film was starting on BBC1. It was *The Portrait of Dorian Gray.* I quickly changed the channel and opened the door.

Kate virtually fell into my arms. Her hair was matted, her glasses were crooked and mascara was smeared around her eyes.

'Thank God', she said. I took a quick look up and down the corridor and helped her inside.

'Are you OK?'

'I will be after some of that', she replied, pointing at the champagne.

I watched her as she took off her coat and let it fall to the floor.

'Does he know about us?' I asked.

'Does *who* know?'

'Mark. Your husband.'

'No.'

The cork popped and I poured.   We clinked glasses and she downed hers in one.

'Give me another.'

She drank the second just as quickly.   I hadn't even touched my glass. She kicked off her shoes and lay on the bed gazing at the ceiling.

'It's all fucked up, Jonny. All of it.'

This was all I needed right now. She held her empty glass out to me and I topped it up.

'The bastard's gone and done it now.'

'What's he done, Kate? Did he hit you?'

'Believe me, if Mark had hit me I'd be in hospital. He's six-four and two hundred pounds. He plays second row. No. He didn't hit me. He's never hit me. Not in that way, anyhow.'

'So what's happ –'

'The fucker's been having an affair.'

I finally took a sip from my glass and Kate sat up.

'He's been banging his secretary – he calls her Miss Moneypenny but I know who she is. She's twenty-three and blonde and she probably sucks his dick all day long. Bastard!'

She threw her crystal champagne glass against the wall and it shattered onto the carpet. We turned to look at each other, eyes wide, like naughty school-children. She started to laugh and it set me off too.

'Can you believe it!' she said. 'After all the times I've fucked around I catch *him* at it and I lose it completely –'

'*All* the times?'

'Well you don't think it's just been *you*, do you Jonny?'

I laughed harder.

'I mean', she continued, 'married to someone for five years who does all-night stake-outs – '

'Why did you marry him?'

'I was in love with him. Once.'

'We're a right pair.'

'At least *your* wife hasn't been banging her secretary.'

I laughed so hard, tears started to stream down my face.

They say that walls have ears, but not at Claridge's. The walls at Claridge's are very thick, so thick that no-one heard us laughing and no-one heard Kate's glass smash against the wall. No-one heard the music from VH1 that we turned up, the late night Dido special, live from Wembley Arena. Even when we made love at full volume and made the bed-springs pop, no-one heard us. We were cocooned in linen and velvet, isolated in room number four-six-three.

It was just as well that we were so well-cushioned against the outside world because less than twelve inches from our bedpost, in room number four-six-five, Chas Mullion was lying in bed with the newest associate partner at Silverman Bach.

My wife.

As I lit a post-coital cigarette, Kate asked me if she could stay the night.

'I have to be up early', I said, thinking of what I had in the safe. 'Very early.'

'So? Does that mean I can't stay?'

I looked at the clock on the bedside table. It was coming up to midnight. I would have to be up at four and at Heathrow by five.

'Of course not', I replied, looking at Kate's long legs and setting the alarm for three-thirty.

I felt remarkably clear-headed for someone who'd only had three hours sleep. The next morning, for the first time, I could understand how those City traders lived, the ones who stayed at their desks glued to their computer screens until ten and were back again at six the next morning. If you had millions to make – or even, say, twenty-two million two hundred and fifty seven thousand – then you reached a whole new level of adrenalin. You reached a different place, the top of the mountain. Chas Mullion had been up there – maybe he was still there – and the buzz was unbelievable. The only difference between what they did and what I was doing was that, technically, what I was doing was a crime and what they were doing was authorized by the Financial Services Authority.

The words *zero-sum game* kept playing in my head. *Zero-sum game, zero-sum game.* Someone wins, someone loses. William the Conqueror redistributed England from the Anglo-Saxons to the Normans. In 1084 he made my ancestor Gawain Berrie an earl and granted him feudal rights over forty thousand acres. The Berries had managed to whittle forty thousand down to zero. As I rode through the darkness of a pre-dawn morning in a black cab towards Terminal One I felt like Robin Hood, stealing from the rich to feed the poor.

I got to Terminal One at ten to five, an hour before the Zurich flight. I'd left Kate under the thick duvet and I'd emptied the safe. All I had with me was my briefcase and I was pretty sure no-one had followed me.

The streets had been empty until we got onto the A4, the old Great Western Road that wound its way over flyovers and old breweries and past GlaxoSmithKline on its way to the busiest airport in the world. The 737 was nearly empty and I decided to fly economy. Once we took off I walked up and down the aisle, stretching my legs but also looking closely at every other passenger for signs that they might be following me. I wish I'd been this paranoid before my university finals. I might not have ended up with a *Desmond*.

We landed with Swiss punctuality right in the middle of the rush-hour and I didn't get to *Bahnhofstrasse* until nearly nine-thirty. I stood outside the blacked-out windows of *JP Chartrier et Freres* with my hand in my pocket, clasped tightly around Genevieve's security device. I looked to the right and I looked to the left. I had an hour. No-one was following me. I pressed the button on the outer door and the light flashed green.

I got through the second door and walked up to the girl on reception, a different one this time. She looked at me and smiled.

'*Guten Morgen. Kann ich Ihnen helfen?*'

'I need to make a transfer.'

'Of course sir. Please take a seat and I will get Mr Rennstein.'

'Thank you.'

I was glad it wasn't Daniel Wesselman today. I looked around, trying to be as casual as I could.

I was the only client in the bank, or that was what it looked like anyway. A man with very shiny hair appeared from a mirrored door and bowed.

'Willie Rennstein at your service sir. I understand you wish to make a transfer?'

'That is correct.'

'Please follow me, sir. The terminals are this way.'

I followed Willie Rennstein as he glided through another mirrored door and into a part of the bank to which I had never been before. The walls were lined in leather and the ceiling was lit by thousands of tiny LED lights. There was a vague whiff of stale cigar smoke. We stopped at a room marked *Everest*. Willie Rennstein keyed a number into the pad by the door and then I heard a click as it swung open.

'Follow me, sir.'

Everest continued the same decorative theme, leather and LEDs. A single desk stood in the middle of the room with a black flatscreen monitor, a mouse and a keyboard. I looked at the screen. It had a prompt asking for the account number.

'Press this button when you're finished, sir', he said, indicating a red button on the side of the computer monitor.

The door shut behind him with a click. I took a deep breath and slipped my mobile phone out of my pocket. I called up the Genevieve ten digit account number and keyed it into the computer terminal. The screen went blank for a second and then an instruction appeared in four languages:

'KEY YOUR TEN DIGIT ACCOUNT NUMBER

INTO YOUR HAND-HELD SECURITY DEVICE, THEN
YOUR PASSWORD'.

I did as I was asked and the little machine prompted me
for a password.   I keyed in V-5-L-V-5-T and a four digit
number appeared. The computer monitor prompted me to key
in this four digit number. My hands were shaking as I did it
and I pressed the keys very deliberately so that there was no
way I could possibly make a mistake.

The screen went black. I turned off my mobile phone and
I looked quickly at my Rolex. It was a quarter to ten. I looked
back at the screen. It was still black. Was there something I'd
forgotten?   Now I saw a little revolving hourglass at the
bottom right hand corner. Ten seconds passed. Why was it
taking so long? I smelt the stale cigar smoke in the room and
saw an ashtray on a side table. I fished out a cigarette and lit it,
pulling the ashtray towards me.   And then something
happened.

The screen flickered momentarily and the words *'Genevieve
International S.A. welcome page – click here to enter'* appeared. I
moved the mouse and I clicked. The next screen gave me a
number of options: balance of accounts, interest calculations,
bill payments and lastly transfers out.

I clicked on *balance of accounts*: there were two, both
denominated in US dollars – Genevieve 'A' and Genevieve 'B'.
I clicked on Genevieve 'A' and the screen flashed up a balance
and list of transactions.

My eyes moved quickly to the top right of the screen with
the running balance. Nineteen million six hundred and forty-
three thousand dollars. There was a God after all. I scanned
the list of transactions and found the one I'd been looking for.
A transfer from a Cayman Island account to Genevieve 'A' in
the amount of twenty-two million dollars and then another in
the amount of two hundred and fifty-seven thousand.   Poor

Jim Kelsey.

I looked at transfers out. About three million dollars had been taken out in one go the week before. It showed up as a cash withdrawal. To think someone had left here with that amount in *cash* was mind-boggling. To think that there was still nineteen million left in the account even more so. I clicked on *'transfer money'*, tapped in *'US$19,000,000'* and then typed in the ten digit number of my account at the same bank. A helpful pop-up informed me that the transaction would be completed on a same-day basis. It would leave six hundred and forty-three thousand dollars in Genevieve 'A' and with a bit of luck they might think that Interpol or the FBI or Kelsey himself had done it. I looked at the *'confirm'* button. My hand was shaking as I pressed it and the screen confirmed the transfer.

I checked my watch. It was five to ten. In ten minutes I'd made nineteen million dollars. Chas Mullion and even Martin Hotson would have been proud of me. God knows what Georgina would have thought if she'd been standing next to me.

My account was multi-currency. The funds would clear today. Maybe they had cleared already? Maybe if I logged out and went in again I could check? I looked back at the screen and clicked to Genevieve's welcome page. Why stop with Genevieve 'A'? I couldn't believe I was doing this. I quickly looked around for cameras but I couldn't see any. Oh my fucking Lord, I was going to do it.

I clicked on the little hyper-text link for Genevieve 'B' and lit another cigarette. Why stop now? The screen flickered for a second and then it seemed like a hundred different account pages were flashing up in front of me in milliseconds. They were flashing up so fast I couldn't read them. All I could tell was that there were a hell of a lot more transactions for Genevieve 'B' than there were for 'A'. The screen stopped moving and settled on the most recent account page. There were about forty transactions just on that page, the last transaction about three months ago for seventy thousand dollars to an account in Panama. As I had done for Genevieve 'A' I looked quickly to the top of the screen for the current balance and then I dropped my cigarette on the carpet.

I took off my glasses, stared at the number in front of me at the very top right-hand corner of the screen and start to sweat. Fifteen minutes ago my stomach had been a twisted ball of nerves and now it felt like fifty ulcers striking at once. I looked at the number again and blinked: US$4,790,865,000.05.

I counted the zeros again to make sure I wasn't dreaming. I wasn't. Four billion, seven hundred and ninety million, eight hundred and sixty-five thousand dollars and five cents. I checked my watch. It was now one minute to ten. Four minutes had passed since I'd cleaned out Genevieve 'A'. What the hell was I going to do now?

I watched the second-hand of my Rolex tick by and thought harder than I'd ever thought in my life. This wasn't Kelsey's money anymore. I scrolled through the account and saw a number of cash deposits stretching back a number of years, sometimes ten million dollars, five days in a row. Khaled Al-Khalim had been so casual the way he wanted to make restitution for his crimes. What was one billion dollars when you had nearly another four in the bank? And how many other accounts were there? More than a billion had been transferred to one in Panama and there were others too. Oh my fucking God. I'd started out the day with three million Swiss francs. What was I going to end it with?

I didn't need four billion.

Christ I hadn't needed nineteen million but I'd taken it all the same. I'd never have to work again. I was rich now but still not as rich as Martin Hotson or Chas Mullion. If I took a chunk of the money that Khaled had stolen from the Jadzik people, did that make me as bad as him? After all, he'd offered to give back one billion.

Think, think, think.

Three things were clear: (1) I couldn't clean out the whole amount; (2) if I was going to do anything it had to be *now* and (3) it had to look like a payment to someone. It had to be something that Tarzi and Jacob and whoever else was in on it could find an excuse for. It had to be an amount that would be missed but not that much. Or did it? I looked at the number again. This money wasn't meant to exist in the first place. It had been meant for the Jadzik people and Khaled had stolen it. If I transferred seven hundred million that would still leave more than four billion in the account. Maybe no-one would notice? Somehow I didn't think that was likely. Maybe one or two million might be over-looked, but then again, maybe not.

Another five minutes passed. I only had ten minutes before I had to get to the airport and I really needed to wash my face. I lit a third cigarette. *'Take the money, keep your mouth shut'*, Sir Wilfred had said to me. A flash-flood of images swept through my brain - Chas Mullion's wedding-cake mansion, Brenda's diamond and Martin Hotson's space-ship of an office. Chas was a banker, Hotson a murderer and Khaled, Attila the Hun. Georgina loved our kids but she loved money as well. And Kate? A girl with great legs who'd passed the bar exam and who I was falling for. How would they all describe *me* if they could see me now? What would Jacob and Tarzi say? What would my mother say? And my kids? Would they even understand what daddy was doing?

I turned back to the screen. I had to be quick.

CHAPTER SEVENTEEN

Martin Hotson was arrested at noon. When I walked through arrivals at Heathrow I saw the BBC pictures of him being led away from his office on Ropemaker Place, handcuffed and smiling for the television cameras, his glossy blond beard glowing under the lights. I turned my phone on. There were two messages. The taxi-rank outside the terminal was full and so I headed quickly for the signs for the Heathrow Express to Paddington. Hotson would have been taken to the police station at Farringdon, Snow Hill, less than five minutes from Ropemaker Place.

The first message was from Martin Hotson asking me to go down to the police station and talk about bail. I could hear loud voices in the background. I'd been right – he was at Snow Hill. I took out a miniature whisky bottle that I'd snaffled from the plane and drained it. It was less than a double measure and I needed steadying.

The second message was from Tarzi, wondering where I was. I called him and told him I was on a train back to London from Yorkshire where I'd had to see my mother - a possible appendectomy. I had a number of pre-purchased open returns to York just in case he wanted proof.

He didn't mention Khaled.

He was more interested in Martin Hotson, telling me to go to the police station right away. I said I was on my way.

My next call was to Jacob. He picked it up on the second ring. I'd never been so pleased to hear his voice. I needed to get back to him and switch security devices as soon as possible.

'Can I see you later Jacob?' I asked. 'I'm going to need your assistance with Martin Hotson today.'

'Naa problem, sir. I'll be 'ere til late.'

'Good. Don't go anywhere.'

It was coming up to one o'clock and my train was approaching Paddington. I grabbed a quick cheese and tomato sandwich from the buffet service and queue-jumped into a taxi to Snow Hill police station. I sat back on the big seat and strapped myself in.

'Can I smoke?' I asked.

The cabbie shook his head and pointed to the 'No smoking' sign right in front of me.

'Can I smoke?' I repeated, slipping a fifty-pound note through the perspex division between us.

My electric window slid down without me touching it and off we roared, up the ramp, over the speedbumps and towards Marble Arch.

It was one-twenty-five as we belted down Holborn Viaduct and screeched left onto Snow Hill. We couldn't pull up right outside because the street was full of police cars and press. I smoothed down my hair and checked myself in the mirror.

'I seen yer on Newsnight', said the cabbie to me suddenly.

He hadn't spoken the whole journey. 'You're the bloke with the Aston Martin.'

'That's right', I said, tossing him another fifty and getting out to a wall of photographers.

'Who've you come for Mr Berry?'

'What are you doing here Mr Berry?'

'You here for Mr Hotson, Jonathan?'

'Where's Khaled, Mr Berry?'

'Is Khaled *here*, Mr Berry?'

I didn't say a word. One hand was on my briefcase, which was empty, and the other was thrust firmly into my trouser pocket, clasped tightly round the Genevieve security device. The police saw me coming and opened the main door for me.

'No Aston then?' leered a giant of an officer into my face, his breath smelling of coffee.

I nodded to him and walked quickly up to the counter behind which sat another giant.

'How can I 'elp you, sir?'

'My name is Jonathan Berry and I've come to see Martin Hotson. I'm his barrister.'

I felt embarrassed just saying the word.

'You're 'im off the telly, intya?'

'I am.'

'You ge' aroun', dontcha?'

'I do.'

He took me downstairs to the holding cells. I looked through the grille.

Martin Hotson was sharing a cell with a gloomy-looking man in a cheap suit.

'Embezzler', said the Detective Constable next to me as he opened the thick steel door.

I nodded sagely.

'Jonathan!' said Martin, rising as he saw me. 'Thank God!'

'You OK, Martin?'

'I'm fine.'

Martin turned to the DC.

'Can I go somewhere private with my barrister?'

The DC pursed his lips.

'Someone's comin' down 'ere to charge you formally, Mr Hotson. I'll take you into an interview room and send our man in when he arrives.'

'Fine', said Martin.

'Fine, said I.

The interview room, like all interview rooms, was smelly, cramped and uncomfortable. They did it so interviewees would want to get out as quickly as possible, to tell the police exactly what they wanted to hear.

'Why have they arrested me, Jonathan?'

'It's beginning Martin. The prosecution have their case and they've considered the risk of flight.'

'So no bail?'

'You're a very rich man, Martin and they know that unless they ask you for everything you've got you could still fly off to South America or...or Panama or somewhere.'

'They're right. I could. That's why I gave you the – '

'We're being recorded here, Martin. I'm sure we are.'

'Oh.'

He suddenly looked rather tired and his beard seemed to droop. I fished out another little bottle of whisky from the plane and offered it to him.

'J&B?'

'Thanks.'

He drank it swiftly.

'Any...progress?' he asked.

I shook my head.

'I think we have to abandon that plan', I whispered.

He stared at me, disbelievingly.

'Really?'

'Yes. Really. And I've been having second thoughts.'

Martin grabbed me by the lapel and jammed his head against my ear.

'I'll want my money back', he said.

'You can have it', I replied.

He looked away.

'You need more?' he asked.

'It isn't the money', I replied, truthfully for once.

'You've done it before.'

'I haven't.'

'You've forgotten Desmond Lyons already have you, Jonathan?'

I didn't reply.

'Oh God', he whispered, rubbing his face as if trying to wake himself up from a bad dream. 'I won't be able to deal with this, Jonathan. I can't go to prison.'

'You said something to me, when we spoke the first time around, something about someone else killing Elspeth. You said it wasn't you, that it can't have been you.'

'That's right.'

'Do you remember exactly when you took the tab of LSD?'

'Not really. I remember I didn't take it straight away. I remember only starting to trip when it got dark.'

'And it was July, right, the party?'

'Yes. Height of the summer season.'

'So getting dark would be sometime after nine o'clock?'

'I suppose so.'

'And you were meant to have strangled Elspeth and thrown her in the pool to drown at, what, midnight or so?'

'Maybe a bit later.'

'An acid trip can last for eight hours, Martin.'

'Mmm?'

'I took some once, at the Edinburgh Festival. I had a *good* trip.'

'What are you saying?'

'I'm saying you're – possibly – beating yourself up about this when actually there may be a completely different explanation of what happened. If you were under the influence of a Class A drug…'

'Yes?'

'Then maybe you are just believing what someone else wants you to believe.'

'*What?*'

'Did you kill Elspeth Huntingford-Smith?'

Martin stared at me and stared at me.

'I don't know', he replied, finally. 'I just don't *know.*'

Just then there was a knock at the door and we both looked up.

'Moment of truth', he said, trying to smile.

'I'm here', I replied. 'We'll be fine.'

The door opened and two large men in plain-clothes strolled in.

'Not interrupting are we?' asked one in a cut-glass accent.

I shook my head.

'This is Detective Sergeant Cummings and I'm Detective Inspector Bowyer. We're here to talk to you about what you're being charged with and the terms of any bail application.'

I froze and the two detectives looked at me as if I were the defendant and Martin Hotson my barrister.

'Jonathan?' hissed Martin. 'What's the matter?'

I cleared my throat and tried out the *Berrie* charm.

'Did you say *Bowyer*?' I asked.

'That's right', he replied pleasantly enough. 'DI Mark Bowyer. Scotland Yard.'

I shook his hand and told Kate's husband my name.

We were finished by three in the afternoon and I set the bail hearing for the next morning so Martin would only have one night in jail. On condition that Martin Hotson was electronically tagged it was very likely the prosecution would agree to set bail at ten million pounds. I also managed to persuade Bowyer to give Martin a single cell. DI Mark Bowyer had been very pleasant indeed but that was probably because we had so much in common. We shook hands and he even gave me his business card.

'Anytime', he said. 'Any problems, just give me a tinkle.'

'I will', I replied, itching to get back to 21 Wessex Yard and away from DI Bowyer.

**

'Tea please, Jacob. A lovely Earl Gray?'

'Yessir.'

He got up and took off his jacket. All I would need would be a few seconds when he did his routine with the tea bag and the milk. Now he was hanging the jacket on the back of his chair.

This was too easy.

Switch one security device for another and then…and then it suddenly occurred to me they might suspect Jacob.

I watched him walk down the corridor with a little skip in his step. That wouldn't last long once Tarzi and Khaled checked the Genevieve accounts. Poor Jacob. He'd set me up and I was going to return the favour.

I walked quickly over to his chair and felt in the jacket pocket. Nothing. Maybe I had the wrong pocket. Nothing again. There was nothing in any of the six jacket pockets that resembled a security device from *JP Chartrier et Freres*. What had I done? They had *my* security device but no account number. I had *their* security device and all the numbers I needed. Maybe Jacob had it in his trouser pockets. There was only one way to find out. As he walked back down the corridor towards me I reached out for the tea.

'Thank you, Jacob.'

'Pleasure, sir.'

I held the cup up to my mouth, took as big a gulp as I could and started to choke. My face turned purple and I spat my Earl Gray all over Jacob's trousers, fairly drenching them.

'Oh god!' I spluttered.

Jacob winced and looked down at himself.

'I'm so sorry, Jacob.'

'S'alrigh' sir. I always keep a spare.'

My eyes followed Jacob as he opened the cupboard next to his desk. There was a pair of trousers hanging there and he pulled them out.

'I'll have them dry-cleaned for you, Jacob.'

'Won't be necessary, sir', he said. 'I've got tomorrow off. I can do it in the morning.'

'You've got tomorrow off?'

'Thassrigh sir. I'm goin' clay-pigeon shootin', sir.'

'You are?'

'Yesssir. Guest of Mr Tarzi, sir.'

He stared at me rather oddly, as if waiting for my head to fall off.

'Up in Yorkshire, sir.'

I paced up and down my room, kicking the cartons of hooky cigarettes in despair each time I passed them. Escape was always an option. I could get back on a plane and head to Zurich but Martin Hotson knew I had a Swiss account. Even though it was unlikely he might have told someone, I didn't want to take unnecessary risks. I moved to my desk, opened my laptop and booted it up. I tapped in the password. I quickly flashed up on the Chartrier website via an external wireless link, bypassing the chambers network. Andorra, Liechtenstein, Zurich, Geneva and Monaco. *JP Chartrier et Freres* had branches in all of these locations and Monaco had a lovely ring to it. I'd never been there - not yet anyhow - and they had a casino and hundreds of private banks.

I'd taken two billion dollars out of Khaled's account and transferred it to my own at the same bank.

That left nearly two billion eight hundred million in the Khaled account and two billion in the account for *Mr Desmond*. As I might never be able to get to *Mr Desmond*'s account again I had no option. I had to transfer *another* two billion from Khaled's account to get back to where I started and then Khaled would be down four billion. I wasn't even thinking of Jim Kelsey now. I just needed to open another account.

I checked my own jacket pocket for the six open returns to see my mother. Yorkshire was becoming an exceedingly popular destination all of a sudden. I had the international flight times in front of me. It was two hours to Nice and then a twenty minute cab ride into Monaco. I didn't fancy the helicopter option at sixty euros, not because I couldn't afford it but because I was scared of helicopters. I had Martin Hotson's bail application at ten the next morning so the earliest I could go would be the one o'clock flight which wouldn't get me there until nearly five o'clock with the one hour time difference. It would be too late. The banks would be shutting.

I leaned back in my chair. Maybe I was over-reacting? Perhaps Tarzi would have the device in his office in Mount Street. Perhaps I could do the switch this afternoon. Perhaps I should go straight there now but then perhaps I'd taken enough risks. I didn't know *who* had it or even if I could get it.

I thought of what would happen to whoever had to tell Khaled that there was no way of accessing his money, that the machine didn't work.

And if I did the switch, I thought of what would happen to whoever had to tell Khaled that his account was short by two billion. What had I done?

Maybe I was *under*-reacting. I could go on the run with US$2.8 billion and no-one would ever find me. I could lose myself in South America or Africa. I could buy a country, just like Khaled had done. Maybe I'd taken things too far. The money had so many zeros it didn't seem real.

I reached for my briefcase and, as I did so, the first bullet caught me in the shoulder, barely making a sound. I fell forward onto my desk, pushing my laptop onto the floor. The second bullet hit one of the hooky cigarette cartons and the window smashed behind me.

'*Down! Down!*' I heard Jacob shout outside my door and then the roar of a diesel engine down Wessex Yard. I managed to crawl under my desk, blood soaking my shirt and the lining of my suit. I'd never been shot before and it wasn't as painful as I thought it would be. In fact, I could feel my eyes closing, almost in relief. God was punishing me for what I was doing. I didn't believe in Him but it was a sign. I heard my door slam open – everything was a little foggy now, dampened – and then someone was crawling over to me on the carpeted floor of my office. I opened my eyes and tried to focus. It was Jacob. I think I tried to say something but I couldn't hear what I was trying to say.

All I could see was Jacob's face, blurred, looming closer and closer to mine.

CHAPTER EIGHTEEN

'They got Mr Tarzi', were the first words I heard.

I turned my head to one side to see who was there and I felt an agonizing stabbing pain in my left shoulder.

'Ee's dead.'

'Jacob?'

'Ullo sir.'

I tried to sit up but my shoulder hurt whenever I moved.

'Did you say Tarzi's dead?'

'I did sir. Just you and me now, sir.'

'What…what…where are we?'

'In 'ospital, sir. You've 'ad some morphine.'

'I feel like shit.'

'They nearly go' me 'n all, sir. I 'ad a bullet through my

winder as well.'

'Who did it?'

'It's the same group wot killed them lawyers in Jadzi…Jadziki..'

I suddenly remembered the death threat on the phone. Me *and* my family. I felt sick.

'My children? Georgina?'

'Police 'ave moved 'em sir. Somewhere safe. Dan't worry, sir.'

I breathed out and even that hurt.

'How…how did they get Tarzi?'

'Bombed 'is car. Got Aziza too. On the way to the airport.'

'The airport?'

'Yessir.'

'There's a little button on the side, sir, if yer want more morphine.'

I moved my head. Resting by my hand at the end of a long plastic tube was a little plastic beeper with a blue button. I pressed it twice and felt a wave of calm sweep over me.

'You'll be in 'ere a week, sir.'

'Where…where is…where are my things, Jacob? My…my wallet, for instance?'

'Nurse put 'em all in there, sir', he replied, pointing to a metal bed-side cabinet. I tried not to stare at it.

'And my family?' I asked.

'I dunno where they are sir. Police wouldn't tell me. They'll want to speak to yer soon I fink.'

'The police?'

'Thassri' sir. Attempted murder, innit?'

I pressed the blue button again.

'I think I'll rest now Jacob', I said.

'I'll be on the mobile', he replied.

I waited for him to leave and then I pressed the little blue button again and swung my legs out of the bed. My shoulder was agony and I felt weak. I must have lost a lot of blood. Two drips – one morphine, one plasma – were stuck into my forearm and they were starting to throb.

I bent down and opened the metal cabinet with my right hand. Inside was my wallet, my cufflinks, my mobile phone, six open returns to York and, last but not least, the little electronic key to Genevieve's vaults. I pulled out my mobile and looked next to my bed. Jacob had even brought in my laptop from chambers. There was a television set across from me and a remote control fixed to the wall by a wire. I was about to turn it on when there was a knock at the door. I got back into bed as quickly as I could.

'Yes?'

Detective Inspector Mark Bowyer poked his head round the door.

'It's me again, Mr Berry. You feeling up to a few questions?'

I closed my eyes and nodded. Better to get it over with

while I still had the morphine drip. He walked in on his own, a pad and pen in his hand.

'I just need to get a statement from you while it's all fresh in your mind.'

I looked at the clock. It said 0935 hours. I'd lost about fifteen hours.

'Can I take your full name please, Mr Berry?'

'Jonathan Peregrine Morgan Berry.'

'Age?'

'Thirty-five.'

'You're a barrister at 21 Wessex Yard? Clerk Jacob Potts?'

I nodded.

'Mr Potts told me you've just got the Hotson and Khaled cases and something for Customs on cigarette smuggling.'

I nodded again.

'Do you know why anyone would want to kill you, Mr Berry?'

'Could...could I have some water please?' I asked.

As he poured me some into a plastic cup and held it to my lips I noticed that the wedding ring he'd worn at Snow Hill police station wasn't there any more.

'Are you alright for me to go on? I can come back, Mr Berry?'

'No...no it's OK. You asked me why anyone would want to kill me?'

'Yes sir.'

'I think for the same reason they bombed Hussain Tarzi and that poor girl Aziza.'

'And why would that be?'

'My clerk told me it was the same group that killed the lawyers in Jadzikistan.'

'That's what the press are saying, Mr Berry but you understand I cannot assume until proven otherwise that the two incidents are related.'

I took another sip of water. What the hell did he mean? Was it possible someone *else* wanted to kill me?

'Where are my wife and children?' I asked.

'They're fine. They're staying with a friend of yours. It's a high-security street – the Greek embassy's just on the corner and there's twenty-four hour protection.'

'The Mullions? Chas and Brenda?'

He nodded and I breathed a sigh of relief. Chas's house was like a fortress. I remembered him boasting about the steel shutters, security cameras and back-up generator.

'We're going to be seeing a lot more of each other, Mr Berry.'

'We are?'

'Certainly. I was on Hotson anyway but now I've been assigned to your case too.'

'Good', I said, trying to smile at Kate's husband.

'I understand you're separated from your wife?'

'Er…yes. It's…temporary.'

'Can I ask where you're staying at the moment, Mr Berry?'

I suddenly felt very ill.

'Why?' I croaked, taking another sip of water.

'Whoever did this to you might try again.'

'Then…then I'll resign from the Khaled case. The terrorists can have their victory.'

'Can I ask where you've been living, Mr Berry?'

I cleared my throat.

'In a hotel. Near Tarzi's offices.'

'Which one?'

I looked at the pen poised over his notepad.

If I told him which one he might find out I'd been checked in as *Mr Johnson* and that there was a *Mrs Johnson* as well. Mark Bowyer was a pleasant-looking chap but he was very tall and he had a thick neck. He could crush me like a snail if he wanted to and I didn't want him to.

'Claridge's', I replied. 'Mr Tarzi was paying the bill.'

'Mr Tarzi's dead, sir. I suggest you don't go back there. You should have the hotel bring your things over.'

'Errm…thank you. I'll ask Jacob. Detective Inspector?'

'Call me Mark.'

'I'm feeling a little tired, Mark. Could we – possibly – finish this another time?'

'Just one more question and then I'm done.'

'Just the one then.'

He reached into his pocket and pulled out a clear plastic bag. Inside it was a battered and scorched *JP Chartrier et Freres* security device: mine.

'We picked this out of the wreckage. Did you ever see Mr Tarzi use it?'

He handed me the bag and I stared at the tiny little calculator. It looked as if it had been damaged beyond repair.

'No', I replied, looking into his eyes unblinkingly, 'I can honestly say I've never seen this before in my life.'

I woke about an hour later, slightly confused. I hadn't even seen a doctor yet, or a nurse. My mobile phone was resting on my stomach. Had anyone checked it? Had Mark Bowyer checked it? I scrolled through the numbers and deleted Kate's, leaned over and opened the little metal cabinet. Genevieve was still in there. I shut it again and turned on the television set. The cardboard folder next to my bed told me I was in the Queen Charlotte Hospital just off Harley Street and the television set announced the midday news on BBC1.

'The Home Office, in a statement released this morning, confirmed that it refuses to bow to what it describes as mindless acts of terrorism.'

The Home Secretary's face filled the screen.

'Nothing', he said, *'nothing will delay the trial of Mr Al-Khalim. Whilst our sympathies lie with the victims of this latest atrocity, we can reveal that a replacement legal team to conduct Mr Al-Khalim's defence has already been appointed...'*

I was off the case!

Jacob hadn't said a thing and neither had DI Bowyer. Maybe they didn't know. Fired by television. I suddenly felt wonderful despite the gaping wound in my shoulder. I felt like a glass of champagne but I took another little hit of morphine instead. Did this mean, now that Tarzi was dead, that I would be taken off the Hotson case as well? I would have to speak to Jacob. And what about Kelsey? With Tarzi dead, surely he couldn't expect anything from me. Certainly not his twenty-two million.

A week, Jacob had said. A week in hospital. I didn't feel that bad now. Just a little tired. The morphine was doing its job. Maybe Georgina would come and visit me. And what about Kate? Surely she'd have heard it on the news…

I turned back to the television set. They were showing pictures of Jadzikistan, the horrible pictures of dead and nearly-dead children, starved to extinction because Khaled had failed to provide for his people. On screen the BBC presenter announced an appeal. A free-phone telephone hotline number - *0800 SAVEAKID* - flashed up.

'*Please give generously*', said the presenter.

'I'll try, I replied woozily, thinking of what was in the little metal cabinet next to me. 'I'll try.'

I checked the little metal cabinet next to my bed about thirty times that day. A doctor and then a nurse came in and told me I was recovering well. The bullet had passed right through me and avoided any major organs. I thanked them and gave the nurse a tenner to buy me a padlock. I tried Chas's home number and Georgina's mobile to tell her I was OK and where I was. I wanted the children to know I was fine but the only person I managed to speak to was Chas's butler. He told me rather stiffly that he'd pass on the message. I didn't dare call Kate, not with her husband liable to walk in at any moment and she hadn't dared call me, probably for the same reason.

Jacob came to visit me later that afternoon, bringing me a bunch of grapes and my clothes from Claridge's.

'I spoke to Mr 'otson, sir', he said, eating a grape. 'Ee got bail this mornin'. I got Mr Macdonald to do the application. Ee still wants yer to act fer 'im on the murder trial. If yer feel up to it. Ee's appointed new solicitors an' they'd be 'appy with you 'n all.'

'I'll need to recover before I can decide, Jacob. I may decide to take…a sabbatical.'

He nodded and ate another grape. I bet it hadn't even registered with Customs that I'd been shot.

'I parked yer Aston in the Temple, sir.'

'Oh. Thank you, Jacob.'

'Anythin' else, sir? Eard from yer wife?'

'Errr..no Jacob.'

'She 'ad this delivered, sir' he said, holding up a large brown envelope. 'Said I should make sure yer got it personally.'

'Thank you.'

'Want me to open it fer you, sir?'

'No thanks, Jacob. I'll look at it later.'

He rested it on top of the bedside table.

'And Miss Bowyer called, sir.'

'Oh?'

'I told 'er you'd be alright. Ou' within a week.'

'Err…good. Thank you, Jacob. I'm feeling…a little tired now, Jacob.'

'Right you are sir.'

'Thanks for the clothes.'

'S'alright, sir.'

'And the car.'

'Na problem, sir.'

I watched as he left, taking one more grape from the bunch next to my bed. I could buy twenty thousand Astons if I could only get out of here. I had two billion eight hundred million dollars sitting inches from me and I couldn't touch a penny of it. I looked over at the brown envelope from Georgina. She'd never been much of a letter-writer. It was marked 'by hand'. I opened the seal with my good hand and poured the contents out onto my bed.

It was a divorce petition.

Lord Marden was not in a good mood. He paced up and down the back corridors at *Velvet*, hands thrust deep into his pockets, muttering to himself. He'd been a fool. A complete idiot. All the strings he'd pulled, everything he'd done for Tarzi over the years was to have been topped-off by the biggest pay-day his Lordship had ever had. But now that Tarzi was dead, I'd been shot and Khaled was in a maximum-security prison the whole thing had ground to a halt. *Who had the money?* was the question his Lordship kept asking himself over and over again. *Who had*

Two years to retirement and more than thirty as a judge. And for what? A pension of eighty thousand a year?

What of the sacrifice?

All those years that he could have been making millions as a QC, all those wasted years earning a tenth of that for the kudos of being a judge.

What a confounded waste! A waste!

His Lordship kicked an umbrella stand in disgust. Many years ago, when Hussain Tarzi first came to London, he'd given the newly-appointed William Marden QC his first six-figure brief. That case had enabled Bill to make the cut for the judiciary and he'd jumped at the chance to be the youngest High Court judge in England. He hadn't done it for the money. No-one became a judge for the money. He did it because...because...he'd forgotten why he did it...but it was so long ago. Now he was a lowly public servant, earning little more than a newly-qualified solicitor at one of the US firms that were all over the City.

That was why the payments to his Panamanian account had been so welcome, but the last one – seventy thousand dollars he remembered – was more than three months ago. When he retired he wanted to do it in style. Ten million dollars Tarzi had promised him, ten million dollars to find Khaled Al-Khalim not guilty by reason of insanity. After the death of his only grand-daughter he'd been at a low point and so he'd agreed. The quarterly payments of seventy thousand had been a sweetener but now they'd stopped and it didn't look like they were going to start again. He gave the umbrella stand another kick. Bloody terrorists. Hanging was too good for them.

His Lordship sat on one of the gilded chairs set at strategic intervals along the corridor and took a deep breath. What about Martin Hotson? He was out on bail for murder as of this morning. He'd heard it on the lunchtime news. Martin Hotson was a member of the club of which his Lordship was president and he was very, very rich.

Maybe he should pay him a visit in their hour of need?

I looked up from the divorce petition to see Mark Bowyer walk into my room again.

'How're you doing?' he asked, smiling. 'Not working I hope?'

I slipped the petition back into the envelope.

'No', I replied, again noticing the mark on the finger where his wedding ring used to be. 'It's just something from my wife.'

'Don't talk to me about women', he said, sinking down onto the chair next to my bed. I did my best to smile in sympathy.

'I came by to give you an update, Mr Berry, if that's alright.'

'On…?'

'The shooting. Your attempted murder.'

'I see.'

'You're a brave man, Mr Berry. You seem to be taking it all quite calmly if I may say so.'

'It's probably the medication', I replied, even though they'd taken me off the morphine drip at lunchtime.

'We're ninety-nine percent certain it was the same group that's trying to kill Khaled Al-Khalim. I understand you're off the case now, which means you're probably safe.'

'Oh. Good. Good. Actually I was thinking of taking a…a sabbatical. You see…' My voice trailed off, I paused - for effect - and then dabbed an eye with the corner of my sheet. 'My wife's divorcing me. She served a petition today. That's what I was reading when you came in here.'

'Oh dear. Hitting a man when he's down…'

'Yes. It's charming.'

I wondered if he had any marital news of his own to report but he volunteered nothing.

'I just wanted to let you know we don't think you or your family need to be under surveillance any more.'

'Oh. That's good news.'

'I thought you'd want to know.'

He took one of the grapes that Jacob had left me, popped it into his mouth and stood.

'You've got my card, haven't you?' he asked.

I nodded and he left just as quickly as he'd arrived.

The day was getting better and better. Being shot and having my wife divorce me were wonderful reasons to go on a long, long sabbatical, perhaps even a permanent one. The only people I'd miss would be my kids. And Kate, even though she was the wife of my investigating officer. Georgina hadn't named anyone in the petition. She'd cited 'irreconcilable differences', that the marriage had 'broken down irretrievably' and that we were living apart. All I wanted was to see my children regularly and she'd even suggested fortnightly visitation rights with alternating Christmas, Easter and Summer holidays. It seemed very fair and well thought out, almost generous. She wasn't even after maintenance. Silverman Bach must have been paying her a fortune.

A plan was starting to form even though I felt drugged and my shoulder was painful. I was only on one infusion and I'd be off that within twenty-four hours. They'd said a week but at this rate I could be out by Friday. I had my clothes which Jacob had brought. I knew where to pick up my car and I had no one gunning for me, at least for the moment. I looked again at the padlock on the little metal cabinet by my bed. I kept the key in a little money-purse which I hid in my pyjamas.

Just then there was a knock at the door and a nurse brought in a tray with what looked like my dinner.

'You're looking perky', she said cheerily.

'I'm feeling much better.'

The nurse left my dinner and I stared at it.

Pork chop, mashed potato and green beans followed by apple crumble and custard, in other words not that different to Middle Temple Hall. I picked up my knife and fork and then my mobile phone rang. It was Kate telling me Mark was divorcing her.

'Irreconcilable differences. Bastard! My husband's on your case, isn't he?'

'Not any more.'

'Can I come and see you then?'

'Georgina's divorcing me.'

253

'Jesus.'

'Exactly. I'm very confused Kate.'

'Me too. I'm thinking of chucking it all in and going off somewhere for a break.'

'Are you?', I replied, looking for the umpteenth time at the padlock on my metal bed-side cabinet. 'I was thinking of doing the same thing.'

A man and a woman traveling together would be a lot less suspicious than a man on his own. And a lot less lonely in the evenings.

'When do they let you out?'

'Tomorrow. Perhaps we could go on a long weekend together somewhere? Maybe even a bit longer than a long weekend?'

'Great. To tell you the truth I've been worried sick.'

'About what?'

'You.'

'You have?'

'Yes. You remember you asked me once if I was in love with you?'

'I do. It was at Claridge's.'

'Well the answer's I *think* so.'

'You *think* so?'

'It's too early to tell.'

That's what I loved about Kate. Her refreshing honesty.

'That's good enough for me', I replied. 'I fancy doing something reckless. Maybe…maybe a spot of gambling. A casino somewhere.'

'Las Vegas?'

'Maybe a little closer to home. Monte Carlo, for instance –
'

'Oh I love it!'

'You've been there before?'

'Yes. I can show you round, Jonny, we can blow a few hundred at the casino and fuck like rabbits.'

'I'm recovering from a bullet, Kate.'

'Oh. Sorry.'

'Look. Leave the tickets to me. We can pick them up at the airport.'

'Fine.'

'Let's talk tomorrow. I've got everything here so I'm already packed.'

'Me too. I'm living out of a suitcase. Letting Mark have the house. It's his anyway.'

'Tomorrow then.'

I deleted the number from my phone's history. I checked the padlock for the hundredth time. Two birds. One stone. I could even afford to give Kate some shopping money. My wound was healing nicely and I was nearly back to normal other than the painkillers and the daily change of bandages. I'd been told that I could even have a bath if I wanted to, as long as I didn't get the bandages wet. I called Jacob and told him I was taking a week off, that I'd go away somewhere to clear my head.

He sounded happy for me.

CHAPTER NINETEEN

Somewhere on the other side of the world, a country was struggling to regenerate and that country was Jadzikistan. There were pleas from the ad hoc Jadzik government appointed by the United Nations for all exiled Jadzik nationals to return to their homeland and to bring with them their businesses, their hard currency and their work-ethic. Khaled Al-Khalim had eradicated all of these things over a seventeen year reign of terror and it would take a mammoth effort to redress the balance, to restore things to even the vaguest semblance of a status quo.

In Tufnell Park, Osama was packing his bags. Back in Jadzikistan, nearly twenty years before, his family had been the proud owners of a chain of restaurants. The business had been a profitable one and the restaurants had served a delicious array of local delicacies, eat in and take-away, which included kebabs. Osama knew he would never be fully integrated into the British way of life. His dress, his accent, the colour of his skin.

He didn't feel at home here, even after seventeen years. And so, when he heard the call of his new government, he decided to do something about it.

His father, nearly eighty years old, was his sole surviving relative. His wife and mother, and his children, had all been murdered by Khaled's forces many years before. He gave notice on the lease of his shop to the local council, gathered what possessions he had, cleaned out his bank account and flew to Jadzikistan where his savings of a hundred thousand pounds would be able to buy him a big house and five restaurants.

The plane swooped down from thirty-three thousand feet in brilliant sunshine. To our right, the Mediterranean, yachts glittering in the water, big white dots growing larger and larger as we descended. To our left, the Cote d'Azur, green hills packed with Hollywood-style villas, golden beaches fringed by palm trees, Cannes, Antibes and finally Nice. We landed over water, the runway jutting out like an empty pier leading to nowhere. The door of the plane opened and I took a deep breath of the fresh spring air. It was a good fifteen degrees warmer than London.

We passed quickly through passport control, hand-luggage only and followed the signs for the taxis. I held the door open for Kate and I watched her slide her long legs into the silver E-Class Mercedes.

'Monaco', I said to the driver. 'Hotel de Paris.'

'*Bien sur, monsieur!*', he replied, watching me get in behind him.

We took the coast road, the one that winds along the *Promenade des Anglais* and past old fishing villages now transformed into playgrounds for the rich – places like *Beaulieu*, *Villefranche sur Mer* and *St Jean Cap Ferrat*, home to the Rothschilds' monumental mansion, the Villa Ephrussi. Kate and I sat silently in the back, holding hands, watching the sea to our right. I wondered what she was thinking. I knew what I was thinking. Today was Friday. No banks today. They could wait for Monday. I'd come out of hospital with one carry-on bag and a lightweight suit, sent the rest of my stuff back to chambers in a cab and gone straight to the airport where I met up with Kate. We were booked in at the Hotel de Paris, Monaco's grandest hotel, until Wednesday. Hopefully that would give me ample time to transact whatever business I needed to transact. I'd taken ten thousand pounds from my account at Coutts on the Strand because I didn't want to use my credit card for anything. Cash is king, as my father used to say, especially at casinos. I tried not to think of what two billion eight hundred million dollars might look like in hundred dollar bills.

We swept into Casino Square at five o'clock in the afternoon and came to a halt outside the magnificent entrance of the Hotel de Paris. Next to it was the famous casino, a large white pillared palace. A gloved hand opened the door of our taxi and a uniformed porter unloaded our two small bags and my laptop. Kate put on her shades and stood with her hands on her hips in the sunshine.

She didn't look out of place at all and I hadn't even given her any shopping money yet.

Straight up the steps, through the revolving doors we went and into an ornate reception hall that was about seventy foot long with a thirty-foot high ceiling painted with nymphs and cherubs, not unlike *Velvet*. To the left, small tables and banquettes for impromptu coffees and a sign for the bar. The concierge stood in front of us, seventy feet away, at the other end of the enormous room. Kate took my arm and we ambled up to him as though we owned the place.

'Mr and Mrs Desmond', I said to him with a smile. 'We have a reservation.'

'But of course sir. A sea-view suite. If you follow Marie she'll show you up there. Your bags will be waiting for you.'

'Thank you.'

'How will you be settling your bill, sir?'

I closed my hand around the Genevieve security device in my pocket.

'Cash', I replied.

'Very good, sir.'

The view was wonderful, the bed was huge and within five minutes we were making love on the thick red carpet. Afterwards, I sat smoking in a wing-backed chair facing the sea, planning the weekend with the assistance of a map of Monaco that very helpfully listed all the banks. I planned to go for the most obscure one I could find for my new account.

The sun started to set and I could hear Kate in the shower. I'd decided to use the hotel safe for my little Genevieve and I hadn't told Kate the combination. I picked up the phone and booked us into an Italian restaurant that Kate said she'd eaten at before - Rampoldi's. It was less than a hundred yards from our hotel.

We headed out of our room at about eight o'clock, ready for a stroll before dinner. We passed through the revolving door, aided by a uniformed footman and we waltzed down the steps, glittering Casino Square in front of us. Everything was immaculate. After dreary London, Monaco didn't feel real. It was almost *too* perfect. Every shop-window displayed jewel-encrusted watches. There were no price-tags and you could eat caviar off the pavement if you wanted too, it was so clean. Diagonally parked around Casino Square were vintage Ferraris, huge Rollers and sleek Astons not unlike the one I had in London. Never had I seen so many Bentley Continentals parked next to each other, not even in the showroom on Berkeley Square. This little oasis dripped money. I belonged here. And so, I think, did Kate.

'Nice, isn't it', she said.

'I like it', I replied, wincing as she squeezed my bad shoulder by mistake. 'Shall we walk up there?'

I pointed up to our left, towards the cinema.

Just before it was another road gleaming with designer shops. Chanel and Prada for Kate, but there were also three banks for me, at least according to my map.

One of the banks was JP Chartrier et Freres where I was planning on making a rather large withdrawal first thing on Monday morning. We passed its blacked-out windows and I resisted the temptation to turn and look. Kate stopped and used the reflective frontage to check out her ensemble for the evening: a pretty knee-length summer dress with a cardigan and heels.

Next to JP Chartrier et Freres was a gleaming Berluti shop and then, as we walked up the hill towards L'Hermitage - another magnificent Monegasque hotel - we passed The Gestattenzee Bank of Geneva. Perfect. Thirty seconds between banks. I could open an account at Gestattenzee and feed the proceeds of Genevieve in there to spread my risk. We passed an Agence Immobilier – an estate agency – and I lingered for a moment.

'Thinking of moving?' asked Kate, holding my arm.

'Nice to look', I said.

I studied what was on offer as casually as I could. For the

price of my old house you could buy a two room apartment. One million euros - seven hundred thousand pounds - for two rooms, a poky bathroom and a view of a wall. A three bedroom apartment with a sea view was four million euros or about the same as the house on Bedford Gardens that Georgina had wanted me to buy, the one that was to be a family home for our children.

I could see their faces - Ben, Mollie and little Amy, and even my darling Sophie's that I would never see again.

It would be nice for them to have their own rooms.

My eyes glazed over momentarily.

'Jonathan? Are you alright?' asked Kate, peering at my face. I smiled and kissed her.

'Just hungry', I replied. 'And my shoulder.'

I re-focused on the window and an advertisement in the middle caught my eye. It was for a five bedroom penthouse with its own rooftop pool, fifty yards from the sea for twelve million euros, about fifteen million dollars. They were open on a Saturday and I wondered if they'd take cash.

Detective Inspector Mark Bowyer had a degree from the London School of Economics, which is where he'd met Kate. Having once contemplated a career in the City or the law, his third class degree had consigned him to the Metropolitan Police and six months' training school in Hendon. When Jim Kelsey telephoned the investigating officer on the Tarzi murder to tell him he suspected Hussain Tarzi had stolen his twenty-two million two hundred and fifty seven thousand dollars, he got put through to Mark Bowyer in Scotland Yard.

'Do you have any proof, Mr Kelsey?'

'No.'

'We've got nothing either', said Mark Bowyer, leaning back in his chair with the battered and burnt bank security device recovered from Tarzi's car still in its sealed plastic sack. The one with two billion dollars in the account that no-one, not even *Mr Desmond*, could touch.

The lithium ion battery had melted and destroyed the insides of the machine just as the force of the car-bomb had stripped the case back to the bare metal. There had been a number of rubber or plastic buttons but they'd melted, the LCD display had imploded and the machine was completely unidentifiable. There were a thousand banks that used this sort of security, Mark Bowyer knew. Even his soon-to-be-ex-wife had one for her Coutts account, like all her rich lawyer friends, except that hers had fewer buttons. They could try and run a search, but it would take someone hundreds – perhaps thousands - of hours to track down possible banks and even then there was no way of finding out the account name or number.

'Have you questioned Jonathan Berry?' asked Kelsey. 'He was Tarzi's barrister.'

'About what, exactly?' asked Bowyer.

'About stealing my money. He knows something.'

'May I ask how you know, Mr Kelsey?'

'I offered him a finders' fee – fifteen per cent – if he could find it. He looked interested.'

'I'll put a note on the file, sir.'

Mark Bowyer put down the phone and slipped the plastic bag containing the charred security device into his pocket. He walked towards the kitchenette along the hallway, suddenly remembering where he'd heard the name Kelsey before.

A rich oilman, worth far more than twenty-two million. Fifteen percent was over three million dollars.

No wonder Jonathan Berry had looked interested.

Mark knew what criminal barristers earned – all legal aid stuff – and it wasn't that much.

He boiled the kettle and made himself an instant coffee, something Kate never did. She didn't drink instant. They'd outgrown each other a long time ago. He knew she'd played away from home many times – with whom he couldn't care less – because so had he. She was never going to have children. It was always career, career, career. Money, money, money. She earned five times what he earned and he never saw a penny of it in their joint account. He wanted to settle down with someone calmer, less driven, someone who wanted children perhaps. Someone who didn't always have a headache.

He walked slowly back to his office so as not to spill his coffee. That poor sod Berry – the one who'd been shot – was getting the boot from *his* wife and he had three children. Lost a fourth apparently. Bad things came in threes. Maybe he'd had his share. He wondered what barristers did to drown their sorrows? What would Kate be doing? He knew she was upset, not about the divorce, but about the fact he'd got in first with a petition. Maybe she was in some smoky bar off Fleet Street talking about wigs or whatever it was barristers did for a good time.

I had lobster and scallop salad followed by a steak. Kate had blinis and the trout. We drank a bottle of champagne and a bottle of Haut-Brion '95, a good year. Rampoldi's was treating us well.

'Casino?' I asked, holding Kate's hand across the table as we sipped our complimentary chartreuse.

'Why not?' she replied, smiling.

We walked up the hill towards Casino Square. There were police on every corner in their blue and white uniforms. There were cameras everywhere. There was no graffiti. I'd heard there was little or no crime, at least not of the blue-collar variety. Monaco was growing on me more and more. We passed Café de Paris on our left, stopping to watch a valet try to slide a Hummer with gold-plated bumpers between a 1960s Ferrari and a Bentley. When he did it, we clapped our hands and he bowed good-humouredly.

I kissed her and we walked up the steps to the casino, arm in arm.

By eleven o'clock Kate and I were sitting next to each other on high stools in the main part of the casino, pumping token after token into the fruit machines. We were on the ten euro game which promised a payout of one million if you hit the jackpot and Kate had managed to win a clear thousand already.

'How about some blackjack?' she asked.

'You mean pontoon? Twenty-one to win?'

'God you're thick, Jon. Let me show you where the high-rollers do it.'

We laughed and as we stood someone brought us two glasses of champagne.

We had to pay twenty euros to enter the high-rollers room and I had three thousand in chips, half of which I gave to Kate to add to her thousand euro slot-machine win. She walked over to the nearest table and sat down whilst I walked around the enormous carpet listening to the languages around me and looking up at the ornate ceiling. I heard a lot of Italian and Russian – we were only ten miles or so from the Italian border. There were some Americans but no British. I looked back at Kate, sitting at the table with four others, two Italian men and two women of Middle Eastern extraction. She crossed her legs, distracting the Italians. The Arabs gave their wives pin money to play with whilst they saw their mistresses. Pin-money to them meant *high-roller* to everyone else. I thought about my own little oil-well, safely under lock and key and accessible in less than 57 hours.

***

Khaled Al-Khalim was furious. With Tarzi gone he had lost access to approximately half his fortune. The other half, thankfully, was in safer hands. He held shares across a wide spread of publicly quoted companies on both sides of the Atlantic, or rather, the shares were held by a nominee company that took telephone instructions from one person and one person only.

Silverman Bach was a private partnership and Khaled was not over-joyed at the prospect of a simultaneous listing on the London and New Stock Exchanges, announced by the BBC that night on the ten o'clock news.

During his time at INSEAD studying for his European MBA he had learnt about the extensive due diligence that companies had to provide to the financial authorities if they wanted a full listing on a major exchange. His account was in the form of a nominee trustee account – a bare trust - overseen by four senior partners at Silvermans and he wondered if they would now be forced to reveal to the authorities that the money held by them as nominees was for the sole benefit of a man who was the subject of a worldwide *Mareva* order freezing all of his assets.

No-one was going to let him use a telephone. The only contact he could have would be with his new legal team, a cold, unsympathetic bunch of grey suits from one of the largest law firms in London. They were too distant to be bribable and he knew within an instant of meeting them that they would be of no help to him.

He had to speak to Chas Mullion.

Chas Mullion was having the best year of his life. The cross-Atlantic float would take him perilously close to billionaire status and he had a water-tight pre-nup with Brenda. They'd married in New York and agreed that in the event of a split she'd get one million dollars for every year of marriage, a suitable family home plus a three million dollar bonus if he committed adultery. They only had one child, Harrison, five. Chas would buy Brenda the house Georgina had suggested to him – the one on Bedford Gardens - and round up Brenda's settlement to a cool twenty million. Even with Brenda's spending addiction she would have enough to live on.

To cap it all, Georgina was divorcing me.

'Nice guy, no instinct for money whatsoever', said Chas, lying in bed next to my wife at Claridge's. 'I'd never have him on my team in a million years.'

Chas had advised Georgina to be generous with her divorce petition against me, not to go after a penny of my money – she would have far more than me anyway after the float – and to let me see the kids when I wanted. She followed his advice and even though I'd been lying in hospital with an exit wound by my left shoulder she hadn't wasted any time.

'Get it agreed before the float', said Chas. 'You know he's been dicking you around for too long. If you lived off him you'd be penniless in five years.'

'He's a good man', said Georgina, 'but it's in his blood. Every Berry in the last nine hundred years has ended up with less than his father. It's hereditary. He can't help it.'

'For a woman who's had three kids you've got a great body', said Chas, stroking my wife's leg.

'Four kids, Chas', replied Georgina, sitting up suddenly, 'four.'

The Saturday morning sun was streaming through our fifth-floor window and I hadn't slept a wink. My shoulder ached and Kate had been too preoccupied with other parts of my body to help me change the dressing on my shoulder. The little Art Deco clock by my bed told me it was coming up to nine o'clock.

I got up, washed my face and looked at myself in the wall-to-wall mirrors. I peeled off the dressing of my wound and covered the hole gently with some *crème de Jonctum*. It stung. I pulled an Evian out from the mini-bar and checked the safe. Everything was exactly as I'd left it. I got dressed as quietly as possible and wrote Kate a short note telling her to take her time, have a bath and that I'd be back before noon. I slipped out of the door and along the semi-circular corridor, down the lift and out through the rear doors where a row of expensive boutiques was just opening.

The estate agent hadn't stopped smiling since I'd walked in and her smile became even broader when I told her I had a lot of money to spend. I didn't tell her how much.

'Hmmm. Do you intend to become resident here or is it more of an investment? We get very good yields you know – '

'It would be for living in.'

'Wonderful to think you might be joining us here in the Principality, Mr Desmond.'

'I'm thinking of practising law here.'

'Really? Did something in the window catch your eye?'

I pointed to the pictures of the twelve million euro penthouse with the rooftop pool and she licked her lips.

'I'd like that', I said with a sigh, 'but I can't afford it. Perhaps a studio flat?'

Whilst I'd been in hospital in London I'd done a lot of research using the wireless aerial on my laptop. Monaco was free of personal taxation as long as you earned your money offshore, i.e. outside Monaco. However, you weren't taxed on deposits, on money held *inside* Monaco. In fact, you were encouraged to maintain as much money as possible in the Principality as long as you weren't trading, running a business. If you did run a business, such as a law firm, you paid tax on the profits of that business just like anywhere else, albeit at a reduced rate. But there was no capital gains tax, no inheritance tax and I loved my children more than life itself. I tried to tell myself I was doing all this for them, for the Berrie inheritance, but I'd never been a good liar, not even to myself.

It was about the money.

Small was the word that I would use to describe the flat on the sixteenth floor of a jerry-built tower block with a small terrace and an oblique sea view. No room for guests here, apart from overnight ones. It was newly refurbished and about forty square metres, one medium-sized room with an expensive pull-down bed sunk into one of the walls. The ceilings were lowish but so was the price, for Monaco at least. I didn't have any possessions to fill it with and I could always move up to something better, in time. When Genevieve allowed.

'I'll take it', I said to the agent at eleven thirty.

CHAPTER TWENTY

It was drizzling on Monday morning and the grey light started to fill the sky just before seven. We'd spent the weekend in the hotel, eating at the Alain Ducasse restaurant, listening to the band in the American bar and making love. Kate slept, I didn't. I told her that I needed Monday morning to take care of a little family business and that we should meet for lunch at L'Hermitage. Kate was planning on spending the morning re-stocking her wardrobe, blowing Mark out of her mind and she had four thousand euros in cash to do it with.

'No credit cards', I'd said to her. 'We're both in the middle of divorces.'

'Smart', she replied. 'You're thinking smart, Jonny. Like a good lawyer.'

'At last', I smiled.

I passed through the revolving doors of the Hotel de Paris at eight-thirty, one hour ahead of London. It was still drizzling but I declined the offer of a hotel umbrella. The bank opened at eight forty-five and it was a one minute walk. My right hand was in my pocket, clasped firmly around Genevieve.

I walked down the stone steps and turned left, the cinema in front of me covered in a giant billboard for '*United 93*'.

I walked round the side of the hotel, over-sized posters of unshaven Arab terrorists with bombs strapped round their chests looming over me and I headed up Avenue des Beaux-Arts towards JP Chartrier et Freres.

The two-stage entry process was the same as in Zurich. Once through the second door I was standing in a marble-floored atrium with a po-faced bank teller to my left, an ATM and a pretty girl in front of me, sitting at a desk smiling at me. The ATM was useless to me because I had a numbered account with no cashcard, no Mondeo or VISA facility and no name.

'I have one of these', I said, holding up Genevieve.

'Of course sir', she said, picking up the telephone. '*Monsieur Richaud, s'il vous plaît.*'

I looked around at the four mini-cams whirring on their steel brackets, scanning the atrium and also my face. A few moments later Monsieur Richaud came out from behind a mirrored door, shook my hand and confirmed that he was the manager of the Monaco branch. I didn't offer him my name.

'The terminals are zis way', he said, opening another mirrored door via a fingerprint recognition keypad.

There were four rooms, each with a little sign above the door.

'We take *Mont Blanc*', he said, opening the door for me. 'Just press ze buzzer when you are finished.'

I nodded and the door shut behind him with a click, leaving me alone with the bank's terminal and Genevieve.

I keyed the ten digit account number into the terminal. The screen went blank for a second and then an instruction appeared in four languages, just as in Zurich:

'KEY YOUR TEN DIGIT ACCOUNT NUMBER INTO YOUR HAND-HELD SECURITY DEVICE, THEN YOUR PASSWORD'.

I did as I was asked and the little machine prompted me for a password. I keyed in V-5-L-V-5-T and a four digit number appeared. The computer monitor prompted me to key in the four digit number. I pressed the keys very deliberately and then the screen went black, as it had before. I tried to remember how long it had taken in Zurich and then I saw the little revolving hourglass at the bottom right hand corner, assembling the pixels for the Genevieve International S.A. welcome page. I moved the mouse over to the '*click here*' button and followed the instructions.

Nothing happened.

I moved the mouse and I clicked again.

Nothing.

I fumbled in my pocket for a cigarette and lit it quickly.

I clicked the mouse again and again and again, willing it to work, but the screen was frozen on the welcome page, an hour-glass suddenly in the bottom right hand corner. My shoulder started to throb. I'd skipped the painkillers this morning. My head was inches from the screen, directed towards the little hourglass as it turned, emptying and re-filling itself with digital sand over and over and over.

I watched the second hand glide round the steel dial of my Rolex. Five seconds. Ten. Eleven. Twelve. And then the hourglass vanished to be replaced by a capitalized message in four languages:

'OTHER USER LOGGED ON – ACCOUNT CURRENTLY INACCESSIBLE. PLEASE TRY AGAIN LATER.'

It was eight-fifty-five. The bank had only been open ten minutes. I put out my cigarette and went over to the door. It was locked. I moved back to the desk, rammed my thumb down onto the buzzer and I heard a click. As I opened the door I heard the muffled sound of another buzzer. I hung back in the doorway as I heard another meeting-room door open and then I saw Monsieur Richaud appear in the corridor. He looked towards me and then towards the open door to my left.

'Gentlemen', he said, raising an eyebrow. 'Is there a problem?'

I turned to the man on my left.

It was Jacob Potts.

***

Jacob Potts was born in Walthamstow on the seventeenth of September 1975. Sixteen years later he left school with four GCSEs. He could have scraped into college to do an HND in financial management but he wanted to make money. He was inspired by an article about Darren Walker in the local paper, a Walthamstow boy with four GCSEs less than Jacob who'd made it as a barrister's clerk.

'*All you need*', ran Darren's quote in the paper, '*is determination, an eye for detail and the gift of the gab.*'

Jacob felt he had these qualities and the article said Darren was making in excess of two hundred and fifty thousand a year. That was an enormous sum of money in 1991 and so Jacob started writing letters using the old IBM machine in Walthamstow library, checking his spelling with a dictionary.

He could never be a lawyer with his qualifications but, like estate agency and door-to-door sales, you didn't need any qualifications whatsoever to be a barristers' clerk.

Jacob wrote to every set of chambers he could find in the Legal 500, explaining how it was his dream to work in the law and that he would do anything – anything – to get a foot in the door. After four months, two hundred letters and one hundred and ten rejections, he was accepted as a trainee clerk at 21 Wessex Yard on a salary of nine thousand pounds a year and three months' probation.

Jacob Potts didn't have a girlfriend or a boyfriend. He didn't drink and he didn't smoke and he didn't do drugs. He didn't gamble either, at least, not at the betting shop.

His first pay-cheque, after tax, gave him enough to pay the rent on his studio flat in Bermondsey in an ex-council block only ten minutes from London Bridge. Galleywall Road had its fair share of criminals, but Jacob avoided them all – the girls selling hooky perfume in the grim steel lifts, the boys selling sawn-off shot-guns down the local pub.

He kept himself to himself and started buying a newspaper every day, the one he'd never understood. Jacob wanted to better himself, and so every day when he got off the platform at London Bridge he purchased a copy of the Financial Times and read it cover to cover.

He started with trolley-work, wheeling tens of files along the pavement to the Old Bailey or the Royal Courts of Justice, trailing behind the barristers in their wigs and gowns. He soon became trusted enough to pick out the relevant law reports for the lawyers to use in court and then, after a year, he was trusted with filing pleadings and running documents to and from instructing solicitors.

He also made a mean cup of tea.

In 1996, five years later and at the age of twenty-one he was promoted to junior clerk on a salary of twenty thousand a year plus profit share, the size of which depended on how much work he got for his barristers and the chambers' total billings for the year.

Profits were paid quarterly and his first cheque was for ten thousand pounds. He was now representing three barristers and a pupil.

He moved to a rented flat in a new development just off Fleet Street and started dealing in shares.

He was very good at it.

Hussain Tarzi was always on the look out for young talent and he paid – or rather, his clients paid – very well.

Jacob met him in chambers in 1998 and a year later Tarzi proposed him for membership of Velvet. Jacob's popularity with instructing solicitors increased rapidly, which meant his barristers were working more, billing more and enabling Jacob to earn a greater and greater slice of pie. Seven years later – in 2006 and only thirty-one years of age - Jacob Potts was earning nearly two hundred thousand a year and had a share portfolio worth in excess of a million pounds. Not bad for an East End cockney with four GCSEs. He was very frugal. Very careful. A good Virgo. He'd only had one under-performing asset but at last he'd managed to turn it around and make it perform for Mr Tarzi. The underperforming asset was me and Jacob felt a pang of guilt that I'd been shot. He'd had someone wash my Aston every day as his penance, paid for out of his own pocket.

Mr Tarzi wasn't meant to die. Neither was Aziza. That was the problem when you acted for terrorists like Mr Al-Khalim. It was a risky business. Mr Tarzi had trusted Jacob enough to keep the little security device for JP Chartrier et Freres whenever he felt he was in danger of being investigated or arrested. Jacob had passed it to Tarzi the day before the car-bomb not knowing it was actually *Mr Desmond's*.

He knew where Tarzi had been going with it and the only other person who knew – Aziza – had perished too. Only Jacob was left and he knew what he had to do. After all, just like Darren Walker before him he had determination, an eye for detail and the gift of the gab.

He'd flicked quickly through the list of flights on Expedia the previous Friday. Mr Tarzi had been on his way to Zurich, so that was out, in case they had someone waiting for him. The bank had other branches though, dotted all over Continental Europe. Any branch would do. He'd have to pick up the duplicate security device and the account number, the one that he wasn't meant to have. By three o'clock chambers was already emptying out for the weekend. He walked to the safety deposit box at Coutts on the Strand in ten minutes. His flat was within walking distance and it wouldn't take him long to pack.

***

It had stopped drizzling and we sat outside a café on a side-street just behind L'Hermitage, sipping coffees. Jacob looked ill and he couldn't stop staring at me. I'd taken a painkiller and I would soon start to feel a little more relaxed, or at least that's what I was hoping. A blue-and-white uniformed policeman, tall and blond, walked past the café and waved to the proprietor. Jacob and I turned our faces away from him. There were cameras even on our side-street. The safest place in the world. Unless of course you were about to commit a crime.

'And we're not about to', I said to him.

'No', he replied, taking another sip of coffee.

I looked at my watch. It was coming up to half-past nine. Three hours before I had to meet Kate and my clerk had stopped addressing me as '*sir*'.

'We've got to be smart, Jacob, haven't we?'

'I 'ad a plan, you know. I still 'ave.'

'I had one too.'

'You tell me yours, I'll tell yer mine.'

'You first', I said, lighting a cigarette.

CHAPTER TWENTY-ONE

Brenda Mullion came away from the meeting with her divorce lawyer, rang the nanny and headed straight to Heathrow. The photos of Chas leaving *Annabel's* with that bitch Georgina under his arm had made her want to puke and she felt like ringing the editor of The Daily Star and telling him he was a prick.

'*Fucking pre-nup*', she said over and over again to herself, '*fuckin' pre-nup.*'

She bought a first class open-ended ticket to New York, boarded the American Airlines 747 and six hours fifty minutes later strode through US immigration control, still fuming. Chas had offered her a twenty million dollar divorce settlement which was more generous than the sixteen she'd be due under the pre-nup. Without the pre-nup she'd be entitled to between a third and a half of his assets which would run to hundreds of millions and Brenda was mightily pissed off. Why had she signed the fucking thing?

Her lawyer said the only way to fight it was to find something that Chas had written to her – a love-letter, for example – where he'd promised her more, where it was suggestible by something he'd written that he might have changed his mind after the pre-nup.

All of her old letters – she kept every one – were at their house on Long Island, Chas's childhood home passed from father to son when Charles H. Mullion II died a widower twenty years before.

***

It was early evening when the New York cab pulled up outside number four-five-two Lawrenson Drive West, Lido Beach, Long Island. It was a middle class neighborhood, nothing fancy, but Chas had kept the house because of a sentimental attachment and Brenda knew where she would find the key, under the flowerpot next to the door. The lock was stiff but she twisted the key and opened the door on the fourth attempt.

Inside it was musty, just as she remembered it. It was always musty because Chas had refused to change anything after his father died. They'd moved into Manhattan soon afterwards and so they only visited in the summer and then only for the odd weekend. Inside it was a monument to the seventies.

A cleaner – Maria – still came once a week so it wasn't dusty or dirty and she flushed the toilets and ran the taps just like she'd been told. She even changed the sheets every week in the master bedroom just in case *Senor* or *Senora* Mullion fancied popping down for a trip down memory lane.

Brenda dropped her Louis Vuitton suitcase on the bed and went back downstairs to the kitchen to fix herself a mint tea.

She wasn't in the least tired because she was a woman on a mission and that mission involved searching every nook and cranny, every cupboard, every drawer and every trunk for evidence that Chas loved her more than he loved twenty million dollars.

It wouldn't be easy.

She started with the rooms downstairs, breaking open the old drinks cabinet with a knife. She found a selection of bills – all paid – stretching back to 1977. There was nothing in the kitchen apart from some ants and nothing in the entrance hall or the downstairs cloakroom. Brenda located a bottle of brandy and poured herself a glass. There were three bedrooms and two bathrooms upstairs. It was now eight in the evening and she wanted to be back on a flight to London the following morning.

There was a whole wardrobe full of Chas's old schoolbooks and college notes. Brenda tore through them quickly, the brandy next to her almost untouched. Nothing. A lot of alphas and beta plusses but nothing Chas did at school had any bearing on his subsequent marriage to the woman now ripping apart his fifth grade science project. What about university? That's when he'd begun his love-affair with Britain, wasn't it? Hadn't he been a Rhodes Scholar at Oxford? He'd won a prize, she was sure of it, but she couldn't find anything in any of the bedrooms.

It was coming up to midnight and Brenda Mullion had gone though four cups of mint tea and two large glasses of brandy. She was getting tired and she sat on the first floor landing in the old rocking chair, the one that had belonged to Chas's grandmother.

'Oh God', she said, looking up to the Almighty, 'oh God'.

In that moment of despair, the despair of seeing hundreds of millions of dollars slip through her fingers to a shit of a husband who'd run off with her best friend, she saw the little hatchway that led up to the loft.

It was dusty and it smelt of damp but there was an electric bulb to flood the beamed roof-space with light. Brenda stood on the top rung of the ladder and levered herself onto a wide beam next to a row of boxes, each one numbered and dated. She couldn't recognize the handwriting. It must have been Chas's father's and the dates went back to 1947. Box five was '1970 to 1980' and box six only had a start date – the fourteenth of July 1980. Brenda pulled the boxes one-by-one across to the hatch and lowered them to the floor of the first floor landing.

Brenda read it eight times, over and over. The certificate was old and slightly ripped in one corner, but it was completely legible. In Marylebone Registry Office on the seventh of August 1975, Charles Henry Mullion III, son of Charles and Henrietta, married somebody called Elspeth Huntingford-Smith, daughter of Roger and Willa.

She poured herself another glass of brandy and searched for the divorce certificate but all she found was a death certificate dated the twenty-fourth of August 1975. Seventeen days of marriage. It was creepy. He'd never mentioned this woman, Elspeth. Ever. He'd never told her he'd been married before. The girl was pretty too, from the newspaper clippings she discovered.

For a split-second she felt a touch of sympathy for her soon-to-be-ex-husband, cruelly robbed of a wife in the first month of marriage. But only for a split-second.

The clippings said some Brit called Winters was charged for her murder. She scanned them quickly. He'd been accused of drowning her in a swimming pool but he'd been acquitted. There was no mention of Chas anywhere. Brenda pulled out all the relevant papers including the marriage and death certificates and stuffed them into her suitcase. She put the boxes back in the attic, replaced the loft-hatch and took a shower to wash off all the dust. Her lawyer could work out what to do with it all now. Brenda was tired and the brandy would help her sleep.

***

Lord Marden sat in Martin Hotson's enormous office with a glass of Scotch in his hand.

'So you see my problem, Martin', said his Lordship.

'I do. And you see mine.'

'Yes. It's very inconvenient for both of us. Will Berry return the money?'

'Unless he's spent it. He says he had nothing to do with murdering Desmond Lyons and frankly I believe him.'

'We can help each other, Martin. We each have something the other wants.'

'You can really do it, can you Bill?' Martin Hotson edged forward on the sofa. 'I'd be enormously…grateful.'

'Of course, my price will be a little higher than Berry's.'

'Of course. How much higher?'

'Ten million dollars for an acquittal or if the case is withdrawn for any reason. I have an account' - his Lordship cleared his throat - 'in Panama.'

Martin smiled.

'Funnily enough, Bill', he said, 'so do I.'

***

We got back to my suite at the Hotel de Paris at ten fifteen. Neither Jacob nor I would let the other out of our sight, even for a second. As I'd expected, Kate was out spending the four thousand euros she'd won at the casino.

'Can yer trust her?' Jacob asked me.

'Can I trust *you*?', I replied.

We sat next to each other at the leather-topped desk by the window with the super-yachts parked outside in the Med less than fifty yards away.

I took two sheets of thick cream-coloured paper from the complimentary hotel stationery and gave one to Jacob. We each wrote a number at the top of our sheet of paper: US\$2,800,000,000 – two billion, eight hundred million dollars.

'Remember what we agreed', I said. 'It's the only way.'

Jacob nodded and started writing whilst I rang the concierge and requested an additional bed for the suite as per our agreement. Kate would understand.

We both breathed a sigh of relief when it came to twelve thirty because that was when JP Chartrier et Freres shut for lunch, opening again at two. Neither of us would be able to clean out the account until then. We walked out of the Hotel de Paris and into L'Hermitage where Kate was already sitting with a glass of champagne.

'Look who I bumped into, Kate', I said, smiling at Jacob next to me.

'It's Jacob, isn't it?'

''Ullo Miss Bowyer.'

'Jonathan?' she asked, puzzled. 'What's going on?'

***

'They're crawling all over us', said Chas across the large meeting-room table in Ropemaker Place, surrounded by his fellow management partners and his right-hand-woman, the one he was sleeping with. She called herself Georgina Whittaker now, her maiden name, even though she still hadn't received the decree nisi and so technically was still my wife.

'Fuckin' regulator's makin' us sweat.'

'Here and the US.'

There was a lot of murmuring as a waitress brought in a tray filled with coffee pots, croissants and chocolates.

'We set for the sixteenth, Chas?'

Chas gave a thumbs up sign, his mouth full of croissant. He signaled for Georgina to give the team an update, the one he'd been through with her last night at the hotel before he'd fucked her brains out.

'Gentlemen', said Georgina, seated, 'the broker indications are excellent. They're pegging us to the top of the range, an opening price of seventeen pounds in London and thirty-one dollars on the NYSE.'

The partners sat there poker-faced, each one calculating what his – and they were all male – individual slice of pie might add up to.

'We're looking at a two-year lock-in on ninety per cent of partner shareholdings', she continued. 'Keeps the underwriters happy and boosts the share price.'

More calculations. This time what ten per cent would be worth on day one and what ninety would be worth in two years. Chas closed his eyes. He would be worth an additional half a billion dollars courtesy of the float and a whole lot more if the share price ballooned. He would be fifty-six years old and a billionaire with a full head of hair. He would share his good fortune with Georgina.

No-one had batted an eyelid when he'd handed in his list of proposed bonuses for his staff.

He was recommending her for a one-off float bonus - payable half in stock, half in cash - of ten million dollars, which was half the bonus he was giving Brenda under the pre-nup.

Poor Brenda.

***

We ordered three club sandwiches from room service and I called a law firm I knew in the Bahamas run by an old school-friend, Roddy Houston. I asked him to sell me an off-the-shelf company.

'Delighted to, my dear fellow', said Roddy. 'Rush job's seven thousand dollars -'

'Fine.'

'...plus an annual five thousand dollar retainer to file the requisite corporate documents in Nassau and set up two nominee trust shareholders. I assume you'll want beneficial control?'

'Yes. Together with someone else', I replied, looking at Jacob, 'on a fifty-fifty basis.'

Jacob stared at me, tight-lipped.

'Can you fax the corporate resolutions to me, Roddy? I'll give you the number of the hotel I'm staying in.'

'No problem.'

'And can you send a courier overnight to Monaco with the original documents for tomorrow morning?'

'Might be better if I send an assistant with them.'

'How much?'

Another five thousand.'

'Fine.'

'His name's Cracken and he'll be with you by ten.'

'I owe you Roddy.'

'You do, matey. Seventeen thousand please, soon as you can.'

'I'll give Cracken a cheque tomorrow morning.'

I put down the telephone and looked up at Jacob and Kate. The club sandwiches lay untouched on top of a silver trolley. It was five to two, JP Chartrier et Freres would soon be opening for the afternoon and I could see Jacob getting twitchy. The fax from Roddy came through direct to our hotel room within ten minutes and the second the confirmation spewed out of the machine we were out of the door.

It had started to drizzle again and Kate put up an umbrella to protect her new Chanel suit. We passed by the front door of JP Chartrier et Freres and straight through the front doors of the Gestattenzee Bank of Geneva three doors down the street. Within minutes we had opened an account in the name of Trueblood (Bahamas) Inc, the company we'd just bought from Roddy.

'We will need a – ha - *deposit* to open the account', said the manager Mr Morelli, a grey-haired man with bushy eyebrows, horn-rimmed spectacles and an Italian accent. 'When do you foresee –'

'Give us 'alf an 'our', said Jacob.

With our new account details we walked back to JP Chartrier et Freres and withdrew one million dollars in cash from Genevieve's account.

The bank even threw in a free leather briefcase.

We sent Kate back to Gestattenzee with the briefcase and the cash to open the Trueblood account, leaving Jacob and me alone with Genevieve.

'You fink we'll see 'er again?' he asked, watching me smoke one of my hooky Customs cigarettes.

'I think so, Jacob.'

'You're testin' 'er, aren't ya?'

'Perhaps.'

We sat and waited within the confines of *Mont Blanc*. It was ten minutes past three and we had less than two hours to make the requisite transfers. All four of them. Jacob and I sat in silence holding our Genevieve security devices, watching the clock. Ten minutes passed.

'Ow long can i' take?'

'Patience, Jacob.'

We'd told Kate everything. Well, nearly everything. I hadn't told her - or Jacob - about *Mr Desmond's* account with the two billion in it that was now too dangerous to touch. I hadn't told her – or Jacob - that *Mr Desmond's* security device was sitting in Mark Bowyer's pocket in an unusable and untraceable state somewhere in Scotland Yard.

I hadn't wanted anything to cloud her mind, or Jacob's. Or mine. Not today. But as the minutes went by I was starting to have doubts. How long could it take? Would Kate's mind have been clouded by the thought of one million dollars in cash in a briefcase? Or was she going to help us with our plan? What about the bank's money-laundering policy? Would Mr Morelli ask one too many questions?

And then the door opened.

'He didn't even ask where the money came from', said Kate, triumphantly handing me a Gestattenzee Bank receipt for a deposit of one million into Trueblood's account.

'Four transfers', I said to Jacob. 'And then we can get rid of these.'

I looked down at my Genevieve Security device.

'You boys need me for anything?' asked Kate. 'Only I wouldn't mind some pin money for the casino.'

I gave Kate fifty thousand euros to go to the casino with, leaving me alone with Jacob and the two little Genevieves.

We didn't know if there were any other little Genevieve devices circulating – after all, Jacob had one and there might be others – so whatever we did we had to do quickly and whatever we did with the funds had to be as clean as possible so there could be no fall-out.

Jacob and I each had our own lists, the ones we'd drawn up in the Hotel de Paris at my desk.

Transfer number one was to get Kelsey out of the picture. We agreed to return twenty-two million two hundred and fifty seven thousand dollars to his account. I didn't deduct the fifteen per cent finders' fee to which I was entitled because I didn't want Kelsey to know I'd found it. Jacob let me use my security device. I also wanted Martin Hotson off my back but I couldn't wire the three million Swiss francs to Halcyon's account – to the same account details that appeared on the bottom of the cheque that Martin Hotson had given me and that I'd photocopied – because then he'd know that the money was from a numbered Swiss bank account under my control. Martin Hotson would have to wait.

We'd talked about *fuck-off* money, Jacob and I, and then he started on the subject of leverage.

'We got a shade under two point eight billion to play with. Done clever, you can make a hundred million do the same job, turned over enough times.'

'What do you mean, Jacob?'

'I make two hundred grand from my job, Jonathan.'

'More than me, Jacob.'

'An' another three hundred from share dealing.'

'Really?'

'Thass my dream, Jonathan. Propriet'ry trading. Could do it here in Monaco. Just need a little room somewhere, five phone lines and a couple a computers. An' a fuck-off wad o' money 'n all fer workin' capital.'

I smiled.

'I think your dream is going to come true, Jacob.'

The second transfer was to the new Trueblood account in the amount of four hundred and fifty million dollars. I let Jacob do it, with me standing over his shoulder.

The third was to a Cayman Islands children's trust – 'The BMA Children's Fund' – which had only three beneficiaries: my children Ben, Mollie and Amy Berry. I was the sole trustee. I'd been busy in my hospital bed.

The fourth and final transfer was to the 0800-SAVEAKID appeal for Jadzikistan. We transferred the balance of Genevieve 'B', all two billion two hundred and seventy million dollars, direct to the appeal's account at the European Bank. That was the one that made us feel good, or at least, the one that made me feel that what we were doing wasn't criminal.

I felt like Robin bloody Hood.

We closed the Genevieve account at four-thirty with a fifty thousand dollar cash contribution to the JP Chartrier et Freres benevolent fund, smashed Genevieve's security devices with the bathroom scales in my room at the Hotel de Paris and threw the unidentifiable bits of metal and plastic into the skip of a construction site just behind L'Hermitage. Our next stop was the estate agency, two doors down the street.

Trueblood paid five hundred and seventy two thousand euros in cash for the studio flat subject to completion within twenty-four hours.

The vendor had been only too happy to comply with our

condition and by seven in the evening we had the keys. Jacob bought two laptops, wireless adaptors and a router for the flat from Fnac in the *Galerie Charles III* shopping arcade. I bought three plastic folding chairs and tables. With one phone call and a new Trueblood credit card I set up a virtual office address for us in the Principality, complete with receptionist to answer all calls and a mailing address. All mail was to be forwarded to the Bahamas, not Monaco. All of our business would technically be conducted offshore via accounts we had yet to set up.

Kate came back from the casino at about half-past-seven with one hundred and seventy thousand euros, more than three times what she started with, and we opened a bottle of champagne whilst another idea was forming. I had a lot of ideas suddenly.

'You're on a roll, Kate', I said to her, clinking glasses. 'Fancy the casino later?'

'I'm knackered', she said, kicking off her shoes wearily.

I got up and walked over to the bridle-leather satchel by my side of the bed. I held it open in front of Kate. Inside was one million euros in neatly-stacked five-hundred euro bills.

'Perhaps not that knackered', she said, crossing her legs.

Jacob and I had done enough for the day and now it was Kate's turn. We ordered dinner from room service – steaks all round and more champagne – and at eleven o'clock we headed for the high rollers room where she'd walked out with a hundred and seventy thousand earlier in the day.

Jacob didn't have to sleep in our room anymore because we'd got rid of Genevieve so I got the hotel staff to remove the extra bed. I looked at Kate, dressed in a figure-hugging strapless black dress, legs crossed, sitting at the blackjack table. I wanted her to myself tonight. I felt good. We had about half a billion dollars between us and our names weren't noted anywhere.   I finally had fuck-off money.

Just like Chas Mullion.

CHAPTER TWENTY-TWO

Chas Mullion was on his fourth cognac, standing in the drawing room of his fourteen million pound mansion backing onto Holland Park. He was alone. Georgina was spending the night with my kids in the house on Abbotsbury Road, the one I used to live in. Chas was pacing the room, making the sort of calculations he hadn't even dared think about in the management meeting earlier that day. Neither the Financial Services Authority in the UK, nor the Securities and Exchange Commission in the US had picked up on the fact that out of the billions held by Silverman Bach for its clientele was four billion held by Chas and three of his colleagues for one Khaled Al Khalim, now on trial for genocide and mass murder.

Khaled would never see his money again. He would never know it had even gone missing. Chas couldn't give it up to the SEC or the FSA, not now. They'd ask Chas why he hadn't done it before, such a large amount. It'd hurt the float price as well. Four billion. It was tempting, very tempting. Was a billion enough? That's what he'd be worth after the float. What would he do with it all?

'Ha!' he laughed out loud, the sound echoing off the walls

of the enormous high-ceilinged room.

The twenty million he was giving to Brenda was nothing. A pin-prick. He'd have to talk to the others of course. Was it two or three? One of them was Harrigan, a greedy bastard. He'd go for it. They'd be able to convince the others it was a worthwhile gambit. Sell Khaled's shares piecemeal and transfer the funds to an offshore investment trust controlled by the four of them. What would Rockefeller have done in his shoes? And those bastards at Murrell Hammond Christie? Yeah, Chas knew what they'd do. Exactly what he was thinking of doing.

**

Anthony Garrett was an old man and he had been a solicitor for nearly forty-five years. He knew he could have retired a long time ago but he had glorious offices set in an Edwardian block in Hans Place in Knightsbridge and he was the most successful divorce lawyer of the twentieth century, possibly also the twenty-first. A letter from him on his firm's letterhead – Anthony Garrett & Co. - would strike fear into the hardest husband or the coldest wife. Anthony Garrett made nearly two million pounds a year. Anthony Garrett was Brenda Mullion's divorce lawyer. He studied the papers in front of him with more than mild interest, although, from his face, you'd never know it.

'These are documents of public record', he said.

'Yeah, right', replied Brenda, letting her ring catch the light.

'Perhaps they should be made public.'

Anthony Garrett looked down at the marriage certificate,

Charles B Mullion III to Elspeth Huntingford-Smith. Marylebone Registry Office. 1975. Then the death certificate. The name rang a bell.

'Nothing from him to you in writing?' asked Garrett, loading his question with extraordinary gravitas.

'No. Bastard never wrote me anything nice.'

'I see.'

'I'm exhausted.'

'You flew back this morning?'

'Yeah', Brenda yawned. 'I need a facial.'

Garrett took off his glasses.

'If he never mentioned the wedding to you, and the unfortunate death so soon afterwards, then perhaps he has something to hide.'

'Like what?'

'I have no idea. But – '

'We go to the papers? Not much of a story is it?'

'Journalists can find the most peculiar things in the most unlikely places.' Garrett put his glasses on and leaned back in his studded leather armchair. 'I could dig around, take some soundings, that sort of thing.'

'Okay.'

'Please don't worry Mrs Mullion, you're not paying me to let your husband off the hook.'

'Friggin' hope not.'

'Exactly.'

'We done?'

'Yes. Leave these with me and enjoy your facial. I hear Mussons do a very good one. They're just down the road on Beauchamp Place.

'Mussons?'

'I go there myself.'

Brenda took her perfectly-manicured and coiffed body out into the hall and Anthony Garrett tapped his pipe against the side of his chair, knocking tobacco onto the Persian rug. He had a remarkable memory for faces, names and places and he knew exactly who Elspeth Huntingford-Smith was. He remembered the trial in 1975 or 1976, the one where Martin Winters was acquitted of murder and the one for which Martin Hotson, same man, different name, was now in the frame again, thirty years on. He slipped the two certificates into a drawer of his desk and locked it. He was a patient man and there was no rush.

***

Outside London's Central Criminal Court, the Old Bailey, the street was swarming with police, press and onlookers. Above the massive stone building sat the golden scales of justice. Inside, in court number four, the public gallery was packed with press and the front four benches of the court were occupied by a total of twenty-one lawyers, two thirds of them in grey, blue or black suits, the other third in wigs and gowns. In the stand was Khaled Al Khalim, his eyes moving from Nicholas Furniss QC - counsel for the United Nations and the

State of Jadzikistan – to the judge, Lord Marden of Winchelsea.

Khaled Al Khalim didn't want to be there and neither did Lord Marden. There was nothing in it for either of them. Not now that Tarzi was dead.

Awaiting trial in his cell at Brixham Prison, Khaled had watched television sixteen hours a day and one programme in particular had captivated him.

'Crown Court' was a series that had been repeated so many times on British television that there was now a whole cable channel dedicated to it. Khaled had watched it religiously in the week leading up to his trial and he even took notes, just like he used to do at the INSEAD lectures in Fontainbleu.

Enshrined in the English criminal justice system was the inalienable right of a defendant to conduct his own defence.

None of his lawyers had mentioned this possibility to him and so he wondered what they would make of the handwritten note that was making its way row by row towards the front of the court and into the hands of his lead counsel, Gerald Waterstone QC.

Lord Marden avoided all eye contact with the defendant. He looked down at his cream note-pad. He had doodled some numbers. One door closes, another opens, he thought, as he doodled the number '1' followed by seven zeros. He wasn't even listening to the charges as they were being read out. He didn't want to hear about the slaughter of women and children a long time ago in a country he'd never visited. He wanted to hear the sound of money, the sound of a more-than-comfortable retirement. The Khaled case would be his last. His Lordship wanted to finish in style, and what could be better than presiding over the most high-profile murder trial this century? Especially as he now had no financial interest in the result.

The court would sit for the next six weeks from ten in the morning until four in the afternoon, with an hour for lunch. His Lordship would only have to spend five hours a day listening to the arguments. He'd read all the documents, of course. He was remarkably thorough and so he'd already written his judgment. Guilty. That would mean life imprisonment in England, but His Lordship was going to recommend that Khaled be passed for sentencing to Jadzikistan, where they still had the death penalty.

They could make a martyr of the murdering bastard if they wanted to. His Lordship would do what he had done for most of his professional life. He would pass the buck.

'My Lord?'

His Lordship raised his head. Gerald Waterstone QC, counsel for the defence, was standing in front of him, holding a piece of paper in his hand and looking rather flushed in the face.

'Yes?' said His Lordship. 'Have the charges been read?'

'They have, my lord.'

'So how does your client plead Mr Waterstone?'

'I am not empowered to say, my lord.'

'Why not?'

'My client wishes to dispense with my services, my lord, and with the services of that of his legal team. He wishes to conduct his own defence.'

'He does?' said His Lordship, raising an eyebrow.

'He does.'

The court was suddenly filled with loud murmuring.

'Is that correct Mr Al Khalim?'

Khalim Al Khalim stood and beamed.

'That is correct, your lordship. And I would like to make a deal with you.'

'*What?*'

'I would like – '

'Silence!' His Lordship peered down at the defendant, manacled hand and foot. 'This is a criminal trial, Mr Al Khalim. You cannot make deals.'

Khaled's eyes bored into Lord Marden's.

'Have you heard the charges before you, Mr Al Khalim?'

'Yes.'

'And how do you plead?'

'Not guilty.'

'This court is adjourned for one hour, at which point the prosecution will open their case against the defendant.'

His Lordship stood and peered down at Khaled.

'And don't think, Mr Al Khalim, that you can turn my court into a circus, or I'll have you for contempt.'

Khaled smiled.

'Please rise', blared a court official as His Lordship exited via the door immediately behind his chair, leaving the defence lawyers to file out of Court Four for the last time and the press to tap out the first big news story of the day, that Khaled had fired his lawyers and would be conducting his defence himself.

'Dear, dear', said Lord Marden to Harry, his long-suffering clerk of fifteen years. 'Dear, dear.'

'Bad mornin', your lordship?'

'Dreadful.'

Harry knew better than to delve too deeply into His Lordship's cases.

'Sorry to 'ear that, your lordship. Cup o' tea, your lordship?'

'Thank you Harry. Most kind.'

Harry left Lord Marden alone in his chambers. His Lordship looked around him at the collection of the Weekly Law Reports and Criminal Appeals Journals adorning the walls. How many times did his name appear in them? Many times, and rarely had a defendant on such serious charges opted to defend themselves. It could double the length of the trial. He looked again at the number he'd written on his note-pad, the '1' and seven zeros. They hadn't assigned a judge yet on the Hotson case. His Lordship didn't care whether or not Hotson was guilty. He hadn't even asked him. All he'd done was to go to him in his hour of need.

***

Brenda Mullion hadn't seen Chas for days. He was busy trying to make himself even more money by floating his precious fucking investment bank. She'd read it in the papers. It galled her that she wouldn't see any of the millions that he would cream off from the float. It galled her that he was fucking her best friend Georgina. He was truly evil. She hated him. And the more Brenda hated him, the more she thought about who else might hate him as much as her, who else might be able to join forces with her in her quest to squeeze Charles H Mullion III for serious money.

Whoever it was that hated him as much as her, whoever it was, she'd give them a cut of what she got. If they could help her of course.

Brenda called my mobile phone at eight in the morning Monaco time, Tuesday. Kate and I were lying in bed with her winnings safely tucked away in my bridle-leather satchel. Kate had had a good night. Four hours-worth of blackjack and she'd won four hundred thousand euros. My satchel was starting to bulge.

'Brenda? How did you get this number?'

'Georgina gave it to me. Before she – '

'OK Brenda. Enough said.' I sat up and Kate watched me, curious as to who Brenda was. 'What can I do for you?'

'Chas is screwing me, Jonathan.'

I winced and it wasn't just my shoulder.

'I think you'll find he's screwing my wife.'

'You and me both, then. Where are you?'

'I'm…' I looked at Kate's naked body lying next to me in our suite at the Hotel de Paris. 'I'm recuperating.'

'Yeah, right. I heard you were shot. Hope you're OK.'

'I will be', I replied, smiling at Kate.

'He's a liar, Jonathan.'

'Really?'

'Yeah. He was married, Jonathan. He never told me he was married. He ever mention it at that club of yours?'

Kate was trying to grab the phone from me and I stood up, naked, and walked over to the large window.

I pressed the button that opened the electrically-operated shutters and the sun poured through onto the bed.

'He's married to *you*, isn't he, Brenda?'

'Yeah yeah. I mean before. Some woman called Elspeth. He never mentioned her. Ain't that weird?'

I froze.

'Yes', I replied slowly. 'That is weird.' Kate was signaling me to cut the call but I moved closer to the window, giving the yachts in the Harbor a good look at my naked torso. '*Elspeth*, you said?'

'Yeah. Could I get him for dishonesty or something like that?'

'Maybe. Do you have any proof he was married?'

'Yeah. I got copies of everythin' I gave to my lawyer.'

'Could you fax the certificate to me at chambers? The number's – '

'I got it right in front of me, Jonathan. I'll send ya both certificates.'

'Both?'

'Yeah. The one for the marriage and then the death certificate. I'm really grateful, Jonathan.'

'What are friends for?' I replied, my mind racing.

I called Jacob's room at the Balmoral, a smallish hotel down a side street behind L'Hermitage. He confirmed we had Winfax at chambers in London and that we could pick up any fax straight off the internet via our virtual private network.

Five minutes later I opened my laptop, logged on and downloaded Brenda's two page fax. She hadn't wasted any time sending it to me. I printed it off on the tiny inkjet hidden in a desk drawer and studied the pages. Kate was in the shower and I heard a knock at the door. It was Jacob, resplendent in Paul Smith check and he studied the fax even more closely than I had.

'Leverage', he said, smiling. 'Information and leverage.'

'Jacob?'

'The float's on Thursday', he said.

'The float?'

'Silverman Bach.'

'But Jacob – we're still on the Hotson case aren't we? This is crucial evid-'

'...know any journalists, Jonathan?'

'Yes...but –'

We both looked round as Kate walked out of the shower

in a fluffy white robe, a towel wrapped round her hair.

'Morning, boys', she said jauntily. 'What's the plan for today?'

CHAPTER TWENTY-THREE

The sun rose over St Paul's Cathedral, lighting its massive silvery dome with a warm orange glow. On the grid of streets below, taxis and unmarked limousines whisked along Queen Victoria Street and Holborn, their passengers mainly money men, bankers, on their way to work whilst the rest of the British population was sleeping.

A few hundred yards from St Paul's, the lights at Ropemaker Place had been burning all night. Three hundred cases of champagne had been ordered – Krug 1990 – and a number of the Silverman Bach partners had spent the night in the small but luxurious overnight pods on the twenty-four floor, talking to their counterparts in New York and Los Angeles, listening to mood music and availing themselves of the Reuters and Bloomberg screens.

The grunts started filing in at six-thirty, chattering, drinking McDonald's milkshakes and eating bagels. It was a big day for them, too. Even the secretaries were in early, the majority before seven. Some of the longer-serving ones would be realizing a long-held dream. Their eyes were bright and there was a lot of fussing in the ladies' washrooms, much application of eyeliner and lipstick.

A memo had gone round on Tuesday warning everyone that there would be a live CNN broadcast from the offices of Silverman Bach an hour after market opening and everyone wanted to look their best. A lot of mortgages would be paid off today. '*Platinum Thursday*', the memo had called it.

***

We'd brought a click-clack sofa, a futon, into Trueblood's new headquarters – the Monaco studio flat - and Kate and I were sitting on it now, watching Jacob at work. He was in front of two plastic tables. On one, two laptops and on the other, five mobile telephones sitting in their chargers. He was standing, nervously, in front of the screens.

'Openin' price looks like nineteen', said Jacob to himself.

'Nineteen? Is that good?' asked Kate.

'It's 'igh', he replied, 'which is just what we want.'

The small flatscreen television was on in the corner and I turned it up. CNN Marketwatch was giving a run-down of the day's big events and the biggest one by far was the opening day of trading for ten pence ordinary shares in Silverman Bach plc, which looked like they were soon going to be changing hands for nineteen pounds apiece. It was six thirty in the morning, which was seven thirty in London.

'We wai' for New York', said Jacob. 'Wall a money ou' there.'

'When's New York opening?' I asked.

'Nine-thirty East Coast time an' we're six 'ours ahead.'

'So we have to wait here 'til three thirty in the afternoon?'

'Naa', said Jacob, forcing a smile. 'We're gonna be 'ere all night.'

I looked down at the pad in front of me, the one with the City-desk contact names and telephone numbers for three major newspapers in the UK and three in the US including the New York Times together with the numbers for CNN and Reuters.

'You know what you're doing, Jacob?'

'Course I do, Jonathan. Luvverly opportuni'y.'

'Come on, Jonathan', said Kate. 'He's screwing your wife, isn't he?'

I looked down at the screen of my laptop, at the two certificates I'd scanned in, the ones I was going to send from my new untraceable Hotmail account after I'd made the call. I glanced at the scrap of paper on which I'd written Martin Hotson's mobile number and the private fax number Kate had given me.

'Yes', I replied. 'I almost feel sorry for her.'

***

It was five minutes to market opening on Thursday morning and the worldwide management committee of Silverman Bach, all twelve of them, were standing looking down at the electronic boards inside the London Stock Exchange building on Paternoster Square.

Grey market trading the previous night had indicated an

opening share price of nineteen pounds ten pence a share, two pounds more than even Chas or Georgina's most optimistic estimate. The mood in the viewing gallery was bullish.

'Great job, Mullion!'

'You too, Harrigan.'

Chas patted him on the back

'It's gonna be a fine day.'

Today would be the perfect day, the float the perfect smokescreen to set in motion *Plan Dromedary*, which is what Chas and his three co-trustees had called the plan to sell Khaled's shareholdings and dump the proceeds into an account somewhere in the Caymans, held beneficially by the four of them.

Everyone would be so busy with the float they wouldn't even notice the sale of hundreds of millions of dollars in each of twenty large-cap companies in which Khaled held stock totaling more than four billion dollars-worth. No-one would be able to link the sales as Chas had given the instructions to sell blind through another offshore intermediary via ten different brokers. The plan was foolproof but it was, as he and Harrigan were painfully aware, highly illegal.

It was theft, but it was theft from the most evil son-of-a-bitch dictator in the world, now standing trial only a mile away, so it was OK. Chas looked over again at Harrigan's greedy face. They'd done worse. *He'd* done worse.

Nothing was going to spoil today, Platinum Thursday. Nothing. He certainly wasn't going to be sharing his good fortune with his soon-to-be-ex-wife, so when Brenda's number flashed up on his cell-phone for the third time that morning he ignored it.

***

The two-page fax came through without a cover-sheet. He knew where it was from because it was printed across the top of each page: the offices of Halcyon Holdings in Ropemaker Place, the flagship of Martin Hotson, currently on bail and awaiting trial for the murder of Elspeth Huntingford-Smith. Normally all contact came through the CPS or the defendant's solicitor or barrister. This was unusual.

Mark Bowyer was thirsty.

He'd been in his office at Scotland Yard for two hours already – he always got in at six a.m. – so he rested the two pages on his desk and went to make himself a coffee, one of the strong instant ones full of imported Colombian beans.

He'd never heard the name Charles Henry Mullion III. No-one had ever taken a statement from him. He had never come forward, neither thirty years ago nor in the current proceedings. He was sure Elspeth had not been married. The suffix made the name sound American.

He could check if the marriage certificate was genuine in a matter of minutes – the Central Register of Births, Marriages and Deaths was reasonably efficient.

Then it was a matter of locating Charles Henry Mullion III and asking him what he remembered about Elspeth, his wife of seventeen days.

The kettle boiled and Mark Bowyer piled in the sugars and the milk. He liked a milky coffee. Despite the mess in his private life – he was counting the days until the court order separating him from Kate – he was very thorough in his professional one. He'd even started to dig around – in his own time - after that strange little bank device, the one they'd found

310

in Tarzi's car, burnt out and virtually unidentifiable. Nothing yet, but his fourteen years in the force - eight as a detective – had taught him the value of the three 'P's: politeness, persistence and patience.

There was nobody left to bribe, there was no advantage to gain. There was nothing he could do with it. The whole world was against him. Suicide was an easy way out, the cutting off of one's own life in order to avoid responsibility for one's actions, but suicide was forbidden by his religion. Attila the Hun would not have contemplated suicide. He would have preferred to die in battle against his mightiest foe and if Attila the Hun had been born in the twentieth century he would have also considered the other factor now weighing heavily on Khaled's mind: public relations.

He would be transferred to Jadzikistan for sentencing, he knew it.

He could see it in the judge's eyes.

He would be hanged and it would be televised for the world to see. They would feel hate, revulsion, and they would breathe a collective sigh of relief. But if – by some miracle – he could somehow make atonement for his sins, if he could show the world that he repented of his crimes and was prepared to suffer for them, then, and only then, would he make *them* suffer.

Hussein Tarzi had set up the trust for him ten years before and had introduced him to one of the partners, Charles Mullion, in a hotel outside Amman Airport in Jordan in 1999. Hussein remembered the man's gleaming face, his shiny black hair and his manicured hands. He was a tall man, impressive and reassuring. A typical American banker now controlling four billion-odd invested in a wide spread of shares in a blind trust held by four Silverman Bach nominees. Silverman Bach was a symbol of Western capitalism. Silverman Bach was revered and respected the world over. And Silverman Bach – he knew from the papers – was going to be the toast of Wall Street and the FTSE. He'd had enough of listening to the prosecution.

It was time to make a statement.

I'd never understood spread-betting. It was one of those mysteries that had always eluded me and I remembered my eyes glazing over when Georgina had once tried to explain to me the mechanics of put and call options and spread-bets.

'Take a football game', she'd said to me in our favourite restaurant in Notting Hill, Kensington Place, back in '97. 'What if Arsenal are playing Manchester Rovers – '

'…United', I butted in, grinning. We were in love then and she smiled back.

'What if Arsenal are playing Manchester *United*, and the odds set by the bookies are for Arsenal to win one-nil but you think there are going to be a lot of goals, say you think it's going to be three-three.'

'Okay…'

'You can place a spread-bet which wins you an amount for each goal scored more than the one that the bookies predict.'

'So?'

'Lots of people do it with shares. Say you've got ten thousand pounds and you want to buy British Telecom shares at three pounds a share because you think they're going to go up. You can buy 3,333 shares at £3 per share and pay the brokers' commission and stamp duty of half a percent. Say they go up twenty pence and you sell. You come away with £666 pounds less commissions.'

'Or...?'

'Or, instead of buying the shares, you can bet an amount of money for each penny the shares go above three pounds. With ten thousand pounds deposited in a spread-betting account and a stop-loss set at, say, ten pence you could bet £500 per point.'

'What does that mean, Georgina?'

'It means, Jonathan my darling, that if the same British Telecom shares go up by twenty pence per share, you make £500 for each point.'

'So a point's a penny?'

'Usually.'

'So?'

Georgina smiled at me and held my hand.

'The shares have gone the way you thought they would in both examples, but in the straight share buy where you physically own the shares you make £666, and with the spread-bet you make £10,000.'

'Christ!'

'Exactly. And the winnings are tax free in the UK.'

'Christmas! Why doesn't everybody do it?'

'Because it's very risky, darling.'

'Oh?'

'If you just bought the shares and they went down by twenty pence, instead of up, and you sold them, you'd lose £666. If the spread-bet went the wrong way, your stop-loss would kick in once you were down ten pence and you'd lose £5,000. Without the stop-loss, you'd lose the whole £10,000.'

'Christ!'

'Christ indeed. We call it leverage, and it's very dangerous unless you know exactly what you're doing.'

I told Jacob I knew exactly what it was I wanted to do and Jacob told me he knew exactly what he was doing.

We had five spread-betting accounts with all the major players in the UK and the money we were using was clean, funneled through Trueblood's new London subsidiary over the last twenty-four hours. We had a mobile phone for each account and they stood, individually labeled, on the plastic table in Trueblood's new centre of operations, our five hundred and seventy-two-thousand-euro Monegasque studio flat. We were ready to play and it was a zero-sum game. If we won, Chas lost, and boy did I want him to lose. I just didn't know how big it was going to be.

Jacob was going to place a succession of down bets on each account, in sterling, up to a maximum of £50,000 per point with a stop loss of twenty points per account. This meant, Jacob assured me, that our maximum loss if everything went wrong and Silverman Bach's share price went up, would be five times twenty times £50,000, or £5,000,000. It was pin-money to us now, but we were doing it because I wanted to hurt Chas. And Georgina. And all the other greedy bankers out there.

I gave Kate a hundred thousand euros from my satchel and she kissed me before she slipped on her shades and headed off to Casino Square to play her own zero-sum game against a different sort of bank.

'Watch the screens', said Jacob, once Kate had left. 'Red is good, blue is bad.'

I did and all I could see was blue.

The price in London had just moved from £19.24 to £19.25.

Blue was bad, red was good.

It was nine-thirty London time and I'd made all my calls within the last thirty minutes, after the market had opened and before the live CNN broadcast from Silverman Bach's offices in Ropemaker Place, the offices jointly-owned by Chas Mullion's bank and Martin Hotson's holding company. Martin had been a client of the bank, I thought, but not after today. Not after the epiphany he'd had on the phone with me the day before where he'd realized the hands he'd seen around Elspeth's neck thirty-one years ago had not been his but those of Charles Henry Mullion III.

Archie Macdonald, the young man I never saw at chambers, had gone straight to Martin's office to take his statement and I'd read it yesterday evening in my room at the Hotel de Paris. It looked very, very persuasive. I wondered what Mark Bowyer would make of it and I hoped Martin had sent it to him this morning like I'd asked him to, exactly one hour after having faxed him Chas and Elspeth's marriage certificate.

He'd told me, in a burst of generosity, that I didn't need to pay him back the three million Swiss francs I owed him.

The Venetian blinds were drawn, letting little strands of sunlight filter through to Trueblood's tiny headquarters.

'All we need's a small movement', said Jacob. 'Fifty pence is fifty points, abou' four per cent.'

He didn't even need a calculator to tell me that if Silverman Bach's share price dropped from £19.25 to £18.75 we would make five times fifty times £50,000, or £12,500,000. It would be a good day's work – more than twenty million dollars – incidentally the same as Brenda pre-nup settlement, the one she wasn't going to settle for.

I turned up the volume of the television and waited.

The champagne corks were popping on the thirty-first floor. The seven hundred London-based staff had all received their float-bonus cheques and the rest of their money was tied up in a stock that was climbing higher and higher. The three-man crew from CNN had had to put up an umbrella to shield their equipment from the spraying of 1990 Krug, more like the end of a Formula One race than the offices of an investment bank.

'Arthur Harrigan?'

'Yeah.'

'Has the float been a success?'

A roar erupted around Harrigan, standing with his arms around a couple of senior M&A guys.

'You heard 'em!' he replied. 'This is a turning point in our history, and I'm just so proud to be able to have played a part in it.'

'Thank you.'

The reporter moved over to Chas who was already miked-up and ready to go.

'Charles Mullion. You're the new CEO. Can you tell us what the Silverman Bach float means for banking in the European and US markets?'

'It's the *global* market-place now', replied Chas, drawing himself up to his full six-two height against a background of cheering.

'Your team look pretty happy', continued the reporter, smiling. Hell, it was infectious. Even the secretaries were rich now. 'What about the clients?'

'They're delighted. This listing enables us to offer an even wider array of high-quality services on a global scale, backed by the Silverman Bach guarantee of honesty, integrity and speed-of-reaction to ever-changing market conditions.'

Georgina stood in the background, holding a cheque for five million dollars.

'Martin Hotson co-owns this building and we're proud to have him as a client', continued Chas, waving him over.

Martin Hotson came forward, smiled for the cameras and handed Chas a large brown envelope.

'Don't open it now', he whispered.

The reporter held his finger to his earpiece, listening to his producer.

'We'll be back shortly', said the reporter to camera, 'but for now it's back to the studio for some breaking news.'

Jacob and I stood next to each other, holding our breath, our hands almost touching, eyes fixed on the little flatscreen TV. Behind us, the two laptop screens were flashing blue.

At the CNN studio a pleasant-faced blonde in a red jacket

turned to camera.

'*We're getting reports from the Central Criminal Court in London of a remarkable development in the Khaled trial.*'

I took a quick look at Jacob.

'*It seems, in a surprising twist to what is the most eagerly-awaited trial this century, that Khaled Al Khalim has this morning revealed the location of substantial secret assets not currently under the jurisdiction of the UN...*'

I stopped blinking. Jacob and I turned to each other, our mouths open, faces white.

'*...and that those assets total some four billion US dollars. Greg?*'

I was shaking. I noticed Jacob's right eye had suddenly started to twitch. A reporter called Greg was standing outside the offices of Silverman Bach. I blinked. There must have been something wrong with the feed.

'*What can you tell us, Greg?*'

'*There's a substantiated report, Mary-Jo, that the funds are being held in nominee accounts at Silverman Bach and that the FSA is sending a team over here now for a full...*'

'*What?*' I shouted at Greg.

'Look a' the screens!' bellowed Jacob. 'Look a' the screens!'

I turned round and I saw red.

CHAPTER TWENTY-FOUR

The view from the wooden terrace was spectacular.

Kate was in the sea in front of me, lying on an inflatable, taking in the last of the afternoon's rays. I was sitting on a sun-lounger, by the door, looking at the calmness of the Caribbean and listening to the crickets. The chattel house had only two bedrooms, was riddled with woodworm and there was precious little furniture, but then we would soon be changing all that.

Our divorces had come through on the same day and we'd cracked open a couple of beers to celebrate. It was New Year's Day, 2007 and even at five-thirty in the afternoon it was well over eighty degrees. We were going to take it one day at a time. If money bought you anything, it was freedom. Freedom from a cold damp room in chambers with the condensation running down the windows. Freedom from the penury of wondering how to pay the school fees. Freedom from feeling inadequate inside your friend's much-nicer house. Freedom from greed. It was funny, but now we were rich, we didn't need to be greedy anymore.

Kate stopped gambling when we moved to Barbados. She was good at it, but it just wasn't necessary anymore. She didn't need an escape.

There was nothing she needed to escape from now.

Real life was exciting enough.

We'd left 'Greed', our twenty-four-metre motor-yacht, in its berth on Grand Cayman, and Jacob was probably still in Monaco, but I doubted he operated from the studio flat anymore. I think he bought the penthouse I saw in the window on Avenue des Beaux Arts, the one for twelve million with the roof-top pool.

He also bought a bank.

That day, the day the news broke, the Silverman Bach share price had stood at £19.25. And just before closing in London Jacob had liquidated all of his positions, at £250,000 a point. Closing price was £8.06 and the shares had been suspended three times in mid-day trading as the hedge-funds unwound their own positions and tried to shelter themselves from even heavier losses.

£279,750,000

Two hundred and seventy nine million, seven hundred and fifty thousand pounds. At current exchange rates, half a billion dollars.

Added to the rest, we had a billion between us.

To cover their positions the spread-betting firms had had to take out a series of complex hedging contracts.

That started a whole new zero sum game and as the spread-betting companies' hedging increased, Jacob spread-bet on their shares falling, which they duly did to the tune of a further £80,000,000 profit for Trueblood.

There was so much money that it didn't matter anymore, although it seemed to matter to Jacob.

I needed to be near Ben, Mollie and Amy, my children, so I bought Georgina a nice five-bed villa on the Royal Westmoreland Estate, only ten minutes from us, and so we shared custody. I took the kids swimming every weekend and sometimes after school. She'd managed to cash her cheque for the five million, but Silverman Bach's shares had been suspended for the last time the following week, so she lost all her shares and then her job.

Chas had had a nervous breakdown and was currently in a mental institution awaiting trial for the crime that he'd confessed to, the murder of Elspeth Huntingford-Smith thirty-two years ago.

He also faced further charges together with his three senior colleagues for the attempted embezzlement of nearly four billion dollars from Khaled's accounts at Silverman Bach. He had been disqualified as a company director and he had been made bankrupt, which had sent Brenda into a deep depression because she hadn't taken the twenty million dollar pre-nup when it was offered and now she had nothing. She'd had to sell her glittering diamond ring in order to pay the legal fees of Anthony Garrett & Co. I think she went back to Lido Beach and was working somewhere as a beautician.

Lord Marden had taken great pleasure in referring Khaled Al Khalim to Jadzikistan for sentencing and Khaled had been hanged on the 1st of October, a public holiday in Jadzikistan.

I could have sworn that I saw Osama from the King Midas Kebab House, beamed to every television screen on the planet, standing at the front of the huge crowd baying for Khaled's blood. Khaled had shopped Chas and the rest of Silverman

Bach but he'd never confessed to Genevieve. Perhaps, I concluded with Jacob, perhaps he didn't even know Genevieve existed.

His Lordship's pleasure in sending Khaled to his certain death was matched by the pain he felt when Martin Hotson declined to pay him a penny when he was released from bail without charge. His Lordship would be spending his retirement a bitter man, although I believe he still retains the presidency of Velvet, an establishment I will not be frequenting again as long as I live.

I received a Christmas card from Jim Kelsey, forwarded to me from chambers in London. I wondered if he suspected anything, if he ever sat down and thought through how it was that his twenty-two million two hundred and fifty-seven thousand was returned to him. But I think I had enough money, enough well-hidden money, to stop being paranoid. Apart from 'Greed', my yacht, there had been no extravagances. I never found out what happened to my Customs case. I think Archie Macdonald has it now.

I wonder if he's started smoking.

Mark Bowyer was promoted and stuck to his diet of milky coffee and leggy blondes from the typing pool.

As the months went by he accumulated enough new cases to start forgetting about the old ones, and the charred remains of *Mr Desmond*'s security device, that held the key to more than two billion dollars, sat in a plastic bag inside a steel drawer somewhere in a basement room underneath Scotland Yard, accumulating interest at JP Chartrier et Freres at the rate of one per cent per annum, in perpetuity.

I did not know what the future held for me and Kate. All I knew is that I didn't want to be a barrister anymore, and neither did she. As we'd agreed, we'd take one day at a time. I could have bought Chas and Brenda's wedding-cake mansion, but I didn't want to. I could have bought a lot of things, but I didn't.

It was so true what they say about money. It doesn't make you happy. But when you're rich, really rich, fuck-off rich, it just doesn't seem to matter anymore.

CPSIA information can be obtained at www.ICGtesting.com
Printed in the USA
BVOW02s2147171214

379869BV00019BA/721/P